An American Saga

"The book is riveting and the storyline captivating. I didn't want to put the book down once I was started. I have never read romance or western novels and I thought this read would be a stretch for me but as I got into the story I immediately became engaged and found myself immersed in each word as the tale, the characters and their lives unfolded."

—*Karen Mayfield, Msc.CC*
National bestselling author of Wake Up Women—
Be Happy, Healthy & Wealthy
and co-creator of the Wake Up Women book series.

"Diverse characters...highly visual prose...a journey of gathering suspense...delicious and devastating results. Rosenthal delivers!"

—Josephine Ellershaw
#1 international bestselling author

What the readers are saying...

The praise from authors and ~~reviewers~~ ~~is thrilling but~~
this book is written for **you,** ~~~~
a few of your fellow readers ~~~~
are saying!

"Better than Louis L'Amour. ~~~~ ~~Louis L Amour.~~"

—*Rhett R., Montana*

"I finished the book last night. It was amazing. If this does not get made into a movie or mini-series for TV, it will be a crime. It is so wonderful. I loved every minute of it and can't wait to read the next one. Yo, dude, you have got the romance thing down. You had my blood pumpin' and even boiling. It is captivating on so many levels and it just kept getting better and better!"

—*Ann J., California*

"Your style of writing captures a reader's attention and won't let go! It stimulates the senses so we can feel, taste, smell, hear and see vivid pictures of the characters and setting, which you so meticulously describe...characters, interesting and diverse with complex lives, become artfully merged with one another to create this really remarkable, unforgettable story.... I'm looking forward to the continuation of the *Threads West* journey!"

—*Nancy K., Colorado*

"My girlfriend bought your *Threads West* book. Then she insisted that I read it. A Western romance? I groaned and thought I would pretend to keep her happy. I did not stop until I read the whole thing. For once, real characters in real situations, with real reactions. A great story, too. I am buying book two, and she will have to get it from me."

—*Tom G., Florida*

"I downloaded *Threads West* and was quickly captivated. Easy to appreciate how some readers have read it front to back at one sitting! It is obviously nurtured in the heart, driven by a love of land and country, and the results are destined to bring great pleasure to many readers. I know this tale will ignite many readers with a forgotten love and appreciation for the heritage of this great country and a clearer commitment to overcome the challenges that lie ahead. There may well have been a reason that *Threads West* should appear at this time!"

—*Ronald L., Colorado*

"I have been completely captivated by your mastery of the art of storytelling. Your wondrous world of *Threads West* is a new adventure in which I want to continue further, learn more about the loves and lives of the characters who are becoming friend and foe and part of my own. This is your passion, painting a visual that is a must-read, and leaving the reader longing for more and the next."

—*Kim H., Colorado*

"Just finished reading book one of *Threads West*. Well done! You have great talents putting in words: emotions, scenery, love and turmoil! But I was mostly impressed at your deep knowledge of history, whether here or in Europe."

—*Joelle B., New York, Paris*

"A breathtaking read...a gallop through literary highs... absolutely thrilling.... Thanks Reid, for re-igniting the American West...."

—**Madelyn F., United Kingdom**

"I had such a wonderful time reading to the seniors at the care facility where my grandmother is, that I will be reading your book again to both men and woman this time....

They love to be read to.... I wish I had my mother's talent for reading but when you have a good story I guess you don't need all the extras."

—*Mitzi H., Oregon*

"I am hooked on your book! I loved it! I would love to have an autographed book or book cover. I will wait patiently for the next one, and I will keep reading the rest of the saga when you finish them. How exciting to travel like that to a new land—and scary at the same time."

—*Linda M., Texas*

"Few books hold my attention. But I was hooked from the first pages of *Threads West*.... I could not put it down and finished reading the entire novel in one day. Don't tell my boss!! When is book 2? Hurry!"

—*Debbie S., California*

"A stunning and brilliant cast of characters with drama and adventure that had me thoroughly captivated from cover to cover. I recommend everyone read the first volume of what will certainly prove to be a great series!"

—*Jeribeth J., WI*

"Can I just say...I love this passage: 'The crimson tendrils of the departing day kissed the tops of snowcapped peaks.' There are many times in your book where the descriptive writing is wonderful but with this sentence, I can feel the warmth of the sun fading on the cool snow. It is great."

—*Ann J., Washington*

An American Saga

THREADS WEST

REID LANCE
ROSENTHAL

ROCKIN' SR PUBLISHING
WRITING DREAM, LLC
Cheyenne, Wyoming

PUBLISHER'S NOTE:
This is a work of fiction. All characters, places, businesses and incidents are from the author's imagination. Any resemblance to actual places, people, or events is purely coincidental. Any trademarks mentioned herein are not authorized by the trademark owners and do not in any way mean the work is sponsored by or associated with the trademark owners. Any trademarks used are specifically in a descriptive capacity.

Also available on NOOK, Kindle, IBookstore and Kobobooks.com

Book Design by TLC Graphics, *www.tlcgraphics.com*
Cover by Tamara Dever; Interior by Erin Stark
Proofreading July 2013 reprint by: WordSharp.net

Photo credits:
train: ©iStockphoto.com/fredrikarnell
train for smoke: 2010 Eric Simard. Image from Bigstock.com
woman: ©iStockphoto.com/duncan1890
London: ©iStockphoto.com/duncan1890
flag: ©iStockphoto.com/Blueberries
leather: ©iStockphoto.com/colevineyard
leather tooling: ©iStockphoto.com/belterz
scrolled leather: ©iStockphoto.com/billnoll
parchment paper: ©iStockphoto.com/ranplett

Printed in the United States of America

ISBN: 978-0-9821576-1-9
Library of Congress Control Number: 2010914165

To my mother June, who, among many gifts, passed on to me a love of, and talent for, writing. To my editor Page Lambert, who taught me just how much I did not know about the wonderful craft of prose. To Jordan Allhands, whose unsurpassed computer and web design skills makes access to this series possible for so many. To Laura Kennedy, tireless Publisher's Assistant and master of all trades. To the characters—my friends—who live in these pages. And, to America, her values, history, people and the mystical energy and magical empowerment that flow from her lands.

An American Saga

Book One

TABLE OF CONTENTS

Threads West
An American Saga

Book Two

Preview

An American Saga

Book One

This is the first novel of the *Maps of Fate* era,
(1854–1875) of the *Threads West,
An American Saga* series.

INTRODUCTION
to the *Maps of Fate* Era Novels
of the Series

THE YEAR IS 1854. AMERICA IS ON THE CUSP OF HER
great westward expansion and the threshold of reluctantly becoming a world power. The lure of the vast
territories and resources beyond the Mississippi cata-
pults the population of St. Louis, gateway to the frontier,
to almost one hundred thousand, an eight-fold expansion from just a decade prior.

One thousand miles to the west lay the Rocky Mountains, the lawless, untamed spine of the continent. The
power of their jagged peaks beckons the vanguard of
generations—the souls of a few adventurous men and
women of many cultures and separate origins, to love
and struggle in the beautifully vibrant but unforgiving
landscape of the West.

America's promise of land, freedom, self-determination and economic opportunity was now known worldwide. Immigrants from many continents exchange the lives they know for the hope and romance of a country embarked on the course of greatness.

These individuals, drawn from the corners of the earth by the promise of land, freedom, self-determination and economic opportunity, are unaware of the momentous changes that will shape the United States in the tumultuous years between 1854 and 1875, sweeping them into the vortexes of agony and ecstasy, victory and defeat, love lost and acquired.

The personal conflicts inherent to these brave, passion-filled characters—the point of the spear of the coming massive westward migration—are spurred by land, gold, the conquest of Mexican territory by the United States, railroads and telegraphs. Their relationships and ambitions are tempered by the fires of love and loss, hope and sorrow, life and death. Their personalities are shaped by dangerous journeys from far-off continents and then across a wild land to a wilderness in which potential is the only known reality.

They begin to build a nation whose essence is in transition, their lives shaken by events and convergences with other souls they could not foresee. An elderly black couple sets their life sails for winds of freedom. An Oglala Sioux family struggles to cope with the foreshadow of lands and culture forever changed. Mormons stream west in the Great Exodus escaping persecution, and searching for Zion. An outlaw vaquero of royal origin from south of the border quests for a sense of self and place and a black-hearted renegade is unknowingly catapulted by his tortured past into possible redemption.

The budding enmity between North and South flares in the winds of war, and the remote fringe of the frontier falls into virtual anarchy as most of the meager army troops are withdrawn to the East. On the Front Range of the Rockies, Cherry Creek has been renamed Denver as the city booms with the effect of gold discoveries in the Pikes Peak area and the Ouray, San Juan and Uncompahgre Mountain ranges. The first newspaper in the West rolls off the presses in Leavenworth and Lawrence, Kansas, and Platte Valley, Nebraska. A Confederate Army mustered in Texas is repulsed by the Denver Militia. Soon, railroads and telegraphs will pierce this wild land. The broken treaties with Native Americans spread into bitter and contagious conflict throughout the West. The "resolution" of the "Indian problem" leaves families and hearts broken, and a dark stain on the pages of American history.

You will recognize the characters that live in these pages. They are your neighbors, your family, your co-workers. They are you and they are us; the threads of many lives—both men and women—from different locations, ancestry, social and financial backgrounds, faiths and beliefs. They are personalities forged on the anvil of the land, woven together by fate and history, and bound by the commonality of the American spirit into the tapestry that is our nation.

The personal conflicts inherent to these brave, passion-filled characters are exacerbated by a country in transition and the accelerating melting pot of diverse cultures that marks this magical moment in American History.

You will recognize the characters who live in these pages. They are you. They are us. This is not only their story. It is *our* story. The adventure and romance of America, her people, her spirit, and the West. It is *Threads West, An American Saga*.

www.threadswestseries.com

May 3, 1854

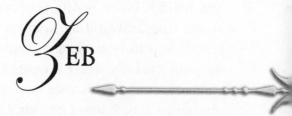

ZEB

THREE HUNDRED MILES SOUTHWEST OF THE UNDULAT-
ing expanse of the Great Plains and the tiny settlement
of Cherry Creek, a small creek rushed and gurgled, feed-
ing a series of beaver ponds along the edge of a large
grove of aspens, alders and willows. The glitters of the
water sifting through the pond's edge of willows and
alders formed points of bright light where they reflected
off the white bark of quaking aspen saplings surrounding Zeb and the stock. Overhead, puffy patches of
clouds flitted across the face of the sun scuttling in hurried billows through a deep blue sky to some unknown
rendezvous to the east.

The sleek, mottled brown and white silhouettes of the
mustang, its thin buckskin-clad rider and the stocky, gray
forms of the pack mules strung behind the horse were
motionless, almost invisible deep in the heart of the
patch of quaking aspen. A .52 caliber breech loading
Sharps rifle lay across the rider's thighs, cradled between

his belt and the saddle horn. Diffused light filtered through the needles of the few conifers interspersed with the ghostly leafless branches of the aspen trees and added to the camouflage of the little band.

Zebarriah Taylor or Zeb, as he preferred to be called, sat erect, perfectly still and keenly observant. One weathered hand slowly stroking a long strand of his thick, unkempt mustache where it tapered off into the graying stubble just above his chin, his eyes probed in every direction and he listened intently. *Quiet. A bit too quiet.*

Slowly craning his neck, he looked back at the three pack mules, each of them burdened with a large bundle of pelts balanced and cinched between the wooden crossbars of the pack saddle frames. Shiny layers of fur protruded on all edges from under the oiled leathers lashed with rawhide over the top of each mound as a protective tarp. The mules stood complacently, though their ears were up. The attention of the mustang was pricked also, and the horse stood like a statue, nose pointed toward the riffled sparkles that bounced off the surface of the several beaver ponds.

Zeb checked the cartridge in the Sharps and then pulled each of the brace of cap and ball pistols from his waistband; tucking them back when he was satisfied they, too, were ready. Leaning far to his left, he pulled the .58 caliber Enfield musket from its belly scabbard, eyeing the flash pan. He left it partially unsheathed, just in case. A split second could be life or death. He carefully swung his left leg over the saddle horn and the horse's neck until he was sidesaddle. Patting the horse's shoulder, he spoke in a whisper, "Easy, Buck, last two traps of the spring season. We made it through the winter—no sense gettin' kilt now."

Slipping off the saddle, he landed lightly on the silent carpet of fallen leaves, brown from the previous autumn and damp from the winter's snowpack. There were still patches of old snow where shade had lingered. Alternating spring-day sun and frozen nights had solidified the once white flakes into little kernels, like frozen corn. This time of year, the warming of each day created a wet film of melted lubricant between the pebbles of ice, and these remnants of a stubborn winter were especially treacherous.

One leg slipped out from underneath Zeb as he was crossing a deeper drift and he almost fell. Catching himself on an aspen branch, he cursed under his breath. He glanced down at the laced-up leather boots that extended almost to his knee. He had fashioned them out of heavy elk hide by firelight over long winter nights in the notch cabin, one of several small log shelters he had built and called home from time to time. *Gonna have to figure out some grippers for these one day.*

Moving with stealth to the edge of the willows that fringed the upper beaver pond, he crouched and looked carefully around once again. *No bears, no wolves, no Indians—for now.* Rising, he positioned the muzzle of the Sharps in front of him and slipped through the thin red branches of the willows until he stood on the edge of the water. On the other side of the impoundment, just a stone's throw away, was the wet, furry head and clear V-wake of a swimming beaver.

Taking a few steps toward a large log, red-brown with sun and rot and perched partially on the bank, he looked down to where it disappeared into the depths of the pond. He could make out his trap just a few feet from shore; his own image superimposed on the surface of the water over the snare.

He took a moment to contemplate his wiry figure, clad in fringed, dirt-stained, brown leather. The lower part of his reflected body was partially obscured by the foot of thin ice that still clung to the shore. A coonskin hat sat above a narrow face with deep-set eyes under bushy eyebrows. The facial features were distorted slightly by gentle riffles stirred by the breeze that wafted down the creek. Even that distortion did not hide two thick purple claw mark scars that descended from below the left eye diagonally down around to the left jawline and neck below the ear. The image grinned at him. *Not very pretty are you?*

Reaching over his shoulder, he drew out the fourteen-inch bone-handled blade that rested in the fringed and beaded sheath on his back. Carefully using the log for support, he sank his arm into the frigid waters up to his elbow and plucked the empty trap from the bottom. He let it lay in the matted winter grass to drip-dry and strode another fifty feet around the pond where he repeated the procedure with the second trap. It, too, was empty. After each action, he paused, peered and deciphered the sounds of the meadow. The beaver he had seen earlier had crawled on the bank and was busily gnawing on the bark of an aspen tree it had no doubt felled the night before. Kneeling, Zeb rested his left elbow on his left knee, taking careful aim at the beaver's head with the Sharps. Pulling back the hammer, he leveled his right eye down the sites atop the forty-seven-inch blued barrel, then hesitated.

Opening both eyes from his sighting squint, he lowered the rifle and gingerly uncocked the firing mechanism. The beaver halted its industrious work and stared at him from across the pond as Zeb spoke to it in a low voice. "Hell, you are a lucky damn critter today. I don't need to make no noise, and I'm not much inclined to unwrap an entire pack for one pelt." Slinging the traps over his shoulder, he watched the beaver for a moment longer. "We'll see you next season. Have lots of young-uns."

Zeb walked with wary caution back to the horse and mules. He stowed the traps in the panniers strung behind the horse's saddle, thrust the Sharps and Enfield deep into their scabbards, mounted and paused once more to scout in all directions. "All right, fellas, time to skedaddle." Wheeling the mustang around, followed by the mules, he picked his way back down the slope, careful not to skyline their figures during the descent.

It was not long until evening, and they still had two hours to the notch cabin. The crimson tendrils of the departing day kissed the tops of snowcapped peaks. Below the snowline of the nearest three mountains, the land had a red cast that mingled with the green of conifer stands. Cooled at higher elevations, the late afternoon air currents whispered gently downslope. His trail led him through grassy plateaus, rimmed by red rock, glowing and pulsing with the low angle of the sun. Stands of trees gathered in clusters wherever unseen springs bubbled to the surface. Here and there were tall, dark, abrupt outcroppings of stone. Bits of white quartz sparkled in the rocks, which stood like sentinels guarding the meadows in the stair-step terrain.

As he rode, Zeb gave some study to his plan. He didn't like towns—he wasn't partial to being in the same vicinity as a lot of other people. Especially white folks. On the other hand, the two trading posts, Bent's Fort along the South Platte, and the others, Vasquez or St. Vrain on the Arkansas River, would only give him a fraction of the real worth of his pelts, gathered during the long seasons of last fall and this spring. He wondered if he could tolerate the sights, sounds and smells of Cherry Creek for the few days it would take to sell or trade the skins.

The edge of night was chasing the last of daylight from the western sky when Zeb reached the cabin. He tied off the mules and put the horse in the rough log corral. Then, patiently rigging the elementary block and tackle he had fashioned to a thick cottonwood limb, lifted the bundles of furs, still attached to the pack saddles, from the backs of the mules.

He rubbed down the animals with straw and threw them some of the wild hay grass he had hand-cut with a scythe the previous fall in the small sub-irrigated meadow by Divide Creek, just below the cabin. "Good job today, boys. I think tomorrow we just might start our trek down to the flats." Reflecting for a moment, he spat the last of his wad of chew to the earth at the side of his feet and added, "Not that I'm all too fired-up about it."

Sliding the long horizontal poles over the heavy log bucks that constituted the jack leg enclosure, he turned and walked a few steps toward the cabin. Before reaching the front stoop, he stopped to regard the shadowed shape of the low-slung structure and rolled himself a smoke.

It had taken a long time using the stock, pulleys and ropes to build the small shelter in this high-country nook. It was only sixteen by twenty feet but he had put great care into its construction. The large hewn logs at the base were well fitted, the walls rising with smaller logs until they disappeared under the sloped cover of the roof. The chink was a mixture of grass and dried mud borne by the mules, pail after pail from the inside corner of the creek a quarter-mile downstream. There the spring runoffs slowed and dumped silt before they made the turn to rush and tumble down the mountain. *Probably need to rechink this coming season.*

Lodgepole pine rafters strung out unevenly below the edge of the roof over the small front stoop by the door. The roof, too, was a mixture of mud and grass, which, except in the worst of the storms, kept the weather from the interior of the cabin. He had fashioned shutters from smaller tree boughs over the four glassless windows, one on each wall. Each had a firing slit. He had never had to use them for defense. The rope-hinged closures kept out the wind and helped retain the heat. The door was thick and sturdy, built of three-inch thick rough-sawn planks hauled from Bent's Fort and Cherry Creek nine years before, the last time he had been to the eastern edge of the mountains.

Drawing deeply on the cigarette he exhaled slowly and critically surveyed the door. Zeb was used to having conversations with objects, his small remuda and himself. Sometimes it was comforting to hear his own voice. "I need to put in a real hinge system," he said aloud. The four doubled-up leather hide strips, their ends nailed to the frame and inside edge of the door, held up for only a few months before they had to be replaced. Zeb stroked his mustache, "Maybe I will get me some of that hardware this trip. Metal ought to last a sight longer than hide." Looking up at the sky, he sniffed several times. *Damp. Smells like snow. Winter's a long time goin' up this high this year.*

In the cabin, Zeb lit the single oil lamp, which—along with one six-pane window—had miraculously made its unbroken way from the flatlands on that same trip almost a decade before. *Need a refill on this lamp oil too. And tobacco and papers. I reckon I'd better make me a list.*

He built a fire in the fireplace that he had painstakingly crafted from creek cobblestones and makeshift mortar. Placing the metal triangle upright and its cast-iron hanging pot close to the flames, he cut off chunks from the salted elk that hung from the ceiling, adding water, and throwing in some wild scallions and previous season asparagus he had gathered during the ride to the beaver ponds.

Lying on the makeshift hide bed on the dirt floor, coonskin hat still on, he supported his head on one hand and watched the fire.

"Yep," Zeb said to the cabin logs that glowed amber from the flickers of flame, "Yep, I think I just might go to Cherry Creek. More money and I can get some things I won't find up on the Arkansas. With luck, I can vamoose out of town in a day or two. That shouldn't harm me none."

THE MORNING WAS HIGH-COUNTRY SPRING CRISP, ALMOST cold, with a dusting of wet snow. The air warmed quickly as the sun rose over the sheer, interspersed, red rock ledges marching up the mountain across the creek and the light of emerging day danced on the riffles of the stream.

Grimacing, Zeb began to roll a smoke and spat the last of his chew, which hit the upright on the hitching post in front of the cabin porch exactly in the center. He glanced out at the horse and the pack mules. "Be with you fellas in just a second."

Turning, he walked back into the cabin, opened one of the window shutters to allow in some light and rummaged for paper. He had learned to write at an early age, though his block print was painstaking. Sitting down on one of the two stumps that served as seats at the makeshift table, he whittled down the point of the pencil with a knife, licked the lead and began to write. The piece of tattered paper he found already had writing on it. Occasionally, on a cold winter night, as skins dried and after chores were completed, he would pencil out thoughts or notions inspired by the eerie groan of the wind as it played on the log corners of the cabin.

Pausing, he stared vacantly out the panes of the cabin's only glassed window, that old familiar melancholy emptiness simmering in his gut again. It was worn far worse on those long snowy nights when the creep of darkness between sunrise and sunset seemed interminable. It was rare that he could pick up a pencil and not think of his family, particularly his mother. She had been a schoolteacher in the small western Missouri town on the outskirts of St. Louis near the farm where he, his brother and parents lived. It was she who had insisted he be literate.

His father had toiled on the one hundred sixty acres they called home. He had been a quiet, taciturn man. Zeb loved and respected him but they were never close. It was his mother, an attractive but rugged woman who looked older than she was, whom Zeb revered. She read him books of faraway places and strange adventures before he could read them for himself. It was the stories of the French and Spanish explorers that intrigued him most. Many nights he would fall asleep in his mother's arms as they read together from the latest book. He loved to watch her teach during the two days a week his father allowed him to attend the one-room schoolhouse. He marveled at her kindness, patience and sincere wish to help others.

Then there was the day his life turned inside out. He had gone into town for supplies. Despite his father's admonition to hurry back, he had spent an extra hour with some friends. His mind had long ago blacked out the details but he could still feel the horror, panic and nausea when he saw the billows of thick gray smoke and heard scattered gunshots a few miles out from the farm. Several bands of white renegades had been terrorizing lonely farms along the Mississippi River north and south of St. Louis. Zeb knew what they did to their victims.

Frantically slapping the lines along the flanks of the old team of horses pulling the wagon, he urged them into a gallop but he arrived too late. The outlaws were gone, with all the horses. Many of the livestock had been shot and those still alive were bleating in terror. His father and older brother lay face down, both shot in the back and scalped. They had obviously made an attempt to get out of the grain field and reach the house, now being consumed in a searing eruption of flame. Every building in the farmstead was burning. Searching desperately for his mother, he finally found her scalped body, dress half-torn away, eyes open and sightless in a pile of bloody hay behind the smoldering hay barn. From that point, his memory went blank.

Townspeople who went out to the farmstead later told him he had fashioned grave markers and buried the three bodies but Zeb had never been able to remember any of that. The bank took the farm and he found a job working for room, board and meager wages for eighteen months at the livery stable, where he learned everything he could from every pioneer, trapper and cavalry man on their way to St. Louis to head west. He learned the renegades that had murdered his family were led by a half-breed who went by the name of Black Feather. He toyed with the idea of revenge but eventually concluded that what he wanted was to leave Missouri, hole up in the Rockies and never return.

Taking two deep breaths, he exhaled slowly, closing his eyes until the scenes in his head faded. He finished his list, held the paper up to the light from the window, squinting and nodded his head with satisfaction. *That ought to do.* He felt strangely cleansed.

Whistling, he headed to the corral to saddle Buck and reload the pack saddles and pelt bundles on the mules.

May 3, 1854

REUBEN

FIFTY-SEVEN HUNDRED MILES EAST OF THE HEWN, SUN-
faded logs of Zeb's notch cabin, Reuben Frank leaned
against the weathered planks of the hay wagon, watching
the languid current of the Lahn River drift past the
great white barn. Upstream lay several fields gridded
by fences and hedgerows. The green, high blades of the
growing grass had a slight remaining vestige of winter
brown. *Some shoots that forgot it's spring.* Watching his
father drive a wagon pulled by two stout draft horses
along one field, Reuben took a deep breath and exhaled
slowly. *I wonder what the seasons will be like over there?*

Lifting thin arms to chest height, his father slapped
the lines to the draft horses with gentle authority. The
large blocks of wood dragging behind the wagon prod-
ded and tilled the manure of winter pasturing into the
fertile earth. Just beyond the river, the rooftops of the
village of Villmar were still glistening with a rare late
season frost turned to dew by the morning sun.

Looking down, he kicked one boot against the other to dislodge mud, his eye noticing an image of himself in the glass surface of a puddle remnant. The young man who stared back at him with worried eyes stood six feet tall with dark brown wavy hair. The image had an athletic frame, not particularly broad-shouldered but powerful nonetheless. Green eyes with a hint of gray sat in a wide face. Stroking his square jaw, his eyebrows furrowed in thought as he leaned against the roughsawn planks. He wondered if he would ever see his family, particularly his father, again.

"Better get this hay out to the heifers," he mumbled in an attempt to distract himself. Drumming his fingers unconsciously on the rim of the wagon bed sidewalls, he stood a moment longer to watch the familiar scene. The table conversation from the night before still rang in his head. *I will miss this simple part of each day.*

They had all come in for the evening meal. Erik, the youngest, was an excellent cook and had taken over much of the domestic duties when their mother had died in 1852, two years prior. Slightly built, scholarly and musically inclined, he wore thick spectacles that were always slipping to the end of his nose before he pushed them back with an impatient gesture.

"Helmon," he said to one of his brothers, "you've been sitting there for half an hour. I told you I would call you when supper was ready. The least you could do is help set the table."

Rising, Helmon fumbled around the kitchen, his large frame seeming out of place as he set out dishes and

looked for silverware. Handsome, although a bit overweight, he was a ladies' man. His general philosophy was
that any problem could be solved by pounding it into
compliance, an attitude he shared with their eldest
brother Isaac.

"Supper is ready!" Erik called in his high voice.

"If you were a woman, I'd marry you," said Isaac,
removing the straps of his overalls from his shoulders
as he came in the kitchen door. There was a bite to his
comment. He was at least four inches taller than Reuben,
with large hands and a florid face. As the senior sibling
of the four, he had taken it upon himself to act as de
facto head of the household as their father's health dete-
riorated, though he often reluctantly deferred to
Reuben's careful reasoning. However, Isaac was a good
farmer and knew how to make the land prosper.

"It does smell good, Erik," complimented Reuben,
helping him place the platters of kosher beef sausage and
boiled potatoes on the table. "Rye bread, my favorite."

"Yes, and the jam is there, Reuben, I know how you
like lots of jam with rye bread," smiled Erik, beaming
at the praise.

All four brothers had taken a seat but were waiting
for their father, Ludwig. They heard his slow but
steady footsteps as he made his way to the kitchen.
He appeared through the low entry and sat down.
Bowing their heads as he said the Hebrew blessing
over the food, they watched hungrily as Erik served
their father first. Then with good-natured jostling,
they filled their plates.

For a moment, the table was silent with the exception of the scratch of utensils on the china place settings.

Sitting back and wiping his mouth with his sleeve, Isaac grinned, "Saw you walking with Hilda the other day, Helmon. She is a fine figure of a girl," he teased.

Helmon had a mouth full of food, and although his answer was indecipherable, his tone of voice was not. They all laughed and respectfully suggestive conversation followed about the girls in Villmar, and who liked whom best.

When they had finished the meal and began to rise from the table, Ludwig motioned them to stay seated. "Erik, would you please clear the table?" asked Ludwig. His voice was soft.

The brothers glanced at one another. An air of expectancy hung over the kitchen. Wincing as he reached behind him, Ludwig placed the rich leather of an old, worn but sturdy leather map case on the now barren surface of the table.

"As you know, we have discussed for some time our inability to expand our land further here in Prussia. The gentiles, though they are friendly, would rather not sell to a Jew. Uncle Hermann in New York and I have been writing back and forth for years. There is trouble brewing in America. There are some who want to keep slavery and others who do not. The government there wants to ensure federal power and settle western parts of the country." Ludwig fell silent and looked around the table. "From what Hermann has written to me and from what I have read in the newspapers, the western part of America is inhospitable, almost lawless but there is land, and where there is land there is opportunity."

He withdrew several large parchments from the map case. The only break in the silence was the rustle of the heavy, beige parchment papers as he unrolled and spread them on the table in front of him. "Helmon, Erik, hold those corners, please." The brothers peered intently at the large sheets.

"It will be a long, arduous journey across the Atlantic to New York and then by train to Chicago and finally to St. Louis." His bony finger traced the route on one of the charts. "Here, from St. Louis, there is no formal transportation. The eventual destination, the Red Mountains in the San Juan Range, is just over three hundred miles southwest of the very small outpost they call Cherry Creek, situated at the confluence of Cherry Creek and the South Platte River, east of a mountainous region known as Las Coloradas or Colorado. It is the western edge of what the United States designates as the Kansas Territory. The man Hermann hired to scout for us has done a good job. Based on his letters, I expected a third map which he indicated would be quite important, but it has not arrived, nor have Hermann and I received any further correspondence from him." Reclining in the chair, he positioned his legs with obvious discomfort.

"It takes three hands to run the farm here. I am of little use. One of you will go on this journey. It will be his job to establish this family in America. The rest of you and your families—if any women will have you," he said, smiling, "may someday follow. I am convinced America is the future."

Giving a slow thoughtful look to each of his sons in turn, his eyes came to rest on Reuben. For a brief moment, pride, love and a vestige of worry clearly etched his face. Then his features turned stern, almost inscrutable.

"Reuben, I have booked your passage on the SS *Edinburgh*. The ship will be launched later this year. Its new condition should make the voyage more comfortable. It leaves Bremen in the evening, on January 16, a little over eight months from now. It makes port for a short time in Portsmouth, steams to Liverpool and then continues to New York. January 16 is a Sunday. You will need to be on the road before daylight that day. I do not wish you to travel on the Sabbath. Erik will take you in and bring the wagon back. Pack light—just one duffel, the map case and one small trunk. I have already sent money in advance to Uncle Hermann. In addition, your work coat is back from our friend Marvin, the tailor. I have hung it in the front closet. There are six diamonds sewn into the hem. The monies you may use as you see fit to buy equipment and supplies and to hire the men that you may need."

Ludwig's deep-set intense green eyes bore into Reuben's. "The diamonds, however, are to be used for one thing only—to buy our land. They are to be used for nothing else."

Wrestling with a mix of excitement and fear, Reuben felt a damp sweat on his palms. "Yes, Father."

Erik smiled at Reuben and nodded, pushing his glasses higher on his nose. Helmon looked lost, as if unsure about exactly what had transpired. Jumping to his feet, Isaac slapped a meaty fist on the table, shouting, "But, Father—"

"Be seated, Isaac." His voice was firm. Looking up at him, Ludwig raised his hand. Isaac broke off in mid-sentence, his mouth still ajar. His usual mildly florid complexion was beet red. He sat with a heavy, angry thud that made his chair groan.

"Reuben, when your evening chores are done, come up to the study. I want to go over these maps in detail with you. I also have Uncle Hermann's letters for you to read. We will review them again before your departure. You have the summer and fall to prepare," Ludwig blinked twice, his eyes watery. "Remember as you say your good-byes around the village it is highly unlikely that you will ever return."

REUBEN'S REPLAY OF THE PREVIOUS EVENING WAS INTER-rupted by a deliberate hard slap to his head. "Do you plan to get that hay out to the cows or have you started your journey a half year early?" snapped Isaac.

Reuben turned to his older brother. *Evidently, the rancor of last night's family meeting has not yet dissipated.* A big man by any standards, Isaac towered above Reuben. He had large thick farmer's hands and his face that morning carried the flush of too much schnapps. Reuben knew Isaac's pride had been hurt.

"The cows will get fed, Isaac."

"Father made the wrong choice. You are not strong enough."

Regarding his brother with steady eyes, Reuben forced himself to remember Isaac's answer to anything was to push, to use muscle. He believed power was merely a physical attribute. Reuben resolved not to get into a fight. *These may be the last months we ever spend together.*

"Father must have had his reasons. I am sure he thought you were too important to keep the farm going here to send you to America."

Isaac's features softened for a moment.

"Do you love me, Isaac?"

His body jerking, Isaac's lowered chin came up, his face wearing a startled expression.

"Do I love you?" he echoed slowly, obviously perplexed. The word seemed foreign to him. "Why would you ask such a question, Reuben? What does that have to do with this conversation or Father's selection of you to go to America?" Isaac fell silent and then added, almost as an afterthought, "Besides, you are my brother. Why would you ask me such a thing?" His tone had turned suspicious and defensive.

Reuben half smiled. "Yes, Isaac, we are brothers. Each of us has our strengths. Your strengths and abilities are important here, helping Father with the farm and getting Erik ready for school. You are Father's right hand. I fear he will not last much longer." Reuben and Isaac looked out at the small figure hunched atop the wagon in the field.

"Yes, I know," said Isaac, his eyes misty.

"Father trusts you to keep what we have. He trusts me to expand upon what is already built and to start something new and different. We each have different talents."

"Are you trying to say that you are smarter than I am?" snapped Isaac, diverting his gaze from the far-off wagon back to Reuben, his voice combative.

Sighing, Reuben shook his head. "No, Isaac that is not what I meant at all."

The two brothers regarded each other warily. "Do you love me, Reuben?" Isaac's voice was harsh and sarcastic.

"I do love you, Isaac. You are my brother. But there are times I do not like you."

Blinking as he thought about the words, the larger man's mouth opened and shut several times. "Well, there are times I do not like you either."

"Wish me good luck, Isaac," asked Reuben, holding out his hand.

Isaac looked at Reuben's hand. Then, shoving his own into his pocket, he snarled darkly, "Good luck," immediately wheeling and walking away.

Standing and watching his older brother's back in retreat toward the farmhouse, the realization that the future of his family and their fortune rested on his shoulders hit him with full force. He found himself imagining the look on Isaac's face if he returned from America a failure.

He looked once more at the wagon out in the field. He loved his father. Ludwig was wise. He had built their enterprise from insignificant to one of the largest in East Prussia. Butchers and breeders regarded their cattle as second-to-none. Ludwig had added to the land and the herd, making improvements to the farm, adding on to their home, building barns, and increasing crops and hay. Reuben suddenly realized that of all of the brothers, he most resembled his father. The thought gave him courage. He took a deep breath and squared his shoulders, straining his eyes to the west trying to see a place he could not visualize nor imagine. He clenched his jaw and balled his hands into tight fists. *I can do this. I will do this, for my father and for my family.*

May 6, 1854

CHERRY CREEK

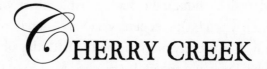

THE FIRST SEVERAL DAYS OF ZEB'S JOURNEY TO CHERRY Creek went smoothly. He followed Divide Creek west as it joined with other tributaries amassing increased current and flow velocity until it reached the Uncompahgre River. Turning his pack string north, he rode downstream to the confluence of the Gunnison. Before daylight the next morning, he had the pack string heading east and north up the Gunnison through rolling sage that turned to patchy aspen. He rode along the south rim of the Black Canyon, its rough jagged walls cascading hundreds of feet down to the silver ribbon of river that twisted through the tortured rock at the bottom of the chasm. The angry white rapids that roared in a rushing free fall down the steep gradient could be seen and heard, even at that distance. Zeb always marveled at the power of this unique piece of the mountains. Past the canyon, the high valley began to rise, the tree cover transitioning grudgingly to conifer as the river gradually dwindled to the tiniest of tributary creeks and disappeared into alpine springs on the high flanks of Monarch Pass.

He made it a point to keep his travel parallel but off actual trails, though he had a habit of stopping on Monarch when he infrequently had occasion to be on the summit. It was early morning on the fifth day of the trip when he, Buck and the mules reached the top of the pass. Veering north from the trail that they had been shadowing by several hundred yards, he rode into a small meadow. Letting the horse drag reins, he hobbled the mules, allowing the animals to graze the grass patches that poked through the spotty spring snow on the south side of the ridge. Sitting on a sun-warmed rock, he began to roll a smoke, taking in the sight of it all.

The craggy tips of glowing snowcapped peaks pointed their rocky fingers at an endless blue sky. Springs percolated on either side of the ridge. Rivulets of water augmented by snowmelt shimmered, the tiny wet surfaces fluttering in the steady westerly breeze. Zeb studied them as they swirled and winked with sunlight. He had always been fascinated with how, at certain high points, water on one side of the divide seemed to head toward the plains and water on the other side flowed in the opposite direction west toward the ocean, which he had never seen.

"Most confounding," he said to himself stroking his mustache. Clicking his cheek slightly, he gave a low whistle, and Buck trotted over from the edge of the meadow. The mustang waited patiently until Zeb col-

lected the mules. Then they were off, picking their way
downslope from the meadow, headed northeast.

The next day, Zeb made his way around the edges of
the western basin of South Park, ascended the treed
ridge known as Trout Pass, and stopped well within the
tree line on the east flank of the pass that overlooked
the broad expanse of high-country flatlands. He immediately spotted the light, bouncing tops of four wagons
still miles away to the northeast in the gentle rolling
sagebrush. Sitting astride Buck for a while in the timber,
still concealed, he watched the small wagon train carefully. This was Ute country. They were not as friendly
as the Arapahoe were. The light cloth tops of the wagons
were bright against the backdrop of gray-green sage and
Zeb was sure Indians had watched them for some time.
He had planned to turn due north to keep in tree cover
until he had to venture east into the open to cross the
great valley toward the final pass and the headwaters of
the North Fork of the South Platte.

He sighed, his eyes on the distant wagons the whole
time. *Damn fools. Gonna get themselves killed sure
enough.* Turning in the saddle, he apologized to the
mules, "Okay, we are going to meet some white folks. I
know you don't see many, so behave."

It was late afternoon when his trail intersected with
that of the small band of wagons. All four were Prairie
Schooners, slightly lighter and smaller than Conestogas.
The lead wagon reined in when they saw him. The driver
was flanked by a rotund woman with a soiled white lace
sunbonnet tied snugly around her double chin. As Zeb

approached, the man stood with an antiquated musket in his hands. "No need for that, pilgrim," Zeb called out. Hesitating, the man relaxed and sat down, placing the butt of the old rifle on the floorboards of the driving seat.

Riding up to the side of the wagon on the driver's right to make it more awkward to pick up and swing the musket, he nodded at the couple. "Howdy."

Rising in the saddle, he peered down at the three wagons stretched out behind. Each of them rumbled to a stop as they came up behind the lead wagon. The couples in the other wagons, all similarly dressed, were craning their necks curiously at Zeb. Peeking from behind one of the drivers were the small, pale faces of little children. The driver just ten feet from him was younger and smooth-shaven. He fidgeted, unsure what to make of Zeb's silence.

"We are Mennonites," he eventually offered. "I'm John and this is my wife, Norma. We're headed to the west part of the Kansas Territory from the Oklahoma Country."

Zeb's thumb and forefinger played at one edge of his mustache. "That's quite a ways."

Again, there was silence.

John glanced to his wife and then back at Zeb. "We're aiming for the plateau country. Supposed to be good soil there. How far, ya reckon?"

"About six weeks in those," replied Zeb, gesturing at the wagons. "Pending weather. Winter ain't quite done yet. You might be there about June, maybe July. Going to be awful dry in the plateau country that time of year."

"You're the first man we've seen since we come over the pass from Bent's Fort."

Detecting a slight movement behind John and Norma in the interior shadows of the wagon, he shifted his gaze to John. "It won't help none."

The couple cast quick looks at one another. "What won't help none?"

"Hidin' the young-uns in there under the goods." Zeb nodded his chin at the wagon.

The couple glanced at one another again; then Norma turned and called out behind her, "Okay children, you can come out." The freckled faces of two, very young, tow-headed boys appeared, their eyes wide with curiosity.

"Are you one of those mountain men?" asked Norma. Her voice was soft and timid, and her hands were clasped tightly in the lap of her long, gray skirt.

Zeb chuckled. "Nope, just Zeb." Looking back over his shoulder toward the higher country where afternoon clouds had begun to boil at the upper tree lines, he warned, "The Indians won't be none too happy to see you. This is Ute country." Noticing the look of fear cross Norma's face, he was sorry he had said anything, though he had ridden out of his way to tell them just that. *Ain't none of your business.*

"Where are you headed, Mister Zeb?" John asked.

"Cherry Creek, and the full name is Zebarriah Taylor."

John's eyebrows shot up. "Zebarriah Taylor? We've heard of you!" John's eyes traveled to the mules. "Quite a few folks are drifting into Cherry Creek. They might even change that Cherry Creek name to something else. Montana City or Denver City. Gonna sell them pelts?"

"I reckon so."

"We stocked up on provisions in Cherry Creek before we came this way. Ran into some people who came from back East. They was dressed mighty fine and seemed book smart. They told the fella in the mercantile that things from the west and leather and Injun keepsakes fetch high prices way back there."

He studied John's face. "Much obliged for the information but Cherry Creek's about all I can handle, and not for long."

John nodded his head.

"Good luck." Zeb dug one heel gently into Buck's side and the horse took a few steps.

"Damn," Zeb cursed to himself under his breath. He backed Buck up a few steps and the horse's haunches collided with the nose of the nearest mule, which set off some stamps of hooves and brays.

Zeb craned around. "Easy, boys," he said sharply.

"If I was you folks, I'd turn around back to the flats—though I venture there's not much chance of that. If you mean to push on, you might want to turn north here."

Zeb raised his arm, pointing to the white peaks of the Mosquito Mountains to the north of the great sage flat. "There's a pass there called Hoosier. Better trail for them big rigs and you can follow that down the other side along the Blue River. There's a small settlement there called Dillon. You can restock, and if you still have the notion to head west, get directions for the National

Trail over to the Colorado River. There will be a few set-
tlers along the river if you need help. Though, if I was
you, I'd find me a place along the Blue further down.
Good dirt and plenty of water. The further west you go,
the less friendly the Indians. They don't take kindly to
that 1850 Treaty being broken. You might think about
trading that thing..." Zeb nodded at John's musket, "...
for one of these," he raised the Sharps slightly. "Get you
five to six more shots a minute with this breech. Could
be handy."

John smiled. "We will pray on your advice. Thank you.
God bless you."

Cantering past the other three wagons, Zeb pointed
Buck toward the bottom of Kenosha Pass, which rose
steeply and suddenly from the valley floor, like a giant
slice in the tall, rugged skyline on the east side of South
Park. Except for the much lower Pine Ridge at the eastern edge of the mountains, this was the last big mountain
barrier before the Great Plains and Cherry Creek.

Thinking about the trail he would take north along
the Front Range to Cherry Creek, he decided that once
on the back side of Pine Ridge, he'd get out to the edge
of the timberline in the foothills and then stick to the
hogbacks.

He camped at the western toe of the pass that night.
By the next afternoon, he was on the east side of
Kenosha, starting down the headwaters of the South
Platte's north fork. He stayed at least a quarter-mile
from the creek as it grew to a river — more when he
had the opportunity. He began to see occasional riders.

There were several small groups of wagons, one headed south and one west, upstream, in the same direction as the Mennonites. Here and there in the far distance, Zeb could see the outlines of homes, and he heard the occasional guttural calls of cattle, none of which had been there nine years ago.

Evening was closing fast on the day as he followed the river as it sliced through the ponderosa, fir and granite of Pine Ridge. Distant glimpses of the broad gold of the plains swathed in sunset pink and purple began to flash through the canyon.

The next morning, he broke into the scattered timber of the last of the foothills above the flat lands. Buildings and ranch houses had begun to get more plentiful. He began to see one or two every hour. He stayed on higher ground to keep better vantage. By midday, he could make out the faint outlines of far-off clusters of buildings and tents. He reined in Buck, astounded. Though still a half day's ride away, he could see at least a hundred distant plumes of smoke rising from chimneys and campfires.

Hours later indigo was creeping into the eastern horizon, and the dark cobalt blue of twilight had begun to steal across the undulations of the plains that stretched eastward. Zeb was just a few miles out from the first cluster of buildings to the northeast. He could make out a camp of Arapahoe lodges, and a large village of Cheyenne tipis further north, their tips rising at the confluence of the South Platte and Cherry Creek. The

Indians did not bother him but Zeb wasn't keen on a ride into that many white people at night.

"It's a damn city," he complained to Buck. *Maybe I should just head up to the Arkansas.* Taking out his tobacco pouch, he crossed one leg over the saddle horn and pondered the matter as he slowly rolled a smoke, careful to shelter the loose tobacco leaves from the wind with his hand.

With the cigarette lit, Zeb leaned down and stroked Buck's shoulder. "Well, fella, we've come this far. Might as well ride the last bit in the morning. Besides, we need those fixins."

He made his fireless camp along some hogbacks, spreading his bedroll on the thin, eroded, red soil and gray, fractured shale between scattered sage, bitter brush and prickly pear cactus.

MORNING WARMTH FROM A BLAZING SPRING SUN bathed the settlement as Zeb, Buck and the laden mules cautiously entered the cluster of various types of structures. The changes over the nine years since his last visit were momentous. There were still tents, and disorganized, forlorn wooden structures but two mud tracks had evolved into two, short, dirt streets flanked by several wood buildings hazy with fine low-hanging dust from the bustle of carriages, wagons, horses and people. Several ladies dressed in finery with parasols strolled along wooden sidewalks in front of a brief line of shops and pointed to the windows. There was an air of excitement and energy and a continual stream of human noise that made Zeb uncomfortable, and Buck and the mules jittery.

"Like too many squirrels in a tree," he muttered to himself.

"Hey there, honey," a shrill voice called out to him from above. "You look like you've been out a long, long time. I like mustaches. Need some company?" Zeb glanced up at a pretty, young girl who leaned from the second-story window of a saloon. Clad only in a low-cut bright scarlet bodice, the white swells of the top half of her breasts bulged above the tight fabric. Laughing, she waved and blew him a kiss. Even from that distance, Zeb could see the heavy rouge on her cheeks. "Y'all come back and see me when you sell them pelts, trapper man."

Fixing his eyes back down the street, he grumbled to Buck, "Womenfolk. I prefer bears."

Leaning over, he asked a man in a brown silk suit with a matching string tie and top hat, "Ya know Gart's Mercantile? It's a tradin' place that used to be around here somewhere." Looking up without a word or a break in stride, he pointed his arm down the street, and crossed in front of Buck.

"Friendly fella, ain't he?" Zeb asked Buck. The mustang shook his head and snorted.

He reined in Buck at the next corner. Another lean, tall, buckskin-clad figure but with a bushy beard, was leaning against one of the uprights supporting the roof over the walkway. Pale blue eyes looked up squinting in recognition. A deep baritone voice boomed out. "Damn, it's been a coon's age."

Zeb smiled. "Jim? Jim Bridger?"

"Damned if I am. Still got that scalp under that coon-skin?"

Zeb chuckled. "I ain't parted with it yet."

"Looks like ya learned what me and Pierre taught ya when you was a pup, pilgrim. Headed down to get rid of those skins?"

"Yep, plan to trade off these pelts. Need some supplies but don't plan to stay long."

Chuckling, Jim reached into his leather shirt and pulled out a suede pouch that hung from his neck, took out a wad of chew, bit off a hearty chunk and offered it to Zeb. "Got in yesterday myself. And I'm leaving early morning. Headed toward the Northwest Territories. These mountains are gittin' way too crowded."

Zeb nodded. "I heard you found that new trail that bypasses South Pass on the Oregon Trail. Saves sixty-one miles, I'm told." Laughing, he added, "and there's talk they're fixing to name the new route Bridger Pass. You're getting to be right famous."

Leaning over, Jim spit down into the dust. "Them papers back East just love writin' up stories but I reckon there's a few folks that's heard of me."

"Did you sell pelts since you been down?"

"Yep, just yesterday. Sold the mules too. Seems it's been a hell of a good year for beaver. Damn skins stacked higher than a tall corral down at Gart's. I wasn't none too pleased with the price. But I got all the basics I need for the drift north, so no use crying. Want to have a shot of whiskey with me before I head out? We can catch up a tad. Did ya hear Pierre got kilt?"

Zeb absorbed the news for a moment. He had spent four seasons with the stocky, jovial Frenchman, Pierre. He'd been a good man and quiet too, which had suited Zeb.

"You don't say. How'd he go?"

"Damn fool Frenchie went out on the grasslands northeast of here. Convinced himself there were bigger beaver. Pawnee got him. That trapper LaBonte found him on his way up to the Laramie's."

"Well, I guess we all die someday."

Jim's head and shoulders shook with a silent laugh. "Yep."

Zeb looked down the street. "I best get to going. Maybe the price of these pelts has gone up since yesterday."

"Not likely. But I wish you luck. I plan on makin' camp outside of town tonight, mebbe over where Cherry Creek comes out of those cottonwoods east of here."

"Sounds better than a saloon."

"Well then, probably see ya round dark. Give a whistle when you come in. I'll be on the trail early mornin'."

Zeb smiled, "Yep," and continued down the street.

Finding himself in front of a square, partial brick, two-story building with a newly painted sign, *"Gart's Trading Company and Mercantile"* over the front door, he let out a low whistle. Nine years before, the trading post had been tents and a lowly, rambling, wooden structure in danger of collapse. Now just a portion of the old wood building and tent structure remained to one side.

Dismounting, he threw two loops of Buck's reins around the hitching post, waited for several people to scurry in and out of the door and then made his way into the mercantile. The interior was buzzing with activity. Closing his eyes, he breathed in the odor of new oiled leather, freshly milled tools and implements, gunpowder, candy and solvents. *One of the few things I do like about town.*

Walking over to a long counter on one side of the store his eyes were drawn by newer .44 and .45 caliber Colt Navy, Dragoon, Army and London revolvers in a display case. Brand-new Sharps, Springfield and Enfield rifles and muskets were displayed on pegs set into the wall. Kegs of powder, trays of paper cartridges for breechloaders like his, shot and Minié balls filled shelves. Two harried clerks tried their best to accommodate six customers. Zeb lingered by the pistols. They were all percussion, and, depending on the model, had cylinders that held either five or six shells. He had only seen them twice and had been astounded at how quickly they could fire. He looked down at the two old single-shot powder and ball Enfield pistols tucked in his belt, and sighed. *Well, we'll see what we get for them pelts. I'd sure like to have me one of these.*

At the opposite end of the counter, a burly red-haired man with a beard barked out orders with an Irish brogue. Walking over to him, the mountain man tapped him on the shoulder.

The man turned, a big smile flashing between the bushy red of his mustache and curly beard. "Zeb, I fig-

ured you were dead. It's been more than..." he thought
for a minute "...five years?"

"Closer to ten, Randy. Where's that brother of yours?"

Randy slapped Zeb on the back, almost staggering
him. "That damn scoundrel Mac is now our wagon master. He brings groups of fools west that want to trade
decent living for this godforsaken dust and dirt. Getting
to be more and more folks."

"Wagon trains? Where do they set out from?"

"St. Louis. How long's it been since you been back
there?"

Zeb racked his memory. "More than twenty years, I'll
bet."

"You ought to see that place now. When you went
through there as a cub after..." Randy hesitated, "...after
the farm was burned out, it weren't much more than fifteen thousand folks. Now Mac tells me they got more
than a hundred thousand and growing every day. If you
think this place is getting busy with three hundred white
folk and near one thousand Indians, that's turned into a
real damn city."

Zeb tried to imagine one hundred thousand people in
one place but couldn't. "Ran into Jim back on the street.
He said you were buying pelts."

Laughing, Randy slapped his leg. "And he told you
we weren't payin' much either, didn't he? Come on back
here; let me show you somethin'."

Following Randy's broad back through aisles of
goods, they came to two swinging doors, which Randy
pushed open. They were in the long low wooden and tent

portion of the original trading post. Every wall was stacked with pelts, almost floor-to-ceiling.

Turning to Zeb, Randy waved one arm around the space. He was suddenly serious. "See what I mean. Never seen this many pelts this early. Mac brings 'em back East on his return to St. Louis. He's gonna need some extra wagons this time."

Looking around, Zeb felt his heart sink. Randy read his mind. "As you can see, we can't pay too much this go-round. And I'm not even sure we'll get 'em all back to St. Louis in just one set of wagons."

Zeb was silent for a minute, twisting the tip of his mustache with his thumb and forefinger. "Well, what is your top dollar?"

"If they're good quality, and I'm quite sure yours are, we're paying twenty cents for each. But I'll be honest with you, Zeb, if you invest a couple months and head east, you can probably fetch four or five times that, particularly if you beat Mac back with this load. With the winter they had back there, he's not going to be here until later this month or thereabouts. Won't head back East with these 'til July or August. I figure he's somewhere in the Nebraska Territory right now headed this way."

Sweeping off his coonskin hat with one hand, Zeb ran his fingers from his forehead all the way through his hair. He put the hat back on. "Let me ponder it some."

"You do that, Zeb. If you want to trade 'em here, I'll be straight with you. But you can get a heap more money eastward. Told that to Jim, too but he was hellfire for headin' north."

ZEB COULD HEAR THE SOFT CRY OF LOONS AND SANDHILL cranes sifting through the twilight, echoing among the thick textured bark of the cottonwoods. Spotting the lonely, intermittent flicker of Jim's small campfire, he urged Buck purposely toward it.

He whistled the warbling notes of the whippoorwill. An identical whistle drifted back toward him, muted by the trees. As he approached the fire, he saw Jim stretched out, propped on an elbow, one knee in the air. He moved a small skillet back and forth in the flames and the distinct aroma of fresh coffee wafted from the small tin pot propped at the edge of the flames. Both of Jim's rifles leaned on his bedroll.

Zeb nodded at the long guns. "Mighty jumpy, ain't ya?"

Looking up from the dinner preparation, his friend smiled. "I'm always jumpy when there's lotsa folks running around."

Zeb hobbled Buck, set out string lines between two tree trunks and tied off the mules giving them plenty of room to move up and down the rope and graze. He patted one on the rump. "Sorry fellas, can't take them saddles off tonight."

Dinner was two fresh trout and a sizable chunk of venison haunch Jim had evidently roasted on a spit for several hours.

"You know Kit got hurt a few years back," commented Zeb, taking a sip of coffee. It burned his tongue but it tasted better than anything he had brewed in months. "Damn, you always did make the best coffee in the Rockies—but how do you carry that infernal kettle around?"

Squatting, Jim poured himself another cup of the thick dark brew and looked at Zeb with a somber expression. "I heard about Kit. He was huntin' with you when that horse spooked, wasn't he?"

"Sure was. Damned mare rolled over him twice. Stomped him up bad. That was five years ago and he's not doin' well yet."

"Bad luck," Jim replied. "I don't demand much, old friend. Good pelts, no people, good meat, my women from time to time," Jim held up the pot, "and great coffee." He laughed. "Besides, I keep my loose stuff and valuables in it. Don't take no extra space. Did you see Randy?"

Picking up a twig, Zeb threw it into the fire. "Yep, I did indeed. Sure enough, he can't pay anything near what these skins are worth. I got nearly nine months in these bundles."

"Did he tell you about them higher prices being fetched back East?"

"Yep. But that's too much ride back and forth. It's more than a month easy, and partly across Pawnee and Kiowa lands with a string of slowpoke mules. Then I get there and have to put up with a big city, full of green-horns and people, sounds like to me."

Jim was quiet. The first crickets of the season had begun their melodic rasps. Mingling with the invisible rushing sound of Cherry Creek, their chirps were carried westward to the dark silhouettes of the Rockies by wisps of eastern air wafting off the plains.

Leaning his head back, Zeb looked up at the sky through the treetops. The gentle wave of their budded branches imparted action to countless pinpoints of stars that hung suspended in an inky void of night sky.

"Well, hellfire," Jim said. "If you really can get four or five times more, what else ya got to do? Gonna be runoff up high. Trapping won't be good 'til August or September anyway. Besides, the way I figure, gittin' that much money for them pelts would be equal to two or three years trappin' if ya just sold 'em here." Pausing, he stared intently at Zeb. "You can't run away from that past of yours back there forever, old friend. Sometimes you need to go back, face it and be done with it."

"Maybe so." Zeb grew silent, weighing Jim's words. He looked intently at his friend, "How come you chose a different course?"

Staring into the fire, Jim spread the embers with his knife. "Zeb, we may think alike but we're different. We both like the high country, don't much care for people, get along okay with most Indians, and are happy alone, just us and the trees. I guess ya heard the wife died. That's the second wife I have lost. Got hitched again to Wakalalie's daughter around 1850, a year after I last saw your ugly scar face. Sent some of the young-uns back East to school. My papooses are gonna be smart and proper."

Jim wiped the blade on the top of his leggings, lay down on his elbow and stretched out. "Tell ya the truth, Zeb, I got anxious feet. I always got to see new places. Those Northwest Territories and what they call Montana and that Oregon place and hell, maybe even that big ocean. I just got to see it. You like space too but you like where you're at. You built four cabins. I never even built one. I've made me a lean-to when I have to—stayed for spells with my wives in their tipis—and I drop down low for the winter. We're just different."

There was a long silence as Zeb contemplated the other man's words. "I guess it might be like three years of trapping all rolled into one. Probably wind up with enough supplies to not come down for a good long spell."

"Maybe, and if you can get them ghosts of yours handled, it just might be you'll shoot two rabbits with one bullet."

Lying back into the grass, Zeb clasped his hands behind his neck, and stared at the sky. Turning his head slightly, he watched the dim form of Buck as his muzzle routed tender green grass shoots on the sun side of a big cottonwood. He questioned the gelding silently, *Up for a long ride, boy?*

Turning back to Jim, he raised himself up on one fore-arm. "Those're good thoughts, Jim. I reckon I just might head St. Louis way in the morning."

Zeb chuckled to himself when there was no response other than a deep snore from his longtime but rarely seen friend.

June 7, 1854

MORE THAN TWO THOUSAND MILES EAST OF THE LODGE smoke curling from the tipis near Cherry Creek, the first light of the new day was filtering through the sheer silk curtains pulled across the windows in an elegant hotel suite. Muffled by glass and fabric, the sounds of New York City echoed up from the street between urban canyon walls of brick. Inga Bjorne had been awake for hours, staring at the window, her long blonde hair tangled from the night.

She could smell his sweat and their sex on her naked, tall and well-proportioned body. She did not stir for fear of waking the portly form that snored loudly on the opposite side of the bed. Moving her eyes slowly, she took in the room. An expensive great coat and silk top hat hung from a finely crafted coatrack in one corner. Glowing in the morning light, the delicately textured walls blended tastefully into the mahogany trim and baseboard. Mahogany wainscot accented two walls, and a large bear's paw clawfoot tub sat next to the half-ajar door of the water closet. Inga cast a longing glance at the bath. Closing her eyes, she took a deep breath focusing on making her escape without having to endure his touch again. *Once was quite enough, thank you.*

First, I shall get my twenty dollars. Then, when he most certainly asks me to have breakfast with him, I shall tell him my other job interferes. I should be able to get out of here by eight. Thank God, I don't do this full time.

Opening her eyes, she fixed her stare above her, following the design of the ornately scrolled ceiling tile. Clenching her jaw, she fought a momentary stab of revulsion. *A girl has to do what a girl has to do.*

She forced herself to look ahead to the evening at the Carriage Restaurant and Bar, which catered to successful businessmen on West 42nd Street. The wages were terrible. But the sway of her lithe, curvy hips and the fluttering of long eyelashes over her big blue eyes always generated enormous tips. It was also the perfect place to choose, study and entice the occasional customer for her secondary avocation. Without stirring her head, her eyes shifted sideways to the client of the previous evening.

His name? She tried to remember but couldn't. The silk sheets mounded over the portly form stirred with his last gasp of sleep apnea. He reached a meaty hand behind him, groping for her. Inga glided from the bed. Opening his eyes, he partially rolled over, catching her glance at the tub.

"You take a bath, girl. Then we can have some more fun and I'll buy you breakfast."

Turning to him, Inga forced a smile, "Thank you but I have errands. I must get back to my flat and get ready for my job this evening. This is the summer traveling season. It is very busy. I shall bathe at home."

The man's eyes narrowed. "You said twenty dollars gold for the entire night."

Inga had begun to dress. Slipping on her under drawers, then her chemise and petticoats, she turned to him, fluttering her eyelids in feigned innocence and smiling radiantly. "So I did, and as you can see," she said, gesturing at the window, "night has come and gone. I very much enjoyed your company. Do you have a card? I would be delighted to see you again when you are next in New York." Her oblique praise had the intended effect.

The man grunted, then chuckled. Sitting upright in the bed, his large belly forming creases in the sheets as they hung around his midsection, he reached over to the bed stand, took a twenty-dollar gold piece and several silver dollars from his money pouch and flipped them on the bed in Inga's direction. He rummaged in the pocket of his pants, draped over a chair next to the bed, then held out his hand with his card, grabbing Inga's wrist when she reached for it. She slipped deftly away, and forced a covering laugh, glancing quickly at the card. *John Altimer, Chairman, First National Bank of St. Louis.*

"Thank you." She shimmied into her blouse. The banker was watching her every sinewy move, occasionally running his tongue across his upper lips.

"Inga," he said slowly, "I am well acquainted with the mayor."

"The mayor?"

"Yes. The new Mayor of New York, Ferdinando Wood." There was a moment of silence. "You are far too beautiful a woman to be engaged in this line of work. You have no need to trounce yourself around 'til the wee hours at the bar, however elegant it might be."

Taking a moment to run her hands down the front of her thighs, she smoothed out the ripples in her pleated wool skirt. Reaching into her reticule, she extracted a silver-handled hairbrush, and walked to the mirror by the tub. She began slowly brushing the tangles from her long golden locks.

She studied the man's reflected figure behind her in the mirror. *Why not?* Without facing him, and careful to keep her voice nonchalant, she said, "I don't see the connection."

Reclining down to his side, he propped his head up with one hand. "I know the mayor has an opening or two on the mansion staff. It is very well organized. The living quarters are quite deluxe and many important people come and go." He paused. "Far more than at the restaurant."

Inga continued to look at him via the mirror, her mind flashing back over the previous eight years. Her grip on the brush tightening, she recalled her shock at the age of eleven when her parents died after their fishing boat capsized in the frigid waters of the Norwegian fiord, the leer on her uncle's face as he grabbed her arm at the funeral, and his intoxicated words, "It is just you and me now, my dear niece. Uncle will take care of you."

Her uncle had taken control of her parent's cottage. It overlooked the village perched on rugged rocky walls, which descended into the deep blue waters of the fiord. She had loved that house. Her uncle sold it for a pittance and then took her to New York, where they lived in a dirty one-bedroom flat.

Brushing her hair more slowly, her chest constricted at the memory of his unwavering gaze, which followed her every move. When she was thirteen years old, he waited for her to fall asleep one night, crept to the couch she used as her bed, and brutally took her, despite her desperate struggle and screams of pain. She had endured his vulgar touch several more times, as she waited for the right opportunity to escape with her few meager possessions. His fat, usually inebriated frame never left the apartment.

Then she had met a much older doctor in the course of her job as a hotel maid. The physician thought her attractive, and with the rationalization that she was no longer a virgin anyway, she had traded two hours of favors with him for a healthy dose of a strong sleeping potion. "Use this sparingly," the doctor had warned. "It is a very powerful drug. Too much could be dangerous." Several nights later, leaving his fourth glass of bourbon half-full and unattended, her uncle stumbled to the communal water closet at the end of the hall. Inga poured the entirety of the vial into the drink. When she was certain he would not wake, she bundled her few clothes and the treasured silver-handled hairbrush she had been given by her father in a tattered blanket and stole into the city night. In a stroke of luck, she met up with some older women, Mary, Dolly and Lizbeth, whom she had met at the hotel. Their fulltime employment as ladies of the night had not bothered her. She was thankful to share their apartment.

The bank chairman's voice cut through her reverie. "Is there something wrong?"

Taking a moment to compose herself, she swiveled slowly to face the banker. "I assume you will expect something in return."

He half-smiled. "I am in town infrequently and always on business. An occasional night when I am in New York is all I ask. At no charge, of course."

With her most demure air, Inga responded, "I would be honored, John, to make such an arrangement if I could obtain a position with the mayor."

"How do I reach you? What is your address?"

"You can find me at the restaurant each afternoon and evening. I work seven days a week," replied Inga, carefully putting away the brush. She began to don her coat.

"Now, girl, give me a kiss before you go and I shall be in touch. I am seeing the mayor this afternoon. My train leaves this evening, and if I have news I shall drop by the bar."

With a provocative twist to her hips, Inga stepped over to the bed, kissing him with pretend passion. He reached for her but she stood up. "I must go. I very much enjoyed our time together. Please do travel safely, John."

Making her way through the large marble lobby, she felt the recognition in the stares of several of the hotel staff. *That used to be me, staring.* She held her head high, looking straight ahead. Out on the street, she walked for a block and then, leaning a shoulder against a building at a busy corner, she breathed deeply, exhaling with a half-sob. Wiping the tears from beneath her eyes with long fingertips, she squared her shoulders and stood erect. *A girl has to do what a girl has to do. I need a bath.*

Inga shook off her disappointment when the banker failed to appear at the restaurant. She had received two offers from well-to-do businessmen that evening and politely declined each of them, taking comfort in this support of her view that her "second job" was simply the occasional necessary financial supplement.

It was late, almost ten, and the restaurant was closing, though the bar would stay open for several more hours. Business was slow but Inga was in no hurry to return to the incessant gossip that always filled the crowded flat she shared with the three older women. She had a twenty-six-block walk. While the restaurant was located in a better area of the city, the last ten blocks of her nightly commute were through more seamy neighborhoods. Putting on her coat, she checked her bag for the location of the six-inch fishing knife she carried and knew how to use, thanks to her uncle's tutelage. She was ready to leave when a smartly uniformed courier strode through the entrance of the bar holding an envelope in one hand.

He looked around carefully. His eyes came to rest on Inga, and without hesitation he walked over to her. "Is your name Inga Bjorne?"

Inga felt her eyes widen. "Bjorne. Yes, yes it is."

"I am to deliver a personal message to you from the Mayor of New York," he said extending the wax-sealed envelope with a flourish. The patrons near Inga who had overheard the short conversation stopped their chatter, turning their attention to the scene. Glancing around, she took the message, shoving it into her carry bag. "Thank you," she said.

The courier nodded. "The courtesy of your appearance tomorrow at four in the afternoon is requested by the mayor." The man turned smartly and left the bar. As the door shut behind him, Inga glimpsed a gleaming black carriage with the flag and seal of the City of New York on the street.

She stood still for a moment, realizing that many eyes were still upon her. Shaking her hair defiantly, she waved one hand, "Have a wonderful evening, everyone." Walking past the maître d,' she squeezed his arm. "I will see you tomorrow, Jack."

"Have a nice night, Inga," he said, immediately returning his attention to several customers about to pay their tab.

Inga could feel the anticipation boiling in her chest. She walked several blocks. A few blocks further would be the end of the new oil streetlamps installed on this edge of the Manhattan area. Their light would give way to the darker shadows of street posts with candle boxes. She could not wait. Standing under a streetlight, she pulled out the envelope. Her trembling fingers carefully opened the heavy, rich, textured linen. The scroll was artistically applied with the finest of thick tip quills.

His excellency, the honorable Mayor of New York, Ferdinando Wood, requests your presence for an interview before the mayor and Chief of Staff of Gracie Mansion concerning potential employment on the mansion staff at 4:00 p.m., the eighth of June, year of our Lord, eighteen hundred and fifty-four.

The letter was signed with the ostentatious signature of the mayor himself above another stamped wax seal. Walking briskly, the letter still in her hands, her mind raced. *Whatever will I wear?*

CHAPTER

5

November 18, 1854

REBECCA

THREE THOUSAND MILES EAST OF THE FRENETIC ACTIV-
ity of New York City, across the endless expanse of
rolling swells of the Atlantic, the early winter rain beat
with a soft drum-like cadence on the glass of the great
bay window. The drops turned to thin, streaming sheets
of water, which cascaded in haphazard fashion down diamond shapes of glass. The runoff slowed and welled
above the finely scrolled diagonal oak mullion, distorting
the image of large brick and stone row houses that
grandly lined the opposite side of the cobbled street.

Drawing her shawl more tightly around her shoulders,
Rebecca Marx gave a petulant shake to her long, dark,
almost-black hair, staring at her reflection in the window. The gentle glow of hissing gas lamps backlit and
softened her wide brown eyes set perfectly above high
cheekbones and slender, beautifully curved figure. Her
hair flowed in slight waves over proud square shoulders
above a petite waist.

"Dreary," she said to the image in the windowpanes. "A dreary day. How fitting for the day I have made the decision to temporarily leave London."

On the street below the window, a bobby, immaculately uniformed even with his oiled slicker, was making his way along the drenched cobblestones, his sodden steps splashing water in droplets that glistened in the flickering sheen of the oil flames from the streetlight boxes.

Sighing, she spoke in a whisper to the empty space next to her reflection in the glass, "Father, you have left us in such a mess. I know you did not intend to. If only you would have listened to me. We did not need those three entire cargos of spices. Now the family honor is at stake and I am to chase halfway around the world, waste the better part of a year and consort with uncivilized peasants."

Feeling the familiar flush of inner anger creeping up her cheeks, she looked up at the ceiling, stomping her bare foot on the shiny walnut parquet floor. *If you only knew. Whatever possessed you to invest in an asset you have never seen in a country that you have barely visited?*

Closing her eyes, she raised a graceful hand, pressing small, delicate fingers to her forehead and slowly rubbed the smooth skin above her eyebrows. *Or did you know? Did you know, Father?*

No image of her father appeared next to hers in the window. There were no answers. All was unknown. The pout of the lips of the woman in front of her turned into a smile. *We shall see if your beauty and wit are as useful across the sea as they are here in England.*

Her mother, Elizabeth, puttered into her room, clucking and mumbling to herself. "Rebecca, this will be such a long, dangerous journey. You don't have to go, daughter. We are not so badly off."

Rebecca walked slowly to her mother. Wrapping her arms around her frail bent body, she gave her a gentle kiss on the forehead and stood back, keeping both hands on her mother's trembling arms.

"Mother, I have made my decision. It will take two months to prepare for a journey of this magnitude. I will have our solicitor make arrangements for me to sail in January." She sighed. "Our condition is unfortunately precarious. Remember, I assisted Father for many years with the business and have overseen it since he passed. His investment in America may likely be our only salvation."

Should I share my extreme doubt that anything will come of this trip or the deed, map and mysterious instructions in Father's will? Her mother's lower lip was quivering and mist was filming in her eyes. Rebecca decided to say nothing.

"It will be fine, Mum." Her mother half smiled at this infrequent endearment. "We shall be back on our feet. And I won't be gone for more than seven or eight months." She patted her mother's hands. "I must get some things out of Father's study. Why don't you go down and have Eve and Sally get supper ready?"

Waiting until she was sure Elizabeth was downstairs, she strode out of the bedroom glancing down from the balcony overlooking a portion of the living room and the entry foyer. Through the sculpted luster of the balusters of the balcony rail, she could see her mother gesturing to their servants, a man, a woman and their daughter, now in her late teens. They were Aborigines.

They had returned with her father from Australia sixteen years prior. *Much to Mother's horror!* Rebecca remembered, smiling to herself. She had taken her father's side against her mother's argument that "this sort of staff was highly improper."

Though they barely spoke, seemed to know little English and appeared disinclined to learn, they were loyal, respectful, hard workers. Rebecca and her father never could pronounce their names. Over the years, they had simply become Adam, Eve and Sally. Sally was nineteen, just a few years younger than Rebecca was and they had developed a mostly silent bond. It was Sally who drew Rebecca's baths, sometimes helped her dress and cleaned her bedroom. Her father had given them their freedom several years before he passed on but they had chosen to stay.

Moving briskly down the hall, she noticed Adam's gaze following her, a somber look on his face. Rebecca had always felt Adam had a strange prideful power, something she could not quite define. Many times over the years, Rebecca had come down the stairs without voicing her need of this or that, only to find Adam at the foot of the last step or in the kitchen, hand outstretched with the exact item she had come to gather.

When she had commented to her father after one such incident, he had chuckled. "I have noticed it too. Coming across the Pacific from Australia, we sighted only three other ships. In each instance, Adam had come to me hours before the watch in the crow's nest spotted sails and pointed in the exact direction the other vessels eventually appeared. At first, I thought he was daft."

Rebecca continued to the end of the open-faced hallway, conscious of the slight swishing sounds her slippers and silk robe made as she walked. Grasping both brass knobs of two great six-paneled oak French doors at the end of the balcony corridor, she swung them open. She stood for a minute enjoying the nostalgia of the still present scent of her father and his pipes. Facing the enormous, intricate oak desk squarely in the center of the study, her eyes roved over the two walls of handcrafted bookshelves that were overflowing with books and manuscripts from every corner of the world, and the red ink ledgers of their business.

Her gaze shifted to the wall that was adorned with paintings of her father, his ships and his travels.

"Your life's history," she whispered, walking over to her favorite. Reaching up with two fingers she very gently touched the textured oil image of the well-proportioned, though not overly tall, figure who looked out to sea, one leg bent, leather boot raised and perched on the bowsprit half-wall of his favorite schooner, the sailing ship *Trader*.

Turning from the portrait, she sat in the rich, oversized, brown leather chair that would have dwarfed most desks. Resting her elbows on the writing surface, she lowered her forehead to her palms. *Father, how could you?* Staring blankly at the window she recalled the sudden bewildering loss of his three-ship fleet, precipitated by the financial disaster of the three simultaneously unsalable cargoes of East India spices. That unanticipated shock had begun the precipitous decline in his health that shortly thereafter led to his death.

Rebecca shook her head. "Enough," she whispered fiercely. *Things are what they are, and I must do what I must do. There is no other way.*

Glancing quickly at the doorway to make sure no one was there, she dropped to one knee between the desk and the chair. Feeling underneath the bottom right cabinet, she found and pushed a hidden wooden lever and slid out a concealed drawer. Only she and her father knew of this hiding place.

Reaching down, she pulled out her father's will and a large piece of tattered parchment that that had been folded down to about one-third of a yard square. Inside the folds of the heavy paper was another parchment: "*Land deed to Henry Thomas Marx of Land Grant by Ferdinand, King of Spain.*" Attached to the deed was a document, in Spanish, very formal in appearance, with the impressive seal of the Spanish Crown in wax at the bottom.

Feeling the rough texture of the paper against her fingertips, she recalled the words of their solicitor when they were alone after the reading of the will; "Milady Marx, I know the family is a bit short on cash. I held Mister Marx in high regard. Perhaps I can assist you and your mother by waiving my fees in return for...," he had paused, gazing into space in pretended contemplation, "...for something. Perhaps the map and deed to the American lands? They are so far away and so desolate."

To this day, Rebecca wondered why she had responded so quickly as she did, "Why, thank you, Barrister, for your very kind offer but I feel bound by my father's wishes." She smiled to herself. *I rejected that suggestion in even less time than I refused his dinner invitation.*

She had dismissed the solicitor's urging to trade expenses for the deed. *He was just being noble*, she had thought but *then again...*her father's last words ran through her memory as her fingertips traced the heavy, textured paper.

Shaking her head, she crouched behind the desk, combing through the will until she came to page fourteen:

"I direct that upon my death, my daughter, REBECCA ELIZABETH MARX, be given this map and associated deed and title to that certain one thousand hectares of land owned pursuant to the attached United States deed, and associated Land Grant of the Spanish crown, and situated approximately at latitude 38°46' north, longitude 107°41' west, east and south of the Uncompahgre River in the southwestern portion of the Kansas Territories of the United States of America, also known as the Colorado District. I further direct my daughter REBECCA ELIZABETH MARX to venture to such lands within three years of my death to explore, ascertain and make best use of the value of such land and its resources, above and below the earth's surface, for the health, welfare and benefit of all descendants named in this will."

Reading the words again, *such land and its resources, above and below the earth's surfaces*, she pursed her lips and looked up at the painting of the *Trader*.

Staring at the figure that stood on the bow of the ship in colored oil, she whispered, "Father, I am sure this is a wild goose chase. Know this, I will abide by your wishes and directives because it is your will, I cherish you and we have little choice. I shall not remain in that unfit out-back with Yankee rebels one minute longer than necessary, nor shall I venture one inch beyond St. Louis. I will do what I must and see what I can to convert this forsaken piece of earth into a few pounds for the family, and then I shall return."

December 22, 1854

JOHANNES

SEVEN HUNDRED SEVENTY TWO MILES SOUTHWEST OF the stately row of houses of London's upper end neighborhoods, the villa perched atop a rocky bluff overlooking a restless blue-green sea. The coarse golden beach at the base of the stones soaked up the white foam of frothy swells crashing on the edge of the sand along the Danish coast. A cool salt breeze fluttered the villa's bedroom curtains, the soft cream taffeta caressing the windowsill. Inside, a huge canopied Danish walnut bed and two fine Belgian walnut armoires, his and hers, nestled against either wall. An expensive Norwegian dresser served as an oak pedestal for a dainty white doily that centered a tall pewter candleholder. A solitary thin candle flickered in the air currents from the open window.

Johannes Svenson's tall, thin, naked body was draped over an equally lanky female form. The woman's eyes were closed, her lips slightly parted. Her chest was rising and falling rapidly, the white creamy skin of her thighs quivering and her body trembling from their love-making of just minutes before.

Moving his fingertips lightly, he traced the perfect curve of her hips, slowly continuing his hands' appreciative wanderings down her inner thighs. "Ah, that was wonderful," he whispered in her ear.

Opening her eyes, she turned a beautiful porcelain face to him, large blue eyes staring back into his. A satiated grin spread from the corners of her mouth. Drawing his head down with a delicate hand, she kissed him passionately.

"Oh, Johannes. I have never been touched like that. Eleven years of marriage and I realize that I have never been made love to before."

Cupping his hand around her breast, his thumbs lightly stroked her erect nipple. "I want to see more of you, my sweet Bente, much more."

They began to embrace, the woman wrapping her lithe legs around his hips. Downstairs, a door slammed. They froze.

Pushing on Johannes' chest, her voice frantic, she whispered, "Quick! Your clothes!"

"Put your ring back on!" he hissed back, vaulting from the bed and searching frantically for his trousers among their combined garments scattered around the floor. "Is there another way out?"

She was sitting up, the sheets fearfully clutched to her bosom, her mouth agape.

Reaching out, he shook her shoulder, "Is there another way out?"

"No!" she said in a breaking voice. There were tears in her eyes.

Studying the bed, he realized it was too high to conceal him. *There must be another place. This will not be the first time I have hidden and awaited a later chance to escape an awkward situation.*

He had his pants partially buttoned, only one arm through the sleeve in his open shirt, when the locked bedroom door shuddered. Bente stared at him, her face whiter than the crumpled sheets, mouthing words without sound. Again, the door shook. The wood in the doorframe splintered and the door crashed open. Two of the king's guards stepped in, broadswords drawn, the Seal of the Danish Crown on their breastplates. Behind them, standing with clenched fists at his side was Bente's husband, the First Minister of Denmark—a short, wiry man wearing a monocle attached by a thin gold chain to his lapel. His goatee was perfectly trimmed and jewels bedazzled his wrists and fingers.

"What's this?" he squealed, his hands gesturing wildly between the two of them.

Johannes began to laugh.

"What's so funny?" demanded the cuckold. His monocle fell out of his eye and dangled around one knee.

Johannes's laugh deepened.

"Answer me, you scoundrel!"

The king's guards looked at one another uneasily. Johannes thought a hint of a smile might be playing at the corners of their mouths. Catching his breath, "I can see, sir, why after eleven years of marriage, your wife has never been satisfied."

The minister's face turned purple. "Take him away!" he sputtered. With a thin, vicious leer, he turned his attention to his wife, still in the bed. "I will deal with you later."

JOHANNES WAS GRIMY AND TIRED. HIS CLOTHES WERE tattered from slightly more than two weeks of solitary confinement in a filthy cell deep in the bowels of the royal castle. Creaking heavily, the door of the dark, tiny cubicle opened. Grabbing him roughly, four guards dragged him in chains from the dungeon up five levels of the castle to the courtroom of the Royal Magistrate.

The magistrate was a rotund man with puffy cheeks not hidden at all by his careful attempts to arrange the locks of his silver-powdered wig. His oversized black robe was more a blanket than a piece of clothing. His chest barely cleared the elevated bench at which he sat. Glancing up from papers in front of him, Johannes noticed a flit of surprise sweep across his features; his eyes flickering in quickly masked recognition. Johannes stared directly back at him.

Johannes knew exactly what was on the magistrate's mind. The two of them had seen and talked with one another during a number of clandestine evenings in the lascivious brothels of East Copenhagen. The magistrate was married.

Clearing his throat, the judge gazed with feigned intensity at his documents.

"Johannes Svenson?"

"Yes," responded Johannes.

"Yes, your honor," came the correction from the bench.

"Excuse me. Yes, your honor," said Johannes.

"You were caught red-handed consorting with the wife of the First Minister, Bente Oslo. Is this true?"

Johannes answered simply, "Yes, your honor."

The magistrate looked down again at his papers. "What do you have to say for yourself?"

"She is a very beautiful woman," said Johannes.

The magistrate looked at him sharply, amusement apparent in the twitch of his mouth. "She is that. You do know that sleeping with another man's wife is a crime?"

"Yes, your honor."

"You know also that this crime is punishable in a number of ways. We can decide to make certain physical changes to your person to ensure that you never make such an error again."

Johannes suddenly felt clammy. His knees trembled and he realized he was swaying.

"The court could sentence you to ten years hard labor," said the magistrate.

"Yes, your honor."

"Or the court could do both."

"Yes, your honor."

"There is one other measure available to the court. I see here you have a distinguished record as an officer in the king's heavy cavalry."

Johannes said nothing.

"Twice awarded the Cross of Merit, correct?"

"Yes, your honor," answered Johannes.

Leaning back into the high purple velour of his chair, the judge clasped his hands across his protruding belly, regarding Johannes studiously.

A minute went by, then two. Suddenly his portly frame straightened. Picking up a quill, he dipped it in ink and began writing furiously, from time to time pausing and glancing at Johannes. *Damn, he is writing out his order.*

Placing the quill down, the judge returned his gaze to Johannes. "In view of your past service to Denmark and the heroism you have shown in defense of the kingdom, I will not order you incarcerated or castrated. You are, however, hereby exiled. You are never to set foot on Danish soil again or you will be subject to arrest and both of the alternative punishments. Is that understood?"

"Yes, your honor."

"As one other condition of this sentencing, you will converse with no one concerning this case or any related matter, ever. You will talk to no one about anything until you are out of the country, and you will have no contact with any public official, any relative of any official, the royal family or ministry of the kingdom at any time in the future. Is that understood?"

"Yes, your honor."

Nodding to one of the six ax-wielding guards who stood at attention on either side of the great doors in the courtroom, the judge barked his orders, "Captain of the guard, take the prisoner to the first available sea transportation to a non-Danish destination. He is not to leave your sight. He is not to speak to anyone. You are not to return until the ship has disappeared on the horizon. Is that clear?"

The captain of the guard clicked his heels and stood at attention. The magistrate looked solemnly at Johannes. His features were stern but Johannes saw one eye dip in a slight wink.

"That is all, Captain Svenson."

January 8, 1855

*T*HE WINDS OF FATE

THE SUN WAS SLIPPING INTO THE WEST AS THE SMALL, enclosed prison wagon rumbled through the streets of the city. Johannes had been denied his request for a bath and clean clothes by the captain of the guard. Swaying with the rock of the wooden wagon, each hand clenched around a bar of one of the tiny apertures, he peered out at the throngs on the sidewalk. The day was over and people hurried home or to taverns, shops and bakeries, glancing at him curiously. *It is highly unlikely that I will ever see these streets or this country again.*

It's been good to me, overall, he mused, absorbing the jolt as the wagon wheels bumped over potholes in the road. *But perhaps it is time to move on. America. The New World. A land with no kings or royalty.* He would need money for passage. "I am certainly glad they didn't check the heels of my boots," Johannes snorted to the unhearing people scurrying along the streets. "Idiots."

Staring absently at the passing storefronts, Johannes thought back over his years in Denmark. His mother had died when he was five, a victim of the great cholera outbreak of the 1830s. She had been buried with thousands of others in a mass entombment of unknown location. He felt a pang as he realized he would never again visit his father's grave, which he had done regularly since his death in one of the skirmishes of the 1848 Revolution, the uprising that had stripped the monarchy and King Frederick VII of much of their absolute powers—though corruption and nepotism had continued unabated. His father also had been a decorated cavalry officer. "Even in death," Johannes whispered into the air between the iron bars, "you remain my best friend. *Farewell, Father. Farvel.*"

He breathed a melancholy sigh. *A hell of a time to be stuck in a dungeon—over Christmas! But I am leaving nothing behind. Twenty-six years old, and I have no love, little money, no family and no property.* Then he half grinned out through the bars, speaking to the crowds bustling in the street, "But I am sure there will be a broken heart or two." He thought of Bente and hoped she had been spared too severe a punishment.

His years in the military had taught him to adapt, mold to change and travel at a moment's notice. Now he drew on that training and experience. By the time they pulled into the docks, the sound of his whistle echoed in his wooden confines. He looked forward to the unfettered adventure of the next chapter of his journey. The rest of the pages of his book of life were blank.

The captain of the guard, a sergeant, unlocked the back of the wagon. Johannes had to scrunch down to fit his tall frame through the opening. He jumped down to the cobblestones, still hunched over, the chain connecting the manacles at his ankles and wrists making a metal chink. The soldier had his cap and ball pistol out. Straightening up, Johannes started to laugh, the laughter intensifying at the sight of the guard's puzzled face.

"Put that pistol down, sergeant," said Johannes. "I am not armed, I'm half dressed in filthy rags, my hands and feet are chained together and you're about to put me on a boat. And we've both been soldiers in the same army."

The sergeant lowered the weapon.

"Would you mind taking these damn irons off, please? I do have to get along with the people on whatever boat you are going to stick me on."

The guard looked at him with distrust.

"You have my word I won't run. I will get on the ship and I won't come back. I swear as a former officer of the king's cavalry."

The guard hesitated, then gruffly muttered, "All right, come along then." Shoving the pistol into the wide leather belt around his tunic, he unlocked the manacles, throwing them in the back of the wagon. The guard kept his hand on the hilt of his sword. The two men walked side by side down the dock. There were four or five fishing trawlers, a sailing ship and a small tugboat.

At each boat, the guard stopped if any crew was visible, calling out, "Ahoy there! When are you sailing and where to?" Not one of the vessels had plans to put out to sea. Several ships had no crew. They finally reached the tugboat.

"Hey, there! When are you sailing and where to?" called the guard.

An older sandy-haired man, his leather face wrinkled and cracked from too many years in the sun and wind, emerged from the pilothouse. Leaning on the rail, he looked down at them.

"What you got there, general?"

"I have a man that needs passage. King's orders! I have a requisition slip here."

The older man leaned further over the rail, his enjoyment of the moment obvious. "You don't say, now. I assume this isn't the king next to you. And what about this requisition slip? I work on cash. I won't take credit, even from God."

Johannes looked at his feet, trying not to laugh but he knew the shaking of his shoulders gave him away.

"And what are you laughing at, Mister Beanpole? Are you some dangerous subversive or a throat-slitting murderer? Maybe I'll just take you out, tie the anchor to you, dump you at sea and then come back and get my money."

The guard stood stiffly through the exchange. He did not appear amused.

"I say again, king's orders! Where are you headed?"

Swiveling his head, the seadog spat again, "Bremen, if you must know." His gaze returned to Johannes without a shift in his body. "You know anything about ships or are you worthless?"

Johannes flashed a broad smile. "I am not a captain but I can do most things a good crewman can."

"Come aboard, then. Maybe if it works out, you'll want to stay on past Bremen. I've been looking for a good deckhand for a year. I've begun to think people don't like me." He clutched his chest feigning hurt.

"And you there, general, give me that piece of paper and write your name on it. If I don't get paid I'm going to come find you, take that sword and stick it up your ass."

The captain of the guard's face tightened. Reaching into his tunic, he pulled out a small rolled parchment and thrust it up to the grinning old man while Johannes was scrambling onto the deck of the tug.

"I am to stand here until the ship is out of sight," said the guard.

"You can stand there until hell freezes over. Don't matter to me." Looking up at Johannes who towered above him, the sailor's eyes squinted, "What's your name, boy?"

"Johannes."

"A soldier at some time, I would wager," said the old man appraising Johannes. "Well, you look more like a dandy now—a filthy dandy, to boot." He gestured at the ropes that secured the boat to the dock. "Cast off those bowlines. We'd better put out to sea. We don't want to waste the general's time."

The pitch of the tug was therapeutic. Johannes learned the captain's name was Olaf LaPierre. Part Dane, part Scot and one quarter French. Though he was an intelligent man, he had a vivid imagination, which he at times applied to his never-ending stories. There were extra clothes on board that were a bit short for Johannes' tall frame but they worked. Olaf had ingeniously rigged a sea shower with a wood-heated tub from which sprinkled warm seawater when a chained lever was pulled.

Luxuriating under the warm trickle, Johannes first bathing in weeks was interrupted by a gruff, "What are you doing in there, boy? Playing with yourself? Those boilers are hungry for coal. Get a move on."

Days later, chugging into Bremen Harbor, the tall young man and short older one stood together on the bridge of the boat.

As their wake washed the shoreline of the harbor, Olaf gave Johannes careful instructions on how to take on needed coal and fresh water. Then the old man put on his faded captain's jacket.

Johannes watched him. "Going somewhere?"

Olaf laughed loudly. "I need my annual man cleaning and just so happens, I have a good woman in this port."

It was midday. The waters of the harbor were calm but dirty with garbage and human sewage, industrial dumpings and waste products from the steam engines of the ships. Johannes had said nothing concerning the reason he was on the boat. He and Olaf had merely talked of travel, the military and women in general.

With dockhands tying off the tug, Olaf turned to Johannes. "Well, boy, I will be back in a few hours." He hesitated, then added, "You're a good hand. Not bad company, either." He looked down at his feet as if embarrassed and raised his eyes back to Johannes.

"Why don't you stay on with me? We go back and forth to Copenhagen, and every once in a while, over to Portsmouth when the season is right. Sometimes I have work along the coast of Normandy. Good-looking women on the coast of Normandy. Fine cognac."

Johannes liked the old man. Putting his hand gently on Olaf's shoulder, he said softly, "Thank you. That is a very kind offer. If my situation were different, I might very well say yes. But I cannot go back. And one who cannot go back must go forward."

Olaf's face fell, and he nodded.

Johannes continued, "I am glad you understand."

"Where will you head?"

Johannes smiled. "I think, Olaf, that this dumb descendant of a Viking is going to America."

"America?" Olaf repeated, his eyebrows rising in surprise. "My boy, that's close to a month and a half's voyage from here. What on earth will you do over there? I hear it's a wild place."

"I have no idea what I will do. That's the fun of it. But somehow, I know that is where I must go. It is where I want to go. A place where I can be me. A new life demands a new land."

Blinking rapidly, the tug captain reached into his pocket, his voice husky. "There are a few ships that leave from here. Damn few go directly to America, I think. But there are several that leg over to Portsmouth or Liverpool and then head across the Atlantic from there. I hear there are several places you can land over there but New York is the biggest. Here..."

Johannes looked and saw money in Olaf's outstretched hand—five Danish twenty-Kroner gold coins.

"You'll need passage and a little bit of spending money to get over there. This will get you at least that far. I think there's a ship making port tonight or tomorrow, The SS *Edinburgh*. She was just launched. I think she's one of them that goes to Portsmouth, Liverpool and then New York."

Smiling warmly, Johannes extended his hand and closed the old man's weathered fingers back over the money. "I have money but I thank you just the same. I think this should stay with you, to keep this man of war going." Johannes' arm swept the length of the tug.

"You have money?" Olaf's head cocked to one side with skepticism.

Reaching down, Johannes pulled off a boot. "Let me borrow your knife."

The old man handed him a small knife he drew from his waistband. Johannes deftly unscrewed the heel from the boot, pulling ten one-hundred-pound English bills wrapped over five twenty-Kroner gold pieces. He winked at Olaf. "I never go anywhere without my boot. I will stay with the boat until you return from your rendezvous."

Johannes had picked up the German language while in the military. Standing on the dock, his shoulders hunched against the damp harbor wind, he listened to the thick German accents as he supervised the water tender and coal wagon workers restocking the tug.

Several hours later, Olaf swaggered down the wharf. "It's always good to find out I am not yet too old to bring a smile to a woman's face," he said, laughing. They spoke for several minutes, shook hands and Johannes stood on the dock waving to the grizzled figure hunched over the wheel on the bridge of the boat as it steamed away.

That night the SS *Edinburgh* arrived. Johannes secured passage in steerage to save money. The next morning he and other passengers embarked. It was a slow process and the dock was very crowded. A long line of people dragged baggage and trunks up the steep gangway.

Halfway up, he heard one of the deckhands shouting at two men in a wagon not far from the ship. "You, in the way there. Get that wagon moving. Be quick about it!"

Each time the queue paused on its way up the gang-plank, he looked back at the wagon. The men appeared to be young. One of them was slight of build. He strug-gled with a trunk in the rear of the wagon and had to be helped by the other. *Might even be a boy.* They stood close, face to face, talking for a long moment, the younger of the two wiping his eyes. They embraced. *Must be brothers*, Johannes mused to himself.

Almost to the deck, he was delayed again. An enor-mously heavy lady and her huge valise had become wedged at the top of the gangplank. One of the crew was trying to pull her through. He tugged on the front of her jacket and she screamed at him in Russian slapping him on the hand. Laughing, Johannes moved his eyes back to the wharf. The wagon had disappeared from sight. The man it had dropped off shouldered a duffel, picked up a leather case and was reaching down for a trunk to drag over to the ship.

The rotund lady in front of him was finally freed but her high-pitched curses were continuing as she waddled down the deck toward wherever she would be housed for the voyage. Johannes hoped it wouldn't be anywhere near him. Stepping onto the SS *Edinburgh*, he asked a sailor the way to steerage. Humming a military tune, he headed down to find a good bunk.

January 16, 1855

JACOB

FOUR HUNDRED THREE MILES NORTHWEST OF THE bustling harbor of Portsmouth, England, a gray and seamy evening cloaked the cobblestone streets of Dublin, Ireland, slushy with dirty, melting snow of a wet winter storm. The brown brick of city buildings stood dull with late-winter grime. O'Reily's Tavern was teeming with the Saturday afternoon crowd. The air hung stagnant with the brown smoke of cigars and cigarettes. There was a boisterous buzz from the patrons crowding every chair and stool and standing shoulder-to-shoulder at the bar. In the far corner, a group of men had gathered around a table centered under a low-hanging chandelier with four gaslights, each with a copper canopy reflecting illumination downward on the soft, green felt covering the surface of the poker table.

This quiet group was intently watching a poker game. Not a word was spoken among the seven players. This was not a friendly recreational round of cards. There was no love lost among any of the men fingering their cards and glancing with suspicion at one another over their hands. A large pile of chips and coins were heaped in the center of the table.

Jacob O'Shanahan was sitting in a chair with his back to the very corner of the room in his usual spot. Wide-set, pale, blue eyes in a square, slightly ruddy face intently surveyed every player. He was not a big man but he was stocky. Hunching his large shoulders forward, he concealed the cards he held in beefy hands with scarred knuckles.

The buxom, red-haired lady of the night who sat on his lap, one leg draped over his thigh, both arms curling around his neck, ran a finger softly over his thin lips. Her once-pretty face was thick with makeup. Glancing up at her, Jacob noticed she was hungrily fixated on the pot. Pushing his cards together, Jacob laid them down upon the felt, picked the top one and threw it face down into the center of the table.

"One," he said with his customary surliness.

The players studied Jacob's impassive features. Several men at the table turned and cast glances at one another.

The tall man sitting to Jacob's right barely moved his head. In an unpleasant tone he said, "Going for the straight, are you now? Or is it a flush you'd be hoping for? Maybe you should have that tart play your cards."

Jacob felt his face reddening. "Stow it, Shawn," he snarled. He commanded the woman, "Get me a coffee, lassie." Watching her walk off, hips swaying in the exaggerated way of all trollops, he muttered, "Just like my mother," and spit on the floor. "Damn whore."

"One," he repeated hitting the table with his fist. "Keep them fingers from my face when I'm playing, tart! The redhead rose quickly to her feet, her features mutating from coy to fearful. Hesitating for a second, the dealer pushed one card face down toward Jacob. The watching crowd drew a collective breath.

He had been the last to draw. Most of the others had seen what fate had dealt them. Shuffling his cards between his fingers, his eyes roved the faces of each player. He did not look at the card. The first player to bet counted out twenty pounds in silver and threw the coins into the pile. The heavy metal pieces made a muffled clang, as they nestled in with the mounded pot.

Cursing, the next man threw down his cards. "I'm out."

The following player likewise discarded his hand to the center of the table with disgust. "Me, too."

The fourth player made no sound and his face revealed nothing. Reaching into the pile of money in front of him, he counted an amount equal to the bet, pushing it slowly toward the pot. The fifth player matched the bet, too.

The sixth man, Shawn, to Jacob's right, laughed without humor. "I think the lot of you a bluffing, and whether you are or not, I'm taking this pot. I call and raise."

Jacob noticed that Shawn's eyes slid up to the redheaded whore who had returned with Jacob's coffee and now stood behind him resting her trinket-jewelry-festooned hands lightly on his shoulders.

Jacob felt yet more heat rushing to his cheek. Peeling just the corners of his cards off the felt, he spread them enough to see all the edges as a hand. He didn't say a word as he matched the bet. The players remaining in the hand did likewise. There were no raises.

"Let's turn them over, please, gentlemen," said the dealer.

All complied except Shawn and Jacob. Jacob had always harbored an intense dislike for the brash taller man and he knew Shawn felt the same toward him. Looking at no one but each other, they turned their cards over one by one. Shawn had beaten Jacob twice in the last hour in close hands, both times for large pots. Jacob's pile of coins and paper money was far lower than when he had taken his seat in the game. They both turned over their last cards simultaneously and Shawn began laughing derisively.

"Well now, O'Shanahan, I guess you couldn't cheat your way into this pot, either. I think a flush beats a straight, doesn't it?" Shawn reached for his winnings, turning his head toward the whore, with a wide grin. "Aye, Miss Redhead, better come over here and sit on my lap, since O'Shanahan doesn't have the money to pay you now."

Shawn's outstretched midsection was exposed as he partially stood, reaching toward the center of the table, both arms outstretched.

"You son of a bitch!" shouted Jacob, launching himself from his chair. Using his body as a ram, his shoulder hit Shawn in the ribs. They tumbled to the floor, both men leaping immediately to their feet. The crowd was shouting and stomping their boots. Rolling chips and coins twirled around the dirty wood planks. Shawn had his fists up, his stance that of a man who knew how to box. Jacob knew he was probably outmatched by the taller man. Bending slightly, never taking his eyes off Shawn, he tugged up the cuff of his trousers and reached into his boot. A stiletto suddenly flashed in his hand. The crowd became silent.

Taking two steps back, Shawn partially lowered his fists, "Don't want to fight like a man, eh, O'Shanahan?" He spat. "I don't have a knife."

The two men circled, wary, much more at stake than a bruised cheekbone or the chips on the floor. The crowd was growing; the outer bounds of the circle of men pressing the inner band forward, narrowing the space occupied by the two adversaries.

"Let's make this even, mate." One of the men in the crowd drew out a knife, and handed it to Shawn. Leaping forward as Shawn stretched for the offered blade, Jacob slashed upward with the stiletto. The blade tip caught Shawn below the ribcage on the left, slicing upward toward his right shoulder.

Shawn cried out. "You bastard! You've killed me!"

A crimson line welling blood appeared diagonally across his solar plexus and chest. Crumpling to his knees, he bent his forehead to the floor. The crowd began to murmur. His eyes darting from man to man, Jacob cut the air with the stiletto. The blade shone a dull gold and red in the gas light. Backing to the table, he grabbed piles of money, which he shoved into his pockets. "Anybody else wants a piece of this blade, step right up!"

Wielding the stiletto, he advanced toward the crowd, which immediately parted. As he neared the entrance to the tavern, he turned and swung the knife back and forth as several men advanced. Then he was out into the night, swallowed by the bustling crowds along Clancy Street.

Jacob's heart was pounding. *That was damn stupid.* Trotting away with glances over his shoulder, his mind raced, *must have been a hundred witnesses. That fat constable Tom Rourk will make it his mission to track me down.*

He forced himself to slow down. *I think it's time, lad, to get the hell out of Ireland.* There was no need to look suspicious. Stopping for a moment on a darkened corner, he mulled the possibilities, then made a decision.

Half an hour later, Jacob was slouching in the dark corners of the buildings by the harbor, out of reach of light from sputtering streetlamps. He studied the fishing trawlers carefully, concentrating on the ones that needed paint or maintenance. On one such vessel, he noticed the crew carrying supplies and making ready the nets. A tall, lean man who wore a dark blue sea coat, white cap and a large beard seemed in command. Skirting the edge of the light, Jacob walked down the dock to the boat.

"Who's the captain here?" he asked. A deckhand looked up. Pointing at the man in the blue coat and muttered something in French. Jacob walked down the dock a bit further, about midships, where he could hail the captain in the least obtrusive way.

"Hello, there. Could I talk to you? You are the captain, right?" Turning, the bearded man peered into the darkness to see the source of the voice. He walked over to the gangplank and came down on the dock with caution.

"Let's step over here," Jacob said, motioning to an even darker part of the dock.

"What do you want?" the captain said without moving.

"Where are you going? When do you leave?"

"None of your business, mate. Who are you?" A definite edge cut the tall seaman's voice.

"I am a man needing a ride and willing to pay for it."

The captain's fingers stroked his beard. "Where, and how much?"

"Portsmouth Harbor would be fine. And how about twenty pounds? That ought to be more than enough." Jacob held up several coins so they reflected in the dimly lit streetlamps several hundred feet away. The captain reached out his hand but Jacob withdrew the coins.

"Why not Liverpool? It is much closer."

"No. Do we have a deal?"

The captain stood silent and still for a brief moment.

"We have a deal. Drop you at Portsmouth. We can fish the channel. I have heard the cod are in the run there, anyway." He paused. "Make it thirty pounds, since we're sailing you half around the British Isles. Where's your gear?"

Clenching his teeth, Jacob agreed. "Thirty pounds it is. I have no luggage."

The captain's eyes narrowed in the gloom. "The law then, is it? What did you do?"

"That's like me inquiring where you're going fishing," said Jacob.

Chuckling softly, the captain pivoted toward the boat, "Come along, then."

———◆———

LONG HEAVY SWELLS ROLLED IN FROM THE SOUTH from England as the trawler rounded the point and left the shelter of Dublin Harbor. The little boat yawed and pitched. Though only minutes had passed since they had hit open water, Jacob had to cling to the rail. *Must have been that damn rotten salami I had in that hole of a tavern.*

"Hey there, bloke. You look green. Never been out in the water, eh?"

Jacob looked up from his slouched position, then shifted his eyes quickly back to the deck. "What's it to you, sailor boy?" he said, his voice strangled.

The sailor was younger and slight of build. His eyes widened at Jacob's tone.

"Aw now, mate, just trying to be friendly. Most people not used to the roll do get sick, you know. It's nothing to get angry over. Here." He held out a thick piece of new hemp, about five inches long. It was an odd amber color.

"What the hell is that?" asked Jacob.

"New hemp soaked in rum," said the sailor. "I have few enough years out here where I still don't feel quite right in really heavy seas."

"You don't call these really heavy seas?"

The young sailor laughed. "No, mate. Trust me; this is a bathtub. Take it. Just chew on it a bit. I don't know if it helps you being sick but it sure keeps that damn taste of your stomach from your mouth."

Keeping his leaning position over the rail, Jacob stretched one arm back. The boy handed over the rum-laden hemp and waited, expecting a thank-you or some acknowledgment. Jacob ignored him. Pulling the rope to his mouth, he began to suck.

"One other thing, don't look at the horizon. Keep your eye on the deck or like you're doing now, straight down in the water."

Jacob barely moved all day. The captain came by and stopped briefly. Craning his neck toward him over his horizontal shoulder, Jacob weakly snorted, "What are you gawking at? Can't you find a different, smoother route?"

"So you'd like to be captain now, would you? I'm not sure you could even stand erect. You're the one who insisted on Portsmouth. If you want a smoother ride, jump overboard and swim. Makes no never mind to me. I've been paid."

Jacob felt his hand tightening on the rail but he was too sick to do anything about the captain's demeaning sarcasm. Long after dark the next day, the trawler pulled into Portsmouth Harbor. Even at that time of night, the port buzzed with civilian and British Navy activity. The calmer waters of the harbor allowed Jacob to partially regain his composure. The trawler made for a point past the end of the wharf toward a beach, perhaps one hundred fifty yards away.

The captain appeared and stood six feet distant, leveling a pistol at Jacob.

"This is the harbor. My part of the deal is done. Over you go." His eyes were hard.

Jacob was incredulous, "What do you mean?"

Cocking the hammer of the pistol, the captain answered coldly, "I mean I'm not waiting in line to moor up for the likes of you. We'll lose half the night trying to get a berth for the minute or two it takes to drop your sorry ass off simply to keep your boots out of the water. After sailing all this way, I don't intend to miss the morning fishing on the inner channel bank."

"But—" began Jacob.

The captain cut him off. "I didn't say I'd deliver you with your feet dry on the dock, mister. Now either over the side with you or it's back out to sea with us. If that's the case, it might be over the side with you out there."

Hunching, Jacob leaned forward to make a move toward the stiletto in his boot. *He's too close and a lead ball is too fast.* Jacob straightened up not trusting himself to speak. Taking a few steps over to the rail, he paused to make sure his money pouch was deep in his pocket, then swung one leg over the gunnels to lower himself into the water.

Moving quickly, the captain shoved Jacob over the rail into the icy cold water. Sputtering as he surfaced, Jacob almost gagged on the reek of fish, oil and sewage. The trawler never stopped moving and was almost past him. He could see the captain leering down at him over the stern.

"Don't drown," the captain called with a flippant wave as the trawler disappeared in the night.

Jacob struck out for shore. He was not much of a swimmer but with a combination of dog paddling and floating on his back, he finally arrived, gasping, at the shoreline. He climbed over large wet rocks, slimy with foul-smelling moss, separated by pockets of coarse sand that felt like dirty paste mortar.

Regaining his breath, he tottered to his feet and looked back out into the harbor. Hissing into the darkness, "Someday I'll run a knife round your throat, you bastard."

Jacob struggled up the embankment to a road of sorts and began walking toward the nearest lights. His boots squished and gurgled with every step. Soaked and freezing, he told himself through chattering teeth, "I've got to find some shelter. Some warmth."

He walked down a very dimly lit street on the outskirts of the town. Gas lamps were spread widely apart. Two-, three- and four-story buildings, some masonry, some wood, virtually all dilapidated, lined the street. Many of the tenements were lit by candles. Only a few people were walking about. Some were sailors off the Navy frigates.

The first door Jacob tried was unsecured. *My first piece of good luck in twenty-four hours.*

Pushing it open, he entered a squalid landing that smelled like urine and wood decay. Stairways led both up and down, with a door to an apartment on either side.

Jacob wrinkled his nose at the odor. *I've always heard the English are a smelly bunch.* He heard some scratching. *Damn, is that a rat?* The tiny tap of claws receded into a dark corner.

Jacob crept down the stairs. He tread lightly but each step squeaked, some more than others. He found a furnace back in a far corner of the basement. It had been stoked not long before. A large pile of coal leaned against the basement wall almost up to the bottom of the opening of the coal chute. It was dusty and dirty but it was warm and dry. Picking out a corner, taking care to keep the furnace between him and the stairs, he lay down on his back. His shivering lessened and he fell asleep.

LOUD VOICES, EBBING AND FLOWING WITH LAUGHTER and good-natured curses, woke him. The sounds emanated from the main landing where Jacob had entered. He had no idea what time it was. *Must be very early morning.* Lying still in the glow of the coal furnace, the only light in the basement, he listened intently.

Come on, man, make a plan, he told himself. *You're safe from the law for now but you need food, clean clothes, shelter and heat. You need to stay on the move.* His hands searched for his money pouch. In the dim light, he could not tell exactly what each coin was but he came close to a total by feel. *About eighty pounds.* Tucking the pouch into his waistband, he walked carefully up the stairs. The boisterous group in the hallway was too engrossed to notice the creak in the old wooden steps. Two men leaned against the wall. One had a whiskey bottle. Five men were kneeling on the floor.

"Playing poker?" he queried with a nod of his head toward the cards on the floor. "Room for one more?" He tried to make his tone friendly.

The men stopped playing and looked up at him, surprised. The two who lounged against the wall straightened up, wrinkling their noses. "Man, what happened to you?"

An oil lamp hung from a long nail protruding from the risers on the stairway. He moved a bit further into the light. "Just me lot in life. I'm Irish," he joked.

They looked at one another and burst out laughing. "A Mick, eh?"

One man smiled in a friendly way despite the slur. "What the hell you do, swim over here?"

Jacob looked down at himself. He was a mess. Caked mud covered his boots. Mud lines stained his trousers halfway up his calves where he had struggled through the filthy sands. He could feel greasy residues in his hair from the harbor water. "I admit I'm in deplorable condition, even for me but would you men mind making room for this poor old Mick?"

"Sure, come on. There's room here at this fancy table," one of the players called out, gesturing to the floor.

"Hey, don't sit too close to me," one man joked. "You smell like the bloody harbor."

Smiling an overly friendly smile, Jacob's experienced eyes roved over the other players for clues. He glanced down at the pot. It was not very large. Maybe three or four pounds. All of the men had calloused hands. Most had thin, worn boots. *Low-level workers, probably at the harbor. Based on their dress, the pot and the run-down neighborhood, they have very little money. This is not the type of crowd I am used to.*

He folded three hands, satisfied just to observe for the price of the small ante. The third hand, he decided to play. His cards were quite good, a solid two pair, jacks and tens, more than enough to take most pots in a game of five-card draw. He most certainly had the winning hand. They went around the circle and each man bet. The liquor bottle had been passed to him three times and he pretended to drink but had not swallowed a drop. The rest of the men, getting tipsy, made small raises, laughing, giving each other good-natured pushes. Jacob matched the bet. The men turned their cards over. There were several players to go but Jacob knew his assumptions were correct. He had the best hand.

Still, rather than turning them over, he threw his cards face down among the others so they couldn't be picked out. "You boys are getting awful good hands. I can't compete—I fold."

The group whooped and hollered. The man next to him slapped him on the back. "Pass me that bottle. Are all you Irish players like that? Bring the leprechauns. I hear they have gold." They all roared with laughter; Jacob made the motions of joining in. For almost an hour, he sacrificed his ante or on a number of occasions even pretended to lose with a winning hand. He wasn't down more than a pound.

When it became his turn to deal, Jacob held himself back. He awkwardly shuffled the cards, making sure he appeared clumsy, even dropping the deck on one deal. He purposefully lost the first two hands he dealt and sacrificed the ante on the third. This group evidently had a rule that each player dealt five hands and then passed the cards on.

As he was dealing the fourth hand, he pretended to fumble the cards several times. With each feigned mistake, his fingers deftly rearranged the deck. He began to deal. "Whoops, sorry mate. I'm an oaf when it comes to this. Let me get you another. I didn't mean to throw that face up."

To his satisfaction, it was clear the other players, even as inebriated as they were, realized that they had just been dealt exceptional hands. Looking down at his own cards, they were just as he intended. The ring of players bet on each card. These were the heaviest bets of the night. Only one player dropped out in the first round and the pot was up to a solid fifteen pounds. The group grew quiet. This was a good deal of money to each of these men. With cards like those that they had been dealt, they couldn't afford to drop out. Jacob was careful not to raise any bet.

"I think I oughta fold," said Jacob with a facade disgust and surrender. He let himself get talked into remaining in the hand, throwing in his money with a great show of reluctance.

On the next round of bets, he again picked up his cards as if he were about to throw them in. "I've had it, mates."

The man next to him put his hand on his forearm. Jacob knew what the man's cards were.

"You're not getting out of this hand, Mick." The other players nodded. "No one gets out of this hand."

"Okay, okay," said Jacob with another show of reticence. He threw enough money in to match the previous raise but no more. It was time to deal the last card. Five of the players were still in. There was very little talk. Each man was raising the previous bet. As the bet went around, to appear even less inclined to stay in, he used body language. He knew the first man to bet held a straight, eight high. Reaching in his pocket for a gold piece, the man called out, "I raise five pounds."

The heads in the circle snapped up. This was a huge bet for this group. Jacob knew the next man had a low flush, nine high. He frantically dug in his pockets, emptying them of every bill and coin and came up with just enough to match the bet. The third man was distraught. Jacob knew he had a better flush, king high. The cards shook in his trembling fingers. He ransacked every pocket and then stood up, pulled off one boot, and extracted some paper money.

"Come on, come on. We don't have all morning. I've got to get me arse to work," said one of the men irritably.

"Easy, mate," said Jacob. "This is a big pot. Give the man time."

The man, whom everybody had been calling Tom, glanced up at him. "Thanks, Mick; that was good of you."

Continuing to rummage through his clothes, Tom's voice cracked. "I just don't have enough. Anybody here want to lend me three pounds six pence? I'm good for it," he slurred in drunken earnestness. All the men shook their heads.

"You'll just have to fold then," urged the man with the lower straight.

"What's that sticking out of your coat pocket?" asked Jacob.

Tom looked up at Jacob's question, startled. He said, "That's me ticket."

"Ticket?"

"For the SS *Edinburgh*. I'm going to America."

Jacob's mind raced. "Tell you what, Tom, you must think you have a good hand, mate. Good hands don't come along often. Why don't I lend you five pounds against that ticket? When you win the pot, you just pay me back. If you don't, I guess I got me a ticket."

Hesitating, the man glanced down at his cards, looking at all the other players. "You'd do that?"

"Sure I would. Men don't get lucky hands too often. I never get 'em. You fellows might have noticed. In fact, to make this fair, I'll just fold right now." Shoving his cards into the deck and discards in the center of the circle, Jacob made sure they were face down so nobody could see the ace high full house he had dealt himself. *Okay, now I am gambling.*

That pushed Tom over the edge. "Okay, Okay." He handed the ticket across the circle to Jacob, who counted out five pounds and threw it in the pot for Tom.

"I counted it. It's five pounds," said Jacob. "Tom has raised." All the heads in the circle nodded. The next two players folded. The last player, sitting to Jacob's right, was a very small man, probably not over five feet high. He was older. Jacob thought him the meekest of this group. Jacob also knew that—besides himself—the man had the best hand, a full house, jacks over eights.

Jacob held his breath. As he had surmised, the old man did not raise but simply matched the bet. "Okay, boys, lay your cards out," Jacob said.

With trembling hands, the circle of players rolled over their cards, muttering curses as each man's good hand was beaten by the next man's slightly better one. Tom's hand was the best thus far and only one player, the older, timid man, remained between Tom and the pot. The elderly player's body shivered. He laid his cards out with unsteady fingers.

"I...I think I won!" he said in a low, quiet voice. Leaning over, the other players peered in disbelief at his full house. Jacob helped the old man spread his cards out so that everybody could see them.

"By God, I think you did." Jacob said. "That's a hell of a hand." He glanced over at Tom, whose face was wide-eyed and ashen.

"I'm sorry, mate" said Jacob earnestly.

Looking desperately around the circle, Tom pleaded with his friends, "Can any of you be lending me the money to buy that ticket back?" The men all shook their heads. Tom turned his attention to the old man, who stared incredulously down at the pot that Jacob had already pushed in front of him. "Harry, can you lend me the five pounds, mate?" he begged.

Shifting his eyes from the pot to his frantic friend, Harry stammered, "I...I don't think so, Tom. There is a rocking chair me wifey has been looking at for a long time. I want to buy it for her, and I'll never have the money to do it again."

Glancing up at Tom, Jacob inquired, "When is that boat leaving?" in a nonchalant but friendly voice.

Pulling out a dented timepiece, Tom tried to focus. "Just five hours from now, at twelve noon," was the desperate reply.

"Tell you what, mate, get yourself cleaned up and I'll meet you back here at eleven o'clock, which will just give you time to make the boat if you can round up the money to buy the ticket back."

"Thank you. You're a fine Irishman." Standing up unsteadily, Tom bolted out the door at the far end of the foyer. The other players stood also. Jacob shook hands with all of them.

"Maybe we can play again sometime," he said following them all out the door. Standing in the chilly, morning sunlight, he watched until they were out of sight, then hurried down the street toward the taller buildings in the city. *I only have a few hours. Need to get some paper, envelope and talk someone into writing a quick note to Cousin Samuel to meet me at the docks. If I can find a British Navy seaman sailing for New York, maybe he will deliver it for five or ten pounds. Those Navy ships are faster than the steamers.* Pausing to catch his breath, he drew out the *Edinburgh* ticket, and holding it to his lips, kissed it. *I need a few changes of clothes and a bath. I want to be at the gangplank at 11:00 a.m., an hour before the ship sails.*

January 16, 1855

THE SS EDINBURGH

ACROSS THE ENGLISH CHANNEL FROM WHERE REBECCA'S six trunks lay open for final packing, gray fog shrouded the slick, dark surface of the waters of the North Sea at the mouth of the River Weser. The quiet of the night had not yet departed. The two Prussian brothers from the Lahn River farmland, eyes straining against the fog, carefully guided the wagon down the cobbled streets of Bremen Harbor.

On one side of the wagon there was the energy of space and the fishy smell of brackish salt water. On the other side were the dark forms of buildings, their corners softened by the thick mist sifting inland from the harbor.

Turning to Reuben, Erik held out the lines. "Hold these lines, would you? I need to pull up my collar against this damp!"

Taking the long leathers, Reuben nodded, "Yes. I am glad we don't live on the coast."

The horses moved gingerly, picking their way down the cobbled streets along the edge of the harbor, their unshod hooves not used to such hard surfaces. They passed several docks, most still quiet at this early hour. The black, looming hull of a steamship appeared out of the soupy, saline shadows of the early morning murk. The big white letters on its bow were unmistakable: SS *Edinburgh.*

The wharf was alive with activity in the now dissipating fog—passengers crowding toward the gangplanks, the crew shouting curses, and rope nets creaking with cargo. Ship's officers barked orders. Seamen scurried on the decks high above the dock. Reuben and Erik sat for a moment absorbing the scene.

"You in the way there! Move that wagon! Be quick about it!" The loud, gruff voice startled them. The two brothers turned to one another, Erik biting his lip.

"Let me help you with your bags, Reuben." Clambering into the back of the wagon, he threw the duffel and the map case down to Reuben. Erik tried to lift the heavier trunk to the side of the wagon but Reuben had to reach in to help him.

"You need to build up some muscle, Erik," teased Reuben, laughing. "I'm sure there's a woman or two who would notice."

"I want a woman who will love me for my mind," retorted Erik.

"When it comes to men and women, Erik, you will find out that there are many important things; the mind is just one of them."

"Is that the voice of experience?" Erik teased. Raising one eyebrow, he grinned. "You think I don't know about Gretchen?"

Reuben slapped his leg. "So that was you up in that tree at the picnic."

Reddening, Erik did not reply but instead jumped down off the wagon next to Reuben. The two brothers embraced.

"I will miss you, Reuben." Erik's voice was thick with emotion, even though muffled in the shoulder of Reuben's coat.

"And I, you, little brother. You will grow into a fine man. Help Father; follow your heart. Don't let Isaac bully you."

Stepping back, the younger brother wiped tears from his eyes. "I know you will be successful, but will I ever see you again?"

Hesitating for a moment, his mind torn between the two thoughts, Reuben mustered a cheerful tone that belied the empty feeling in his gut, "Of course you will." He studied the features of Erik's face to keep the memory with him, embracing his smaller sibling again.

"I love you, Erik. Say goodbye to Father, Isaac and Helmon for me. Tell them I will write when I can. And work on that violin. You have a real talent."

Breaking off their hug, Erik smiled a sad half-smile, tears still running down his cheeks. Wheeling quickly, he walked back to the wagon.

Reuben stood looking after the wagon until it vanished. Hefting the duffel, he picked up the map case and struggled simultaneously to drag the trunk toward the gangplank. A long line of passengers were shuffling in a haphazard queue in front of him. Up toward the top of the gangplank he spied a tall figure, at least a head taller than everyone else, with bright blond hair that was hard to miss. *Now that is a tall man.*

Ludwig had booked a tiny middeck berth for his son. The compartment was miniscule but Reuben was glad to have it. He stowed his gear, wedging the map case and his work coat far against the wall under the single bunk, then shoved the duffel in against them. Making certain they were concealed, he checked the locks on the cabin door.

He felt for his money pouch inside his jacket. It was gone! *Damn.* Other than some British currency, everything had been in coins. Sure he had strapped the leather bag to his waistband, he searched again but to no avail.

Thinking for a minute, he decided to go up on deck and look there but he knew it was futile. *No doubt, somebody is slapping himself on the back at his rare good fortune. What an inept way to start a trip. No matter—I have enough money for the voyage if I am careful, and it is but a small setback. I have some additional money in my pockets and trunk.* "I will need to be frugal," he muttered.

Making his way up to the deck, he saw the crew had drawn up the gangplank. It seemed the ship was about to get under way. Leaning on the rail, lost in thought, he felt a light tap on his shoulder. The tall man with the bright shock of blond hair, whom Reuben had glimpsed when he was about to board the *Edinburgh* hours earlier, was standing before him.

"I am Johannes. I believe this is yours," he said with a smile and a heavy Scandinavian accent. Reaching into his pocket, he withdrew and handed Reuben the change pouch he had lost. A mischievous twinkle emanated from his eyes. Reuben knew immediately he was a rogue but liked him anyway.

"Where did you find it?"

"Ah, my young friend, you did not tie it securely to your waistband. This was with it," Johannes responded, holding out the twisted leather fastener. "If you wish not to be parted from your money again, try a double loop."

Hefting the pouch, Reuben was surprised—which he hoped he hid—that it seemed to be all there. This tall, blond man with steady blue eyes, gregarious smile and roguish aura could be trusted.

"Thank you. My name is Reuben Frank. I realized it was missing when I unpacked. Where are you from?"

The man's grin broadened, his tone taking on a mysterious air, "Call me Johannes Svenson. And I'm from Europe."

"Europe? I know you are from Europe but where? You appear Scandinavian."

Johannes laughed. "North of Italy."

From that moment, Johannes and Reuben talked frequently sharing lunch and supper together as the ship steamed towards Portsmouth. Their conversations were casual, generally discussing other passengers, their expectations of America and the unsavory food served on the ship. Except by general reference, Reuben avoided giving details about his plans, and he noticed Johannes was quick to change the subject any time the talk drifted to the past. Nonetheless, the young Prussian grew more impressed with the mysterious tall, blond Scandinavian. As the *Edinburgh* forged her way through the tempestuous waters between Prussia and England, an idea began to stir in Reuben's mind.

January 17, 1855

FORETOLD

SEVENTY FIVE MILES NORTHEAST FROM WHERE RATS scurried through the coal dust in the dark basement where Jacob slept, Elizabeth's voice floated from the hallway "Rebecca! Rebecca Marx. I have the china all laid out. Do you have room in a trunk, my dear? This china must be wrapped." The question cut through the fog of Rebecca's annoyed self-pity.

Rebecca turned to see her mother at her bedroom door, wringing her hands. "I will get it packed, Mother. Thank you for sorting it out."

"Rebecca, do you know that this will make six trunks? This amount of luggage will cost a fortune in porters and handling." There was a now-familiar half-wondering, half-querulous tone in her mother's voice. Her trembling speech pattern had emerged shortly after her father's death one year before.

Smiling at her mother, she kept her tone reassuring, "I shan't be spending any time outside of cities." She sighed. "I remember a time when incidental costs like baggage handling were of no concern to this family. Now, let's get that china properly wrapped! I must get some sleep—tomorrow will be busy."

January 18, 1855

BLINKING AGAINST THE LAST REMNANTS OF SLEEP, Rebecca partially opened the heavy, pleated curtains at her bedroom bay window, peering out at the mist of early morning gray fog that clutched the street. *Well, at least it's not raining.*

Looking slowly around the room, Rebecca fought the lump in her throat. It was formal but large and airy, with nine-foot-high ceilings. A dark, cherry, carved, four-poster bed with a filmy canopy suspended from the rounded tops of the eight-foot vertical posts perched against one wall, flanked by rich cherry nightstands. The plaster was colored off-white, offset by carved trim, an ornate ceiling, and corner mulligan and wide baseboard. The bamboo floor, imported by her father from the Philippines on one of his trading vessels years prior, shone dark blond. The planks contrasted with the deeper hues of the cherry furniture but blended with the wood trim accents. An ornate, oversized, cherry dresser was settled against the wall opposite the foot of the bed next to a matching armoire. Large antique jade jewelry boxes, also imported by her father on yet another trading mission, sat on the dresser, perfectly centered between large candles on wrought-iron holders with thick curved legs. The muted, mottled colors of a plush Persian rug, given to her by her father just before he died, spanned most of the distance on the floor between the dresser and the bed.

It will be at least six, perhaps as many as ten, months before I again sleep in this bed. The realization that she would not see this space that had been hers since birth crystalized the reality of the enormity of her undertaking, overwhelming her. Walking over to the dresser, her fingers gently stroked the smooth-grained edges of the jewelry boxes. Blinking, then again, she involuntarily wiped a corner of one eye. "You'll do no such thing!" she said in stern self-reprimand.

She breathed in deeply and exhaled slowly, straightened her shoulders and walked to the door. "Mother," she called, "we need to start the staff moving the trunks to the front foyer. My carriage is due in two hours. I have to be in Portsmouth by ten to board."

"Yes, dear," her mother's voice floated up the wide curved oak stairway that Rebecca could see from the threshold of her room.

She hurried from the bedroom to her father's study. Crouching behind his desk, she opened the secret drawer, placing the deed, will and map in her traveling satchel.

"Rebeccaaaa! Rebeccaaaa!" the tones of her mother's voice wavered distantly up the stairwell. "We have everything in the foyer. What are you doing up there? Are you ready?"

Sliding the concealed drawer quietly back into place, she walked quickly down the balcony hall toward her bedroom. "I will be ready shortly, Mother. We still have an hour before the carriage is here."

"Do make some haste, daughter."

Passing the bathroom on the way back to her bedroom, she paused, casting a long wishful look at the tub that Sally had filled for her. Thin wisps of steam still curled from the water. Rebecca had been to sea with her father on short trading voyages to Europe and Ireland. She well knew the confined quarters of shipboard. She had procured one of only two staterooms with private baths available on the ship headed west across the ocean to the place they called America. She had bathed the previous evening. Rebecca sighed. *I shall bathe tonight when settled in my room.*

Back in her bedroom, slipping on silk drawers with a split crotch, she laughed to herself. *Thank God I don't have to take all these layers off when the need for privacy arrives.* She wiggled into her silk chemise, then struggled with the corset, fastening the metal bucks in front. *That was such a good idea to remove the whalebone—far softer and suppler.* Eyeing the stiff, dome-shaped crinoline, she hesitated. *Four of my best petticoats will be far easier to travel with.* She rapidly but meticulously donned the petticoats and fine dress she had laid out the previous night. The light blue satin fabric set her dark hair off smartly and fitted her form perfectly with its billow at the bottom of her hips descending to just inches above the floor. She carefully fastened diamond stud earrings and lovingly draped her favorite emerald pendant around her neck, with its gold heart-shaped picture box carrying the painted image of her father. The large pear-cut jewel hung down to the top of her cleavage, which barely peeked round and smooth above the half-moon edge of the upper portions of the frilled bodice that accentuated her breasts. She took one last look at herself in the mirror, perched her color-coordinated traveling hat at a jaunty angle on the flowing mane of her slightly wavy hair and let down the thin veil from the hat brim.

Smiling to the mirror she announced, "America, the lady Rebecca Elizabeth Marx is about to visit." Adjusting her hat slightly, she took a last critical look, "But only very briefly," she added.

Then, Rebecca descended smoothly down the staircase, dark-blue rain parasol in one hand, and her matching small traveling satchel containing her necessities and her father's map, deed and papers in the other.

The large, glossy black, arched, double-front doors leading to the street were partially ajar. The black carriage, shiny and immaculate with red spoke wheels, had arrived and the servants were moving the trunks from the curb to the rear baggage compartment. The Aborigines huddled with subdued expressions toward the back of the carriage.

"At this rate, you'll never meet a man, be married, have grandchildren for me and live a proper woman's life." Rebecca faced her mother. The old woman's arms shivered with nervous emotion, her eyes had a pained worried glaze and she was wringing her hands. "This is wrong, daughter. School, then business, those voyages on dear Henry's boats, now this."

Taking the few steps to Elizabeth, she corrected her softly, "Ships, Mother, not boats."

Reaching up with shaking hands, Elizabeth tried to straighten the already perfect square pads in the shoulders of Rebecca's dress.

She gently took her mother's fidgeting fingers from her shoulders and held them. Looking directly into the wrinkled eyes, she laid her palm tenderly against her mother's cheek. "Mother, I know what I am doing. And I am doing what I must. It is father's wishes and an unfortunate necessity for the honor of the family. Proper is simply a state of mind. We can certainly never be proper or keep our position in London secure if we do not rescue our fortunes."

"But—"

Raising a finger to her mother's lips she shushed her. "Mother," she said firmly, "do not despair. I shall not be gone long. And as for men, I have never met one yet, other than Father, whom I respect. If I never do, so be it. I may never marry. However, be assured, my dear Mum, that your daughter loves you and I will always be there for you."

Elizabeth began to sob. "I have lost dear Henry and now I shall lose you too."

Folding her arms around the frail heaving body, Rebecca drew her close. Bending her neck, she kissed the top of her mother's silver gray hair, breathing in the matronly scent that had become so familiar over twenty-one years, and then stepped back.

"I must go." Rebecca walked briskly down the marble steps to the street. The door to the carriage compartment was open and the white-gloved, uniformed driver was holding out his hand to assist her.

Rebecca spun to face the house staff.

The Aborigines were nodding their farewells. Tears rolling silently down Sally's face, she ran up and gave Rebecca a brief hug. Eve curtsied smartly. Adam walked to her and stood silently.

"Goodbye, Adam," said Rebecca. Raising her eyes over his head, she smiled at Sally and Eve. "I will see you all in a few months. Take care of Mother."

Adam, his voice deep and low, said in almost perfect, though heavily accented English, "It will be a different life mistress but you shall prosper."

Staring, Rebecca took a half-step backward, unsure whether his English—more than she had heard him speak at one time in the fifteen years she had known him—or his words, surprised her more.

"Adam, I am impressed by your English. And thank you for your good wishes but I shall return before next winter."

Adam's dark brown eyes looked deep into hers, and he half-smiled with a look of sad wisdom. "The power of the land and the man will hold you," he said quietly.

Rebecca stifled her laugh. "See you all in late autumn. Do stay well. Sally, be sure Mother has her potions every night."

Waving at her mother, who clung to the edge of the door, her head and shoulder resting against its edge for support, she called out, "I shall write, Mother. Wish me luck."

Taking the hand of the driver, she stepped up into the carriage and sat, pulling one ankle across the other and clasping her hands in her lap. The driver looked up at her through the still open door, "I understand, milady, that we're bound for the docks in Portsmouth? The SS *Edinburgh*, I believe it is?"

"Yes, driver. The SS *Edinburgh* it is, indeed. Let's be off."

January 18, 1855

$\mathscr{P}$RINCESS IN PORTSMOUTH

THE DEEP TONES OF THE SHIP'S HORN AND THE LESSEN-
ing pitch of the waves of the English Channel woke
Reuben. He dropped one arm off the bunk, rummaging
for his timepiece. Seven a.m. He had overslept. He rushed
to get dressed. He had never seen England, and they were
coming into Portsmouth Harbor.

It was a bright and chilly day. They had already sailed
into the strait between the Isle of Wight and the English
mainland. Gusty winds were blowing up the channel,
their blustery music causing whitecaps to dance across
the waters of the great harbor. A vast array of vessels,
including frigates of the Royal Navy and several passenger ships like the SS *Edinburgh*, were either moored at
countless wharfs or engaged in slow, watery waltzes with
one another. Tugs and barges scuttled back and forth
like ants attending to their queens. The scene verified
all Reuben had heard about the British Empire.

Sidling up next to him at the rail, Johannes slapped
him on the back. "Quite something, eh?"

"Good morning. Now this is a harbor. I have never seen anything like it!"

Johannes gave his shoulder a good-humored shove and laughed deeply. "No, I would imagine a farm boy from the middle of Prussia wouldn't have."

"It's amazing. The Americans must be some tough people to have twice defeated this kind of power and commerce."

"I suppose we will soon see."

Surveying the ship, Reuben had an idea. "As I understand it, we are only in port for part of the day. Long enough to pick up some supplies, top off coal and water and disembark passengers from the continent to the British Isles. I presume there will be additional passengers from England coming on board on their way to America. I think we are due to sail for Liverpool at one p.m."

"Then let's see if we can go into Portsmouth for a few hours," suggested Johannes. "Maybe you can spend some of the money in that pouch and buy a proper breakfast for us. And we can see if there are any tall thin blondes for me, and good-looking dark-haired women for you."

Reuben felt himself start, "What makes you think I like dark-haired women?"

Chuckling, Johannes winked at him. "I can tell. You're definitely a dark-haired woman type of man."

Looking out over the harbor, Reuben was suddenly transported to the heat of a late spring day at the synagogue's celebration of Sukkot, a year before. Gretchen's hair had been dark brown, almost black, and shoulder-length. He swallowed, remembering the feel of her soft curves as they moved passionately underneath him, the heat of her breasts pressed against his chest and the musky, sweet smell of her on his fingers and body.

Catching the look on Reuben's face, Johannes laughed harder. "I hit the mark, eh?"

"You did at that," admitted Reuben, feeling himself flush. "I don't think we have time to get into the city and back. I'll tell you what, though, let's compromise. I will buy us breakfast and a flask of English ale somewhere near the wharf. There should be a restaurant or tavern. I think the English call them pubs. We only have a few hours, and that way we don't have to worry about missing the ship."

"You don't think they would dare leave without us? If you make that two flasks, you have a deal!"

The passengers embarking in Portsmouth had begun to make their way up the gangplank. Stepping onto the long wooden walkway, Reuben saw the figure of a dark-haired woman ascending. She was dressed in finery unlike any passenger on the ship. The rich, light blue clothing clung to the sinewy curves of her figure. She was holding the hem of her dress and petticoats above her feet, her eyes fixed on the slatted wooden surface rising from the dock, as she gingerly picked her way up toward the ship. Backing up to let her pass, he bumped into Johannes, who let out a quiet whistle.

"A princess!" he said in a low tone that hinted of sarcasm. "And dark brown hair, too, Reuben," he whispered.

Stepping up onto the deck, she lifted her face, her eyes sliding momentarily across his. Reuben felt himself involuntarily take in a breath. Oblivious to anyone and anything, her chin stiffly elevated, she turned, gliding down the deck toward the direction of the only two staterooms on the ship. Behind her, six porters were huffing and puffing, carrying an array of trunks, valises and assorted baggage.

Looking at one another, Johannes and Reuben both raised their eyebrows.

Letting out a long appreciative whistle, Johannes chuckled, "Let's go get that ale!"

SEVERAL HOURS LATER, THE PLEASANT WARMTH OF THE English ale and delicious fish and boiled potatoes under their belts, they returned to the ship. Most of the new passengers had arrived and boarded. There were few people still milling at the bottom of the gangplank or on the walkway itself. The coal and water wagons were empty.

Johannes and Reuben had begun to board, when a stocky man with dirty blond hair shoved in front of Reuben. "You trying to cut me off? You must be a high and mighty Prussian!"

There was a definite challenge in his tone. Looking into the man's angry face, he felt his own jaw tightening and that strange tingle in his iris he had come to recognize as his eyes turning gray. He remembered his father's words, "Never back down but always choose your fights."

"Please, you first," Reuben said, his voice icy.

"You'd better make way for Jacob O'Shanahan." Shooting a smug leer at Reuben, and throwing a last contemptuous glance at Johannes, the stocky towhead stormed up the gangplank.

"Not a particularly nice fellow."

Johannes' usual jovial countenance was strangely serious; his eyes following Jacob's figure. "Far worse than that, Reuben; he's far worse than that."

CHAPTER

12

January 19, 1855

 ARAH

TWELVE MILES FROM THE RIVER MERSEY AND LIVER-pool Harbor, five counties north of the seedy, foul smelling hallway where Jacob had fleeced Tom of his ticket, the gentle mounds of the entombed bodies lay close together. A smooth mantle of new snowfall, not yet grimy with the ever-present residue of Liverpool smoke-stacks, flowed over the graves reducing the space between the two areas of raised earth to a barely dis-cernible, small depression.

Stooping to lovingly wipe the week's layers of soot from the lines etched deep in the small marble tomb-stone, Sarah's eyes lingered on the encryption: *Nancy Bonney, adoring wife of Richard and loving mother of Emily and Sarah, 1818–1853.* Closing her heavy tweed-wool coat and rewrapping her scarf, which fell open as she tenderly cleaned her mother's headstone, her eyes moved to the companion grave: *Richard Bonney, devoted husband of Nancy and dedicated father of Emily and Sarah 1816–1851.*

"I wish we could talk," whispered Sarah.

Forcing the tremble in her lips into a soft, wavering smile, she placed a small delicate hand on one, then the other of the headstones. "Even in death you hold one another's hands. I hope I find the love that you did."

She gazed out over the cemetery, a place of solitude and quiet in the middle of the city bustle. She loved to come here, to contemplate life and talk with her parents. Blinking back tears, she looked skyward. Light from the late morning sun elongated the shadows of leafless tree limbs, casting an odd mosaic across the white blanket punctuated by hundreds of grave markers. On the other side of the brick wall crowned by cast iron surrounding the cemetery, she could hear the never-ending noise of the city. It was somehow remote, distant, a part of the past. Tipping her head back, so that the sun could reach her face, she noticed how its rays shimmered auburn across tendrils of red hair that hung in curls across her shoulders.

Her eyes were drawn to the west where the sky was seething with the excitement of departing clouds, a powerful antidote to the sorrow and loneliness that had gripped her moments before. "A good omen," she whispered to herself.

Taking one long last look around the cemetery, she again gently touched the rounded top of each of the headstones of her parents, wiping tears from her eyes with the alternate sleeve of her coat.

"Farewell," she murmured, "it is unlikely that I will ever see you again but know that I am with you and you with me, always."

A short while later, she walked back through the door of the shop that she shared with her sister, Bonney's

House of Sewing and Design. The shop had been founded by her mother twenty years earlier, just prior to Sarah's birth. Her sister, four years older, sharing the same petite curves, lustrous blue eyes and flowing red hair as Sarah, looked up from the cutting table at the back of the shop. Sarah thought Emily's hands clenched a bit more tightly around the silk fabric she was working with. Her lower lip quivered.

"Mom and Dad are doing well. I know it," said Sarah. "I shall miss them and you."

Rising from the table, Emily walked quickly to her and the two sisters clutched each other in a tight embrace. "Are you sure you want to do this?" asked Emily, her voice tinged with an equal mixture of hope and resignation.

Stepping back but allowing one hand to linger on Emily's arm, Sarah gazed fondly around. "Something calls me, dear sister. I must find out what it is. Aunt Stella's letters make America sound so intriguing, and working with her will be a bit like having a piece of Mom with me again. There is opportunity there. One day, I will open my own shop, you'll see."

They turned toward the bells tinkling at the front door. Two middle-aged ladies entered, swathed in finery. Thin veils descended from the brims of their hats and they were engaged in animated gossip.

"Misses Kristy, that dress does suit you, and Misses Gale, that design is perfect for you," beamed Emily at the two women.

Bobbing their heads in a flattered fashion, they returned the smile. "Now dearie, they were your suggestions after all, and there is no doubt in our minds that your needles are the finest in all of Liverpool," cooed Misses Kristy.

Misses Gale's ample cheeks were shaking with agreement, "Everyone at our tea parties has asked us where we get our clothes. I have declined to tell them. You girls are so busy that any more customers and we would have to wait months for our next designs." The two ladies cackled.

Scurrying across the shop with attempted flair, the heavier of the two women put her arms around the shoulders of Sarah. "And you, my dear—I hear you are leaving us."

"Yes, my lady, later this evening in fact. My ship comes into port late today and sails almost immediately thereafter."

Blinking, Misses Gale stepped back. "This afternoon? Oh my. And to where are you headed Sarah?"

"I am going to work with my Aunt Stella, in her seamstress shop in New York City. I am going to America." She felt the smile on her face growing and a surge of excitement coursed through her as she said the words.

Cocking her head to one side, the matron regarded her with a dubious look, "You do know my dear that you're leaving your poor sister Emily in a terrible situation. Why, even with two of you, the shop barely keeps up with its current wonderful business. What is Emily to do without you?"

Sarah felt her back stiffening and that familiar rush of heat to her cheekbones. *My freckles are most certainly showing across the bridge of my nose.* "Misses Gale, your concerns are most appreciated but Emily and I discussed this at great length. Emily will be taking on some very talented help, which I have trained over the past several months. She will be able to maintain the schedule and quality; I am quite sure. At this time in my life, I must follow my heart. Also, my Aunt Stella now expects me."

Misses Kristy chimed in, "Well, this is all very courageous, young lady, off to see the New World and such and it appears that you and Emily have worked out the business of the shop quite nicely. With whom will you be traveling, my dear?"

Clearing her throat and thrusting her chin a little further forward, Sarah responded, knowing in advance their reaction. "I will be traveling on my own, Misses Kristy. I am quite capable of looking after myself."

Exchanging looks, both women clucked with disapproval. "That's hardly proper. It's quite enough that you're leaving your poor sister and traveling half around the world to wild lands inhabited by rebels against the king and savage Indians. I have read the accounts in the *Telegraph*. But for a single woman to travel alone is simply unheard of. There are many evil people out there just waiting to take advantage of a young girl, especially one as attractive as you are. Perhaps you should delay your trip so that you can find a suitable traveling companion or two. I'm sure there are other women who, for whatever reason, wish to see America."

Drawing herself up to her full height until she felt almost as if she were standing on tiptoes, Sarah spoke slowly and carefully, "I am used to being on my own. I have a good head on my shoulders and I believe I am a better than average judge of character, even if just from my interaction with the different customers of this shop." Realizing those last words had a bite to them, she steadied her tone, "Father saw to it that I had an education. I have the experience to handle myself capably and most properly in any situation that may arise. I will not delay my trip. My ticket is purchased, my bags are packed, my aunt expects me and I shall go."

Misses Gale shook her head and Misses Kristy coughed loudly.

Purposely allowing their attention to be diverted by a new bolt of cloth that leaned against a wall, they fingered the material, made some further small talk, and left the shop with a cheery but hollow, "We will be back tomorrow, Emily. Good luck in America, Sarah dear. We will miss you." Their heads shaking negatively at one another, they engaged in animated conversation as soon as the shop door closed behind them.

Sarah glanced at the ornate wall clock and caught her sister's eye. They hugged again. "My carriage will be here shortly. Be well, Emily. I love you. I will write often."

"Wait, Sarah." Running to the back of the shop and shooting a furtive glance at the windows to make sure that no one was watching, Emily opened the locked drawer built in a recess below the cutting table. She returned with eight five-pound silver coins and a small revolver.

"You have a pistol?" Sarah was incredulous.

"I never told you, Sarah but I have had it here for protection since a few years ago. It is one of the first revolvers to be manufactured. I don't think I have touched it since I stuck it in the drawer, and I have only the five bullets that are in the cylinder—see how dusty it is? Take it. Put this extra money that I saved for you and this pistol in that secret compartment that you sewed in your satchel."

Sarah began to protest but Emily raised a finger to Sarah's lips, shaking her head firmly. "Take it."

She took the weapon and the money, set her satchel on a chair and carefully opening the secret area that she had sewn into the bottom of her bag. The hard board bottom of the heavy cloth completely concealed any evidence of the additional space.

Embracing again, both tried hard not to cry. A traveling coach pulled to the curb outside the shop windows. Biting her lip, Sarah walked through the doors of the seamstress shop, turned and waved her hand.

Jumping from the driving seat, the driver bowed to her while swinging open the door to the cab.

"Thank you so much for being prompt."

"My pleasure, milady. I understand you are headed to the harbor?"

"Yes, I must board my ship...to America." Sarah felt that surge of excitement again.

Smiling, the drive cocked his head. "America? That is quite an adventure."

Helping her up the steps of the carriage, he fussed for a moment and made sure she was comfortable. With the door half-shut, he leaned his head in slightly. "I shall have you there in due time, milady. On what ship are you making the voyage?"

"The SS *Edinburgh*."

January 26, 1855

$\mathcal{O}$N THE HIGH SEAS

THE LAYOVER IN LIVERPOOL HAD BEEN SEVERAL HOURS during which another two dozen passengers boarded, as stevedores and dockhands were loading cargo.

With no opportunity to get off the ship, Johannes had decided to sleep rather than come on deck. Reuben liked the open air and was curious to see this new harbor, which was considerably smaller than Portsmouth. He had found a spot that he liked on the main deck just a quarter of the ship's length from the bow. There was a bit less wind than further forward and it still felt to him as if he were at the forefront of the voyage.

As he focused on the organized commotion of the harbor, he sensed he was being watched. Looking around, his eyes found the gangplank connecting the center of the *Edinburgh* to the wharf. A slender, shapely woman with unmistakable red hair and a finely tailored billowing dress was ascending the gangway, looking directly at him. As she paused, the three passengers behind her bumped into one another.

Realizing her stare was being returned, she looked down quickly and almost tripped as she resumed her ascent up the ramp.

Reuben watched her disappear onto the mizzen deck. *Now that was interesting.*

THE PLUNGING BOW OF THE *SS EDINBURGH* KEPT rhythm with the surging, gray-green swells of the open ocean, mesmerizing Reuben as he leaned against the rail more than a week into the voyage. Raising his face to the sun, he grinned to the sky. Relishing the lick of salt spray on his face, and the way the sea air tossed his hair. Most of the other passengers who had boarded at the various ports were wretchedly seasick. To Reuben, the pitch of the deck underneath his feet seemed the perfect separation between the cramped and crowded world he was leaving, and the promise of space and freedom of the new land he was heading toward.

The alluring dark-haired woman who embarked in Portsmouth stood further up the deck toward the ship's bow, the wind pressing her long woolen skirt and petticoats seductively around her legs. She didn't appear sick. Reuben sensed in her reserved manner a curious mixture of disdain and a masked kindred excitement about things to come.

He had met her briefly after the *Edinburgh* departed Liverpool, when the rock of the ship made him lose his balance, causing them to brush against one another as she joined the queue of passengers lined up for dinner.

Even before he'd realized who had bumped into him, Reuben had sensed a strange current as their shoulders briefly touched.

Reuben had turned, "Excuse me, I'm..." The words died in his throat. Large brown eyes looked back into his with a reproachful stare.

Tossing her head back and lifting her nose, the woman said in a cold voice, "You're excused." Then she moved on without looking back.

The others in the line pushed him forward, snapping him from his preoccupation. He asked a friendly old Frenchman with whom he spoke occasionally, "Do you know her name?"

"Rebecca," was the response. The old man raised his thumb, middle and forefinger to his lips and blew a kiss with them up toward the ceiling. "She is something, that one, *oui*?"

Reuben's forearms rested against the rail. Shaking his head, he felt a self-amused smile crease his lips as he recalled the scene. *She doesn't even know I exist.* Straightening up, he looked again at where the dark-haired beauty had been but she had vanished. *No matter*, he thought. *There will be women in America, if I have time.*

STANDING BELOW THE BRIDGE, SARAH'S EYES ROVED THE main deck below her.

Brushing away strands of red hair that blew across her face with several slow strokes of her fingers, she felt a deep wistfulness at the sight of the well-proportioned man on the deck below her. He was leaning on the rail fixated on points beyond the bow. She had learned that he would be at that point along the rail most middays and occasionally in the evening as the sun died in a scream of color on the horizon of ocean. She found herself drawn by the confident, introspective smile on his square-jawed face. *It begs for the stroke of a woman's hand.*

There is a certain energy about him. She felt her cheeks grow warm remembering how she had stumbled when he returned her stare as she was boarding the ship.

JACOB WAS CHEWING ON THE STUB OF AN OLD CIGAR, deep in the crowded, smoke-filled, foul-smelling, steerage compartment near the hold.

Barking at one of the other equally unkempt men sitting around the bunks playing cards, he extended a meaty hand, "Pass me that bottle." Jacob swilled the cheap whiskey. A dribble of it ran down his chin adding to the stains on his shirt. Throwing down his cards, he reached for the pot.

One of the other players began to say, "But I have a—"

His sentence was broken off by Jacob's glare. "Anyone else have a problem with me taking my winnings?" Glancing at one another, several men shrugged. No one said a word.

"Good," spat Jacob, raking the money, a pocket watch and a silver flask toward him.

Several of the men stood up, each of them offering a stuttered excuse about some important task. The game was over. Taking another swig of whiskey, he spit part of it on the floor, where it mixed with a dried pool of old vomit. He put his winnings in his change pouch, shoved the pocket watch in his britches and filled the flask he had just won. *I need some air.*

Ascending the eight flights up to the forecastle, he walked out on the platform. A very attractive redheaded woman was staring at something down on the main deck. Taking a position behind her, he studied the thin, though shapely figure.

Licking his lips, he grinned at her back. *I'd like to get her below deck for a little fun.* The woman was still oblivious to his presence. He walked up quietly behind her until he could almost feel her warmth. She turned, her face reddening apprehensively at his unflinching gaze.

"You ought not be up here alone," he said. "I am Jacob O'Shanahan, gentleman and world traveler."

"I...I like the sea," she stammered.

His gaze roved from her feet to her eyes, lingering around her hips and breasts.

"I'll be happy to get to land," he said. "And you are?"

"Sarah Bonney." With a nervous smile, the woman added, "I have to get out of the wind."

Taking two steps to the door that led to the interior of the ship, he opened it for her with a mock bow, placing himself so that she would have to pass very close. She hesitated, pivoting her body sideways to squeeze between Jacob and the doorframe, then walked quickly down the gangway.

February 27, 1855

THE REDHEAD

THE FOLLOWING NOON, REUBEN WAS AGAIN AT THE rail. Taking a deep breath of the ocean air, he thought of what was to come, the people he might meet and the unknown look and feel of the land toward which fate propelled him. Then there was that woman, Rebecca. *Always attired in finery and never missing the chance to make it clear that she was from a class above everyone else.*

Reuben kept his family's stature to himself, dressing in comfortable clothing with peasant white or light colored garb similar to that of most of the other passengers. His father had sternly advised him to make no demonstration that he was of landed gentry or Jewish.

Hearing the whisper of footsteps next to him, he turned and was startled by a set of huge blue eyes above a nervous smile on a pretty face. Reuben liked the way sunlight played on the folds of red hair.

"Do you think we'll be coming into port soon?" the woman asked, a nervous tremor in her voice. Like his father, Reuben was usually able to size people up instantly. *Attractive, strong but a far softer soul than mine...from moderate means, though she tries to project something more than just average with a dress that has been carefully designed and well-stitched.*

Smiling warmly, he introduced himself, "I am Reuben Frank."

Returning his smile, her eyes fixed on his lips, she said in a slightly distracted tone, "I know. I'm Sarah Bonney. You are from Prussia?" she asked.

"Yes, Villmar on the Lahn River."

Moving her focus to his eyes, she tilted her head back slightly, "I love the country too but I am from Liverpool." There was an awkward pause. She stared at him intently.

Reuben saw Rebecca further down the deck over Sarah's shoulder, her gaze flickering from Sarah to him. There was a look of aloof superiority on Rebecca's face each time her attention returned to Sarah. Reuben's eyes met hers for an instant. She abruptly turned away. There was something in that last glance that Reuben couldn't quite decipher. Shaking his head, he returned his attention to Sarah. Her concentration on him had obviously never wavered.

"Does that mean, 'No, it won't be soon?'" *She mistook the shake of my head for a negative response to something she had murmured but I missed.* Recalling her original question, he laughed, embarrassed.

"Do you mean, when we're going to land?" Smiling, the redhead nodded her head, obviously eager to have the conversation back on track.

"Yes," Reuben said. "I think we will see the shores of America within a week." Like an omen, for the first time in over four weeks, they heard a sudden screech in the sky. Looking up, they could see two seagulls circling the masthead.

GLOWERING ABOVE ON THE MIZZEN DECK, JACOB watched them converse, saw the look on Sarah's face as she gazed up at Reuben and felt a surge of jealous anger. Though he and Reuben had not exchanged a word during the voyage, he had seen Reuben around the ship and instinctively disliked him since their encounter on the gangplank. *We are opposites.* He kicked the railing, muttering at the two figures below him, "You, Mister Prussian are not quite the immigrant you pretend to be. And you, Miss Sarah Bonney—I am going to have you," his words were whipped away by the sea breeze.

March 2, 1855

AMERICA

WAITING IN THE SERVING LINE FOR LUNCH, REUBEN'S attention was diverted by a palpable murmur of excitement spreading through the ship. People were running down the passageways headed to the deck.

Grabbing the sleeve of one young boy who hurried past him, he shouted against the hubbub, "What's going on?"

"Land!" screamed the lad, scampering off toward the stairway. Throwing his tray down on a table, he sprinted for the stairs. Food could wait. He didn't want to miss the first glimpse of the continent that would be his new life.

Jostling and pointing, people crowded the foredecks of the *Edinburgh*. Far off in the sea haze, above the languid swells, a distinctive mass of land could be seen. AMERICA! Ships were within sight all around them now, some under sail and some belching the black smoke of steam power. A flotilla of three American Navy ships, two ships of the line and a frigate made way in single file for the open sea.

They were near enough that Reuben could see the sailors scrambling on the decks and gesturing, blue-uniformed officers shouting orders to the crew. He could clearly read the names on the bows. The Frigate was the USS *Brandywine*. The two ships of the line were the USS *Independent* and the USS *Pennsylvania*. The *Pennsylvania* was enormous. Reuben stopped counting cannons in the four armament decks when he reached one hundred.

The older man from France, swaddled in threadbare wool coat and with gray stubble after a month in stowage, was standing next to Reuben.

"*Vive L'Amérique! Oui?*"

"Yes," Reuben replied in halting French. "It is grand!" Smiling broadly, the old man unexpectedly kissed him on both cheeks.

Rebecca appeared in a doorway to the side of the excited crowd. She turned, smiling brightly in his direction, and then suddenly vanished into the throng. Reuben was stunned. For a moment, it was as if there was no one else on the deck, the friendly push and shove of hundreds of others unnoticed. He was snapped back by a soft, warm hand on his.

"Isn't it wonderful, Reuben?" breathed Sarah.

"It is far more than that, Sarah. It is the future!"

Standing on the deck together, they watched the scene below. Tugs were pulling aside the SS *Edinburgh*. Luggage was being offloaded to be transported to Castle Garden. Ships polka-dotted the glassy waters of the harbor. Several other sailing vessels were also disembarking.

The seamen gathered everyone on deck as the medical officers came aboard to inspect each of them before being transported to quarantine. Captain Kennedy stood at the forecastle waiting for the gangplank to be lowered. He was a large man with a rough beard and kind eyes. Reuben had liked him since they met. The captain was always accompanied by his huge Newfoundland dog, Sam. Legend had it that Sam had rescued fifteen passengers from frigid waters a few years previously when the sea master's last command was the first rescue ship to arrive at the sinking SS *Scotland*.

With quick understanding, Reuben watched the captain gesturing frantically to some crew. Emigrant ship captains often accepted passengers above the limits set by European laws regarding the numbers a sailing ship was allowed to carry. This led to excessive deaths on board due to overcrowding, disease and starvation. Many passages on older vessels lasted six to eight weeks. It was fortunate that this voyage had taken only five weeks in a new ship, particularly for those in steerage, a miserable place with wooden plank pallets covered in straw, and the stench of seasickness and unwashed bodies in the small spaces that sloshed with vomit mixed with seawater and urine.

Only a few unfortunate souls had died on the voyage. The captain kept record of each. Names, ages, occupations, country of origin and expected destination were duly listed on the manifest.

One family, the Callahans, had endured a string of tragedies on the *Edinburgh*. Cathy Callahan had watched helplessly as her husband and all six of her children had died from fever. Cathy had nobody left. Reuben had attended the shipboard funerals, trying to comprehend what it would be like to lose a child, feeling gut wrenching empathy for the inconsolable mother as the last of her children was given a fathomless grave in an unforgiving sea, wrapped in a cold, canvas, winding-sheet.

"Look, Reuben! There's Castle Garden!" Sarah exclaimed, bringing him back to the present. She was pointing to a large round building with wings to either side. "Did you know that Castle Garden used to be a fort? It was originally constructed as a twenty-eight gun Southwest Battery and was abandoned as a fort in 1821, then deeded to the city of New York. Captain Kennedy told me."

Laughing at her earnest recitation, he looked over her head for Johannes but couldn't find him in the flow of the crowd. He caught another glimpse of Rebecca, followed by a number of crew who were struggling with her vast array of luggage. Turning to Sarah, he lightly touched her arm. Looking into his eyes, her lips parted slightly and Reuben thought he noticed a flush creep up her throat, the freckles scattered across the bridge of her nose becoming more pronounced.

"I hear they separate the men and women at this point for immigration and medical check. I am going to go find Johannes, get our bags and get off the ship," he said. "Do you need assistance?"

"No, Reuben; I can manage."

He turned to go but she caught his elbow. "I'm so glad we sailed into America together."

Nodding agreement, he walked away, looking back over his shoulder once. Sarah stood watching him, her eyes blinking rapidly.

March 2, 1855

CASTLE GARDEN

THE BALANCE OF LUGGAGE AND CARGO WAS TAKEN from the hold while Sarah's satchel and the hand baggage of other passengers were being inspected by customs officers. She was helped onto a large barge for landing at the pier where passengers were inspected by a medical officer as each disembarked from the makeshift ferry.

The *Edinburgh* passengers, along with immigrants from other ships, were directed to the main depot. The central rotunda was large and circular. There, the milling throng was divided into English-speaking and non-English-speaking sides of the room. It took most of the rest of the day before the requisite immigration steps were completed by government officials. Each person had to register, giving an intended destination and a contact name in America.

Immigrants could purchase train tickets directly from railroad representatives, and currency exchange was also available. Sarah had sent most of her money ahead to

Aunt Stella but she wanted to convert what she carried into U.S. currency. Seizing an opportunity to slip into the bathroom, she furtively opened her satchel's secret compartment in a private stall, taking out the English funds. Then she went to one of the Currency Exchange Broker's windows.

She felt a light touch on her shoulder, which lingered a bit too long.

"Perhaps I could assist you with the exchange transaction," suggested a man behind her.

Recognizing Jacob's voice immediately, she willed herself not to turn around. *The less he knows about me and my funds, the better.*

"Yes, will you be exchanging too?" she asked in an even tone, attempting to mask her feeling of discomfort. *He has obviously searched for me in this crowded depot.*

Shaking the money pouch in his pocket so that his coins jingled. "No, I like metal." Becoming officious, he smiled slyly. "I would be pleased to assist you, Sarah. You don't want to be cheated by these money brokers."

She suddenly had a hunch. "How kind of you to offer," she said in a soft voice. "Here is the paperwork, Jacob. Would you review it for me?"

Furrowing his brow, he undertook a clearly pretended glance at the papers still in Sarah's hand, finally muttering, "Looks fine. Just fine. I need to find a water closet—drank too much water. Excuse me." Sarah felt a grim satisfaction. Jacob did not know how to read.

"Surprising," came the smooth, sarcastic voice behind her. It was Rebecca, dressed, as always, more appropriately for a formal ball than the activity at hand.

"You are surprised that he cannot read?" Sarah asked.

"No. I am astounded you handled the situation with such alacrity." Rebecca's voice was like cold silk.

Rebecca had not spoken a single word to Sarah during the voyage, though they had made eye contact several times. On each occasion, Rebecca had looked quickly and aloofly away, as if unwilling to acknowledge Sarah's existence.

Sarah felt her teeth clenching. Counting to five, as her mother had taught her, she decided not to respond except for a slight nod of her head. Pivoting abruptly, and without a backward glance, Rebecca walked to the next exchange window.

Finished with the transaction, Sarah sat down on a stiff wooden bench, clutching her satchel tightly in front of her. Muffled conversation ebbed and flowed all around her. She absently watched lines of immigrants, some with wailing children, taking drinks from the iron ladles at the water taps on either end of the large room. Other people, many of whom appeared gaunt and pale, were patiently standing in groups at the tables where rolls, cheese, butter and small cups of coffee were available for fifteen cents.

Closing her eyes, she let her mind drift to Aunt Stella. Her mother's sister, her mother and she bore a remarkable physical resemblance to one another. Aunt Stella had traveled to America ten years earlier while in her early thirties. She was now a widow. Her husband, a gentle, well-educated man, had died soon after their arrival in New York from fever contracted during the passage. Sarah was looking forward to seeing her aunt's shop and the new treadle sewing machine Aunt Stella had written about so often. From what Sarah could glean of the transoceanic correspondence, which took months to arrive, the Singers—just invented in 1851—were increasing production two-fold.

The group of women and children were beginning to grow impatient. Finally, an official shouted above the commotion. "All right, listen up. Except for the names I call, the rest of you are clear to head over the timbered drawbridge behind me to the dock." Swinging his shoulder, he pointed to the span that stretched several hundred feet over the slightly roiled, filthy waters of the harbor. "These men to my right will move your trunks for five cents per item, if you wish."

Sarah was pleased at the immigration officer's announcement. *That is a splendid idea. I will not have to soil my travelling dress or struggle with my larger baggage.* Digging in her purse for a U.S. silver half dime, she made the arrangements and then, excited to get her first glance of the city, joined the crowd of people trudging across the wooden link between Castle Garden and Manhattan. Looking uneasily behind her, she was relieved to see no sign of Jacob. *Good, I've lost him.*

Catching a glimpse of Reuben on the docks, her heart did a strange lurch. She started to make her way toward him in the crowd.

REUBEN LOWERED THE LONG CANVAS DUFFEL FROM HIS shoulder, carefully setting down his father's leather map case. Lowering the one side of the trunk he had dragged, he stopped, taking in the scene. Next to him, Johannes did the same. Even in these first few seconds, he sensed a current of life that no longer flowed in Europe. As he spotted Sarah working her way toward him on the dock, he felt a presence behind him. Turning, he was startled to see Rebecca planted squarely in front of him. Over her shoulder, Johannes was smirking. Cocking her head coquettishly, her eyes looked directly into his. She pushed her breasts out with a look of combined amusement and challenge, a slight flush coloring her cheeks. He felt his loins stirring.

"Your name is Reuben Frank, is it not? I'm Rebecca Marx but I'm sure you know that. Could I ask you to help me with my baggage or are you waiting for that redhead?" Rebecca's eyes flickered toward Sarah, still some distance away in the mill of people.

Reuben held her stare. There was a very long moment of silence during which the color in Rebecca's face deepened.

"I would be delighted to assist you. Where are they, and where do you need them to go?"

"Johannes, would you stay with our duffels? I will be back quickly." *She has not acknowledged that Johannes exists.*

CAUGHT IN THE SURGE OF BODIES CLOGGING THE wharf, Sarah saw Rebecca approach Reuben, watched him turn and the two of them begin to converse. Sensing a connection between them, she stood stock still, occasionally bumped by another passenger in the moving throng. Her eyes slightly misty, she turned away, and took a half step, walking into Jacob's barrel chest.

Surprised, she tried backing away but the crush of the crowd hampered her, and suddenly, Jacob's arms, held her close. Her breasts were pressing firmly against the lower part of his upper torso. Jacob looked at her intently. "Where are you going?"

"Oh, I...I am going to stay with a relative. I am sure their carriage is out front."

"Well then, let's find that coach of yours." Picking up her trunk, he balanced it on one shoulder, took her hand and led her through the crowd.

Sarah was not quite sure how to handle the situation. *I want to be away from this man but what gracious way can I employ to separate? And now he has my trunk.* Weaving through the multitude of people, she looked back for Reuben. *Perhaps he will realize I need assistance.*

"What are ya lookin' for, lassie?" said Jacob over his shoulder.

"Nothing, nothing," replied Sarah, "I was just trying to see if that poor woman who lost her children disembarked yet."

Reaching the street, Jacob looked up and down the thoroughfare. "Where is that carriage of yours, Sarah?"

Fidgeting with the folds in her dress and clutching her valise tight to her stomach, she craned her neck as if to search the long line of wagons, carriages and buggies. She knew her face was pale when she turned back to Jacob and said, "I don't see it."

Jacob grinned. "Well, then, no sense leaving you stranded here in the cold. My cousin Samuel should be here with his wagon if my letter got here before the *Edinburgh*. He delivers milk, so he must know the city. We will drop you off. If he doesn't show, I'll find us a carriage for hire. Where did you say you were going?"

"I didn't say. I am sure my aunt will be along."

Jacob had not lowered her trunk. "You can sit in the wagon with us until she arrives. We'll wait with you. I'm too much the gentleman to allow a beautiful woman to be alone in an unknown crowd in a strange city."

Though sensing the disingenuous irony in Jacob's tone, she could come up with no choice but to follow him.

Walking down the line of carriages, Jacob suddenly raised his free arm and waved. "Yo there, Samuel."

From the mill of horse-drawn transportation, a man raised his hand in response. The weathered wood of the side panels of Samuel's milk wagon had ragged holes where pieces of the planking had fallen out. Empty milk crates were piled in the wagon bed. A film of grime covered the wagon. Two thin horses were hanging their heads listlessly and appeared not to have been curried in months. Samuel resembled Jacob but older, with a huge potbelly and the florid complexion of a heavy drinker.

He grunted, "'Bout time. You're damn lucky. That limey Navy sop just delivered your letter yesterday." His eyes fixed on Sarah. "Didn't write nuthin' 'bout no woman."

"This is Miss Sarah Bonney. We met on the ship. Isn't she a delightful wisp of a redhead?"

The eyes of both men roving over her body, Sarah felt a hot blush rise in her cheeks and a queasy feeling in her stomach.

Twenty minutes elapsed. Sarah continuing to pretend to search for her transportation. Far down the line of carriages, she saw Reuben helping Rebecca with her luggage.

"She must have gotten the date wrong."

Following her stare and line of sight to Rebecca and Reuben, Jacob looked at her thoughtfully. "Well, let us drop you off. We can't leave a lady here alone with no ride, right Samuel?"

Raising bleary eyes to Jacob, Samuel slid them to Sarah and grunted. "What's the address, then, lassie? We'll get you there safely."

Feeling trapped, Sarah could still think of no plausible alternative or excuse. *Besides, he has my trunk...and Reuben is...busy.* "I am headed to my aunt's shop. She is a seamstress. I will be working with her and will live with her in the apartment above the store."

"Well, now, that is all fine information lass, but we need an address if we are to get you to your aunt."

Glancing back at Rebecca and Reuben in the distance, she felt a pang of jealousy mixed with apprehension. *What harm can it do?* She rationalized with herself. *I shan't see him again anyway.*

Without looking at Jacob, she said, "East 42nd Street, off 7th Avenue, please."

Smiling strangely, Jacob winked at Samuel. "You heard the lady. Let's get this sorry crate rolling."

17

March 2, 1855

THE MAYOR'S CARRIAGE

STOMPING HER FOOT WITH IMPATIENCE, EYES DARTING
up and down the line of coaches, Rebecca complained,
"I am soooo irritated."

Standing to the side and slightly behind her, Reuben
smiled at her outburst while allowing himself to soak in
every detail of her figure and clothing. In disregard of
the fashions of the day, Rebecca had replaced the flared
skirts for one with a smooth-fitting front. Her small
waist eliminated the need for a corset. The wide pagoda
sleeves of her dark, wool, traveling suit were trimmed
with black satin braids. This contrasted with the narrow
fitted under-sleeves of black, gathered at the wrist,
which matched the small collar. She wore a knee-length
black, velvet, traveling coat, lined and trimmed at the
edges with fur. It secured with heavy brocade hook-and-
eye closures in front. She was beautiful.

"My father and Ferdinando Wood conducted shipping
business together years ago, until Mister Wood was elected

to their Parliament over here, and recently became mayor. One would think a mayor would be better organized."

"Congress," Reuben corrected. "The Americans call it Congress, and I am quite sure neither the mayor nor anyone else could forget you, Mistress Marx."

Rebecca wheeled to face Reuben. With glittering eyes, she snapped, "It is bad enough, Mister Frank, to have to deal with leaving England for this ragged frontier...," she paused to give the city and harbor a sweeping look of disgust, "...without your impolite sarcasm. I am simply not accustomed to waiting."

For a beautiful woman, she certainly has a sharp tongue! Reuben continued to watch her when she turned back to the street to resume her search. He glanced behind him at the four men who had each lugged a trunk or two, amusing himself with the thought that Rebecca's collection of luggage was so monumental it must have constituted at least half the storage in the hold. A number of carefully crafted valises sat near the six huge ornate trunks with intricate hand scrolling and silverwork. Together they spread out nearly five yards along the curb.

"There it is! That is my carriage!" Rebecca gestured above the crowd out to Bowery Street, where a carriage replete with flags, the coat of arms of the city of New York, two plumed horses and a uniformed driver was prancing toward them.

Turning to Rebecca, he laughed. "Should have brought some mules with you, too." She stared at him blankly. He laughed again, more deeply.

Rebecca shook her head. "I don't quite understand. Explain yourself please," she demanded in a petulant voice.

She seems intrigued by my voice but I sense I annoy her. "Haven't spent much time in the country, have you?" queried Reuben, straining under the weight of the first trunk.

"No," said Rebecca. "The country lacks the culture of the city."

Casting a sideways glance at her, he spoke quietly. "Land, not people, is the root of culture."

Reaching the rear of the carriage, he levered the first trunk on board, then frowned at the driver who hadn't lifted a hand to assist. "Tie off that line, and help me with the lady's trunks."

The driver, startled at the directive, shot a questioning look toward Rebecca.

Following a surprised glance at Reuben, Rebecca gave a nod.

Together they loaded the baggage while Rebecca watched. The assorted pieces filled the carriage to overflowing.

"Be careful with that; there is china in there!"

Snapping his eyes toward her, Reuben shook his head incredulously. "China? You mean as in teacups and saucers?"

"Of course. Thank you, Reuben."

"Where are you headed?"

"I am afraid that after some time as the guest of the mayor, I will have to leave the city to take care of some matters." She sighed with resignation. "My father recently died and left some business interests here that I am forced to attend to..." she caught herself, "...in this place." Sweeping her arm, she looked around with an air of scarcely veiled contempt.

"What type of business and where?" pressed Reuben. "Are you staying in New York?"

Rebecca's face stiffened. "No, slightly west of here," she said curtly, offering nothing further.

Taking her hand, he bowed from the waist, raising her wrist to his lips. The shadow on her features vanished, replaced by a rose hue.

Reuben flashed a broad grin. "I sincerely hope that our paths cross again."

Smiling faintly as she turned, she said without emotion, "I suppose anything is possible, though I would doubt it." Raising her long skirts, she stepped up into the carriage with Reuben's assistance.

March 2, 1855

*U*NCLE HERMANN

THE CARRIAGE ROLLED AWAY. THE MAYOR'S COLORS snapping smartly in the wind, the two meticulously groomed black horses prancing with streamlined precision. Their plumed heads bobbed each time their hooves struck the street with the shallow reverberation of horseshoes on stone. Rebecca sat stiff and erect, her back several inches from the rear of the seat, her profile outlined by the opposite carriage window. Reuben thought she slid her eyes toward him as the coach pulled away from the curb but he couldn't be sure.

"Colder than an ice block in the milk house," he muttered to himself and then headed back to the dock where Johannes was waiting with their duffels and the map case. He wove his way through hundreds of people who milled and moved in every direction, staggering under the burden of luggage, trunks and satchels of every size and description.

"Sorry that took so long," Reuben said to Johannes when he finally reached him.

"I could see glimpses of the two of you and her entourage whenever this throng parted or whenever there were short people in front of me.

"She is undoubtedly the most aloof, most arrogant—"

Johannes cut Reuben off, "You mean you like her."

Reuben's head snapped up and he felt that familiar tingle as his eye color began to change from green to gray, "I don't mean any such thing. I will never see her again, anyway."

Catching the mischievous twinkle in Johannes eyes, he realized his friend's solemn expression was feigned. He relaxed. "You'll get yours, Johannes. Now come on; we have other things to do."

"We?"

"I thought you might like to accompany me to my uncle's home. It will be an hour or more carriage ride but I understand the house is quite comfortable. He left the farm when he was twenty-two and joined the army. He was an officer in the cavalry but was wounded and discharged. He moved to America with my aunt eleven years ago, though she died soon thereafter. Uncle Hermann and I have to discuss the trip west and some other family matters. I'm sure you would be most welcome."

Johannes smiled, shifted from one foot to the other, and his eyebrows arched. "The Prussian cavalry was well-known." Clearing his throat, he looked down the street. "I was just going to sling my duffel and walk from the docks until I found a good, cheap, rundown hotel. I thought we would simply meet up later sometime."

"No sense in that. Besides, I have an idea I want to discuss with you. Come on; grab your stuff. Let's take in our first taste of America."

Johannes and Reuben hauled their gear to the street, hailing a small surrey that was waiting for passengers in a long line of other similar commercial carriages. Reuben noticed few of the immigrants solicited a ride. Most were walking off in various directions, struggling with bags.

They loaded their duffels in the carriage. "157th Street, off Kingsbridge Road, please," Reuben called out to the driver. The driver leaned down and peered back into the surrey window. "That's a long ways from here, mate. Not gonna be cheap."

Reuben waved his hand. "You'll get paid."

The surrey bounced and clattered on the cobblestones. Occasionally the hard pavement would end in a long expanse of dirt or gravel. Johannes was leaning half out the window as transfixed as Reuben by the sights, sounds, buildings and energy of New York City.

"Have you ever seen this many people in such a hurry?" Reuben wondered aloud.

"Can't say I have. Looks like coronation day for the king."

"And what country would that be the king of?"

Johannes shot him a dour but good-humored look and then returned his eyes to the passing streetscape.

The first part of the ride was through a seamy section of the city. People were dressed crudely, street urchins played and screamed in the street, and the signs on the shops were mostly weathered and in need of paint. Then they turned on Broadway and traveled through an area of higher buildings, many of them of newer brick or stone. Storefronts with the latest fashions and large glass windows lined the sidewalks; women in fine dresses and men with top hats and suits scurried from one mysterious destination to the next.

Eventually, they were moving through much less imposing sections of the city. The buildings were lower, few over two stories. There were trees here and there and the walls of the structures were separated by several feet of space, rather than connected along an entire face of city block. The city-like feel of neighborhoods began to change, brightened by the green of occasional small yards. The blocks became clearly more residential and a three- to five-yard separation became commonplace between the houses.

The carriage turned off the Kingsbridge Road onto 157th Street. The lawns were larger; well-kept masonry homes were set back five to ten yards from the curb, and rows of mature, perfectly spaced oak and elm trees lined both edges of the narrow, gravel street surface.

"I think this is it, driver," Reuben called out. The driver tightened up on the lines and the horses came to a halt in front of a two-story brick home with large stone ledgers under tall, arched windows with panes separated by bright, white, painted mullions.

They unloaded their bags, and as Reuben was paying the driver, the front door opened. A man with a build similar to Reuben's and the same wavy hair but peppered with gray, walked out on the covered porch with a noticeable limp.

"Is that your uncle?"

Straightening up from the bags, Reuben nodded. "Uncle Hermann," he called out to the man who now stood outside the front door.

Uncle Hermann waved and then beckoned at them. Reuben smiled when he spoke in German, "Good to see you, Reuben. You were no higher than my thigh the last time I visited. I see you brought a friend. Good. Good. Come in."

Reuben and Johannes lugged their bags through the front door. The home was comfortable but not ostentatious. Fine, distinctly European furniture and stuffed chairs in medium floral designs, along with several woven rugs, were scattered about. Subdued oil paintings of Villmar and the farm adorned the walls. One portrait was of Uncle Hermann and Ludwig standing with their arms over each other's shoulders on the banks of the Lahn. It hung in a scrolled gold frame over a brick fireplace with a heavy, dark stained, oak mantel.

Introductions were made. Johannes walked back to the front door to move the duffels. Reuben noticed Uncle Hermann studying Johannes carefully, his uncle giving the slightest nod of his head as if satisfied with the answer to some internal question he had posed to himself.

Since the death of Uncle Hermann's wife, Gertrude, he had lived alone except for one servant, a very heavyset Negro woman, Mae, who was cheerful and attentive. Mae prepared a huge dinner of pheasant, mashed potatoes, gravy and corn bread, and stood off to the side of the table with a broad smile as the three men consumed huge quantities of food, occasionally smacking their lips, raising their eyes up from their plates, and nodding approval to her.

After dinner, Reuben turned to Johannes as they were getting up from the table. "Johannes, I need to spend time with my uncle to review some family matters. Can you keep yourself amused?"

"I think I will take a walk through the neighborhood to see the sights and sounds. Perhaps there will be a tall, blonde-haired, blue-eyed maiden out there for an evening stroll."

Reuben and his uncle spent a half hour talking in the parlor over cognac. Uncle Hermann finished his third snifter, reached over and put his hand on Reuben's knee. "Ah my boy, you do remind me of my brother in many ways. It has been wonderful to hear the news of the farm but we have business to attend to. Come up to my study."

Uncle Hermann's study was almost identical to Ludwig's. Floor-to-ceiling black walnut bookcases crammed with volumes occupied three walls. Three great, overstuffed chairs were gathered around a walnut coffee table. A roll top writing desk was centered under the one window. Reuben felt a nostalgic pang. "Uncle Hermann, this reminds me of home."

Sinking down in one of the chairs, Uncle Hermann chewed on the stem of his cherry pipe, peering sharply at Reuben. "This country is now your home, nephew. Now, tell me what you know. What has your father told you?"

He listened intently to Reuben's understanding of the family's aspirations for expansion of the cattle business in America, and they pored over the maps. Then his uncle fell silent.

Paying studious attention to the bowl as it tapped against the ash box, Uncle Hermann knocked the ashes from the pipe. He finally looked up. "It is a very dangerous and unforgiving place that you are going to," he said quietly in German. "There is no law. There are great tracts of land but there are Indians, extreme weather, thieves and men without conscience. I fear this country may come to arms over the slavery issue. The conflict could spread even to the remote west. No one has adhered to the Compact of 1830. There are many who want to extend slavery north of the 30th Parallel, which the compact set as a boundary for legal use of slaves in commerce. The 1854 Kansas-Nebraska Act passed just last year and has merely stirred a deeper rift over the issues. There has been violence in the east half of the Kansas Territory over the last six months.

In addition, the government has already broken the Indian Treaty of 1850, and there have been accounts in the paper of raids and killing. This will not be the gentle pasturing of cattle on the lush green fields of Villmar. You will need your wits and all your strength and courage, and once you have chiseled out the family's place, you may well have to fight to keep it."

"I know." Reuben leaned forward. "I am ready."

Uncle Hermann again deliberately emptied and refilled his pipe. Reuben realized his boots were tapping with impatience and willed his feet to be still. "I feel as if you are probing whether or not my character is strong enough."

Uncle Hermann's eyes flicked to his for a moment, then back to his pipe. "Ludwig wrote me more than two years ago that he had chosen you. He wanted only to wait until you were twenty-one. Neither of us doubts your ability—only your experience. You would be foolish to travel alone, Reuben. Everyone needs a trusted friend to cover his back. Two sets of eyes are far more powerful than simple bravery."

"I know, Uncle. I agree. I have decided to ask Johannes to accompany me. I believe he will."

"That is wise, nephew. I had hoped you would do that. There is a strength in him behind the devilish attitude. It would not surprise me if he has had extensive military experience."

"Now that you bring it up, Uncle, that would certainly explain some things I have noticed. Johannes carries himself a certain way. I'll ask him."

Motioning to Reuben to remain seated, Hermann rose. "There is also something you must have," he said. He limped from the study, reappearing minutes later with a .54 caliber Sharps long rifle and the monies Ludwig had steadily sent across the ocean. Reuben could not keep his eyes off the long-range gun. The gold and silver breech offset the splendid walnut stock. He eagerly took the weapon when his uncle extended it, turning the Sharps slowly in his hands. It was heavy and solid. He swung the brass butt plate easily to his shoulder and then lowered the rifle. "There is a perfect heft and fine balance in the swing of the muzzle. It's beautiful, Uncle Hermann."

"I will show you how to use the breech-loading mechanism tomorrow. With practice, eight to ten rounds a minute are possible. I also had some custom work done. The gunsmith added on an Enfield adjustable ladder sight, as you can see. There are steps in one-hundred-yard increments up to four hundred yards. The adjustable flip-up sight that I had him add extends the accuracy of the gun to between six hundred fifty and twelve hundred fifty yards, depending on wind and how solid a rest you have. British Marines...," a dark look crossed Uncle Hermann's face, "...are designated marksmen if they hit a two-foot bull's-eye seven in twenty times at six hundred yards." He tapped his pipe on the ash box with several particularly hard taps. "I trust you will shoot far more accurately than Her Majesty's Red Coats."

"Thank you. I am sure it will properly defend me and put meat on the table."

Leaning forward, his uncle's reply was terse. "Yes, it is beautiful but it is more than that where you're going. It's a weapon, perhaps at times the most important tool you will have. Remember, nephew, sometimes the best way to defend is to attack."

"That sounds rather grim." Reuben set the rifle down.

"It is simply as it is. One more thing. Did Ludwig tell you we never received the third map?"

Reuben nodded.

"Based on the last note from our scout's brother, which might not have yet reached Prussia before you left, I have reason to believe the missing map may have indicated the possibility of gold near where you will establish the ranch."

"Ranch?" Reuben cocked his head quizzically.

Hermann smiled, "Yes, ranch. That is what Americans call cattle farms out west. Have you decided on how you will travel to the West?"

"I plan to leave Thursday, the day after tomorrow, by train to St. Louis via Chicago. Father told me the river steamship routes are too complicated and slow."

The older man nodded. "So they are, my boy. So they are. St. Louis is a boomtown. The population has gone up almost eight times in the last ten years. It is the primary gathering place for adventurous souls headed west into the frontier." He sighed deeply. "In many ways I envy you."

Rising, he tousled Reuben's hair. "I am tired, nephew, and I must rest my leg. I will leave you to your preparations."

Reuben stood, reaching out to shake his uncle's hand. He was surprised when, ignoring his outstretched hand, his uncle took a step forward and hugged him tightly. "Yes, you are much like my brother, Reuben. Ludwig was right to choose you. Now take the rifle. Do not hesitate to use it when you must."

You and Johannes should get a carriage down to Wiggins and Booraem Mercantile tomorrow. It is located on Pearl, north of Wall Street. Ask for Wallace, and tell him you are my nephew. Buy two Colt revolvers. I prefer the Navy models in .36 caliber. The Squareback is the best of the two Navy styles. They are a bit more accurate than the .44 Dragoon or Army models. They swing quickly, point well and have the six-shot cylinder." He looked out the window with a vacant stare. "If we had had those, I think we could have defeated the British." His eyes returned to Reuben. "But we didn't. Good night, nephew."

Johannes returned and joined Reuben who sat in the parlor lost in thought, the Sharps on his lap.

"How was your walk?"

Johannes eyes twinkled. "Other than a lack of female Vikings, quite pleasant." He whistled appreciatively. "That is a hell of a rifle. Many think it is the best in the world. And I see you have elevation ladders on the sights. Very impressive."

Reuben punched him playfully in the shoulder. "So, women *and* rifles, eh? And I thought you only had a one-track mind. But, besides that, there's something I want to show you."

Opening the leather map case, he carefully withdrew the maps he and his uncle had studied and spread them on the table. "I told you on the ship that my plans were to head west and establish a cattle operation for the family. However, there is much more. We are here," he pointed at New York. "There are trains that run from here to Chicago and St. Louis."

Reuben unrolled the larger of the two maps. While crude, it clearly showed St. Louis, the Mormon and Emigrant trails west, the Kansas Territory and a great range of mountains far to the west.

Pointing at a label on the extreme western side of the map, Reuben looked firmly, solemnly into Johannes' eyes. "Montanas Rojas, a set of three peaks in the mountain range known as the San Juans in Las Colorados, the west edge of the Kansas Territory. That's where I'm headed, Johannes. It is my family's future."

"Sounds exciting, but why share all this with me?" His friend's tone was nonchalant but Reuben noticed a keen interest in the blue eyes that had not left his.

Reuben cleared his throat. "Would you like to join me?"

Studying the map, a broad smile spread across the tall blond's features, and he nodded his head slowly. "The San Juans, eh? Not very Scandinavian. There's much you'll need to teach me about cattle."

"Yes. Well, perhaps you can teach me about women," Reuben snorted, "if there are any where we are headed." Laughing, the two men shook hands.

"We start day after tomorrow. We must outfit ourselves and you will need one of these." Reuben held up the Sharps. Johannes hefted the rifle. His facial features turned impassive and hard. Handing it back to Reuben, he shook his head firmly. "I think instead I will choose the slanting breech carbine from Sharps. It is shorter and lighter than yours and better for use while on a horse."

"How do you know all that?"

Johannes sidestepped Reuben's question. "We will both need pistols, too, and I would like a saber."

"Uncle Hermann suggested pistols but a saber?"

"They can be useful."

"Are you familiar with the use of sabers?" Reuben pressed. "They are mostly military issue, aren't they?"

Johannes expression remained inscrutable. "I have used one a time or two."

"But—" began Reuben.

Standing suddenly, Johannes extended his long arm and stretched. "I am tired. Time for some rest. Good night, Reuben, my friend." He turned and strode from the room. Reuben felt his eyebrows arch as he stared after Johannes, now more curious than he had been before.

March 2, 1855

GRACIE MANSION

As HER TRANSPORTATION DEPARTED THE WHARF, Rebecca made sure her sidewise glance at Reuben was not revealed by any turn of her head. Playing back Reuben's orders to the driver, how his green eyes coolly appraised her and the hint of condescension in his smile, she pursed her lips. *He is really rather an upstart for the commoner class...though his tone was even, not overbearing but one of someone used to being in command.*

Thrusting back her shoulders, she forced herself to think ahead to her introduction to the mayor. Her father had intimated he was a rogue. The interior of the carriage gave some hint about the splendor he enjoyed. Plush, pleated, leather, burgundy seats faced each other. The floor was of polished oak in a herringbone design, carefully crafted and fitted. The cab walls were finished in rich burgundy velour; black braid trim was carefully placed at each seam and traced the curve of where the interior walls met the ceiling. The carriage windows had glass, a luxury Rebecca had not often seen in carriages in England. Small latches halfway up the windows could be pulled out to lower the top half of the window.

They quickly left the neighborhoods in close proximity to the harbor, turning down Broadway, and then Fifth Avenue. "My, my, I had no idea," Rebecca said aloud, as she looked out the window.

The sidewalks were of carefully laid stone. Expensive shops with the latest fashions in the windows lined the street, and uniformed bellmen stood outside the doors of residential buildings and hotels. Well-dressed pedestrians turned, pointing at the carriage and craning their necks in an attempt to see if the mayor was inside.

The horses turned into a semicircular drive on East End Avenue and 88th Street. The clip-clop of their shoes echoed almost in unison off large wrought iron gates bearing the sign *"Gracie Mansion."* They were opened without hesitation by two uniformed policemen dressed smartly in blue tunics, with big badges, beige trousers and blue caps, which had crossed rifles embroidered on their crowns. The mayor's mansion was set well back from East End Avenue. The drive was paved with red brick and the grounds were immaculately manicured. Surveying the building carefully as it came into clear view, Rebecca decided the architects had tried to imitate European flavor, somehow blending the continental with aspects of American creativity. The huge home was of imposing height. An oversized portico extended from wide entry steps that rose to entry doors. The driveway widened under the covered entry and the brick pavers were set in herringbone.

The carriage came to a halt near the bottom of the steps. There was space under the portico for a number of large carriages. The white Gothic-style columns that supported the cover cast linear shadow designs across the front entry. Intricate latticework rimmed the entire second floor. Two members of the mansion staff were rapidly descending toward the carriage. One was a large, athletic, Negro man who went immediately to the carriage's rear cargo well. The other, a very tall, slender, beautiful woman with long blonde hair, stood demurely as the driver assisted Rebecca with perfect etiquette and form as she stepped down from the coach.

"We welcome you, milady Marx," the blonde woman curtsied smartly, spreading the gray pleated skirt of her uniform to both sides with either hand, and bowing low into the white lace hemmed into her bodice.

Rebecca nodded. The woman appeared to be around the same age as she was. It was not often that she encountered another female whose beauty rivaled her own. The servant's English was impeccable, though there was a noticeable Scandinavian accent.

"My name is Inga. I assist Mayor Wood with guests, and I will be your personal attendant during your stay with us. We have been looking forward to your arrival."

Turning to the Negro, she smiled, "John, could you please secure milady's bags and bring them up to her suite."

John looked at her with a startled expression, pointing to the rear of the carriage.

Walking over to the rear of the carriage, Inga looked in the baggage compartment, which overflowed with

Rebecca's trunks. "Oh, dear! John, I think it best that you get some assistance in moving this luggage. I'm sure milady will need items from her bags immediately to freshen up to meet the mayor."

Rebecca smiled. "A lady must have her comforts, and I insist on traveling prepared for any occasion. The three trunks in silver leaf can be stored in a safe, dry place. They have both valuables and breakables; so please handle them with care. The other three trunks and the three valises, I shall need. If you could have your helpers put them safely in my quarters, that would be greatly appreciated. What is your last name, Inga?"

"Yes, milady. Inga Bjorne. I'm originally from Norway."

"Thank you, Inga. I am pleased that you've been assigned by the mayor to assist me. With your European culture and your obvious good grace and manners, I feel welcome already. I'm sure we will get along quite well."

Inga acknowledged the compliment with a reserved smile.

It took John several minutes to assemble two younger, and likewise muscular, mansion staff to assist with Rebecca's heavy trunks. Rebecca felt a start of surprise when Inga gave the newcomers orders in fluent French.

Returning to Rebecca's side, Inga directed extrication of the final trunks. "We know, milady, that traveling can be tiresome. If you would follow me, I'll show you to your room so you can freshen up."

Leading Rebecca into the foyer, she stopped, sweeping her arm around the room, "Welcome to Gracie Mansion, milady." The semicircular floor of black-and-white marble stretched in a pattern of diagonals and squares many meters from the front doors across an elliptical receiving area with a great volume that rose to the second floor ceiling. Stairways of oak at least three yards wide curved upward around either wall to a balcony two stories above the entry floor. The black curved handrails floated with perfect synchronization in their sweep up the stairs atop intricately milled glossy white balusters. Behind the railing of the balcony, a number of white-paneled doors were visible.

INGA WAS NOT ENTIRELY SURE WHAT TO MAKE OF Rebecca Marx. There was something familiar about her, her name, mannerisms and pattern of speech, but Inga could not place exactly what gave her the feeling.

She had grown accustomed to a wide variety of guests and visitors to the mansion, and she had unabashedly taken full advantage of her looks with the mayor and her innate ability to organize and charm. In just months, she had been rapidly promoted from the janitorial staff to the reception staff.

She usually assigned herself to attend the visiting males. She took special delight in achieving a fine balance between their interest and the strict prohibition against male touch or sexual interaction she had imposed upon herself in her new job. *At least this guest will not have to be fended off*, she thought to herself, walking toward the bottom of the right-side stairway, Rebecca several meters behind.

Inga came to an abrupt stop as the mayor's voice echoed from the other side of the room. "This must be milady Rebecca Marx."

Inga pursed her lips slightly. *His voice is so much higher-pitched than one might expect from a man in a position of power.*

Bustling across the floor, a wide smile cemented itself between the tremors of his pudgy cheeks. His rotund frame and average height were accentuated by knee stockings that clung to stocky calves until they disappeared at the bottom of leggings that ballooned in an upward taper from his knee to the top of his thigh. His long-tailed vest was open to a starched, white, ruffled shirt. The bright, green fabric was too tight around his shoulders and imparted a peculiar twist to the dark gray of the wide lapels, where they flared wide at his collarbones and tapered to a mere point of fabric at his hips. Though no longer the style of the day, his cheekbones showed a hint of rouge.

Looking down at the floor, Inga tried to hide her inward snicker as he approached Rebecca, his eyes moving hungrily from her feet to her shoulders. *He has certainly chosen his attire unwisely for this occasion.*

She glanced at Rebecca, who was facing the mayor with a forced smile. The mayor was not much taller than Rebecca's five foot four inches. Bowing forward clumsily, he grabbed one of her hands and raised her wrist to his lips.

"Milady Marx. Ferdinando Wood, mayor of the great city of New York at your service. It is truly such a pleasure to meet you. I was appalled to hear of Henry's untimely death. He was a God-fearing, successful, adventurous soul. Though he often talked of you, I had no idea his daughter was so radiantly lovely and charming."

Inga started at the mention of Henry Marx's name. *Could this really be his daughter?* Perhaps that would explain the vague sense of recognition.

March 2, 1855

*C*OMMON GROUND

WATCHING THE EXCHANGE CAREFULLY, INGA AMUSED herself with thoughts of how few successes the mayor had with the opposite sex. *Though he fancies himself quite the ladies' man.* Occasionally, he enjoyed couplings due to his money and power but Inga had never seen true attraction on the part of any woman. Shifting her gaze to Rebecca, Inga empathetically studied the contrived smile pasted on her face, her unnaturally stiff posture and her free hand firmly in front of her abdomen.

Graciously, Rebecca allowed the mayor's lips to linger on the back of her wrist before withdrawing her hand. Fluttering her eyelids, she crooned in just the right tone, "I did not expect such gentlemen in the New World."

Inga was impressed by the dark-haired woman's perfect blend of aloof, yet coquettish, manipulation.

"The New World?" The mayor chuckled. "My dear, my dear, this is America. We are no longer the New World. We are modern." He gestured with both hands around the room, rolling his shoulders from side-to-side on feet that did not move an inch.

Picking up on the cue, Rebecca responded, "Your mansion is most impressive, mayor. Visits here were the highlights of my father's excursion to America. He enjoyed the shipping business he conducted with you prior to your election to Parliam...to Congress in 1852. He spoke very highly of you."

Beaming, the mayor stuck his thumbs in his vest pockets, bouncing several times on the balls of his feet. "Well, your dear father was always one of my most respected and welcomed guests and trading partners. His pride in you was evident, and I can see why."

Batting her eyelashes again, Rebecca kept her half-smile frozen in place. "You are too kind, mayor. I very much look forward to hearing more about Father's visits."

Reaching forward, he took one of Rebecca's hands in his, then covered both with his other. "I'm sure your long voyage must have been most tiring. I hear the disembarkation and immigration processes leave much to be desired, and that gentlemen and ladies are not separated from the rest of the rabble, whom I'm told are quite rough. I'm sure you need a bit of rest and to freshen up. How long shall we enjoy the honor of your company? Perhaps I can talk you out of going further west, though I understand from your solicitor's letters that was your original intention."

Rebecca's eyes were fixed on her small delicate hand sandwiched between the mayor's meaty digits. Inga was sure Rebecca was fighting the impulse to pull away.

"We shall see, mayor. I had planned to take the train to St. Louis several days from now. My hopes are that I would not have to travel beyond that. Your kind offer to grant me some time to rid myself of the weariness of the trip is accepted. I'm very grateful to you for putting Inga..." Rebecca turned, smiling genuinely at Inga, "...at my disposal. She seems quite competent and attentive."

Glancing briefly at Inga with an absent look, his eyes involuntarily soaked in the curves of her figure. "Of course, of course. Inga is our very best, just as you deserve milady. Inga, take milady Marx to the Green Suite." He turned back to Rebecca. "That is the corner accommodation, the very best in the house, with two large windows looking out over Hell's Gate and the grounds."

Inga started to say, "Your excellency..." but her words died in her throat at a sharp glance from the mayor. *Milady Marx had apparently just been upgraded.* She gave some thought as to how quickly she could get John to move the trunks from the smaller suite originally assigned Rebecca, to what the staff termed the royalty suite. *I shall manage*, she thought to herself. Smiling sweetly back at the mayor, she curtsied. "Yes, your excellency, right away."

The mayor returned his stare to Rebecca, again not able to control the slide of his eyes from her face to her breasts and then to her hips. "Would you like some refreshment, milady Marx? Tea? Bread pudding? I could have the kitchen staff put together whatever you wish."

"You certainly think of my every need, mayor. Some tea would be excellent. If it could be brought up to my room, I would be most grateful."

Spinning, the mayor raised an arm and snapped his fingers twice. "John," he called out to the same big Negro who had greeted the carriage and now stood with his hands clasped before him at a far-off door. "Please tell the kitchen to prepare a pot of tea." He turned back to Rebecca. "I know the English like milk and honey?"

"Just milk, thank you."

"And milk, John. Let Inga know when it's done so she may bring it up to milady Marx."

The mayor glanced at the huge grandfather clock that rose against the wall next to the stairway. "Would you do me the honor of dining with me tonight? It is almost four now. Perhaps seven o'clock? Would that give you enough time?"

Widening her eyes, Rebecca smiled, "I was hoping that you would ask me for dinner, mayor. We have much to talk about. I wish to know all I can about the New... about America."

"Yes, yes my dear. I am sure we will find many topics for discussion."

"Thank you. I shall look forward to seven o'clock.

Grinning delightedly, he again rocked back and forth on his toes. Turning to Inga, he gestured, "Please escort milady Marx from her chambers to dinner. The staff will serve supper in the blue room."

"Of course, your excellency." Inga curtsied, smiling down at the floor. The blue room was centered at the back of the mansion. Its windows faced all directions from the round half-wall that extended out from the flat wood structure. It overlooked ponds, the flagstone terrace at the heart of the grounds and Hell's Gate. Inga knew from the mayor's occasional unsuccessful attempts to lure her to his bedroom that he considered this dining area to be the most romantic in the mansion.

"Excuse me, then." Bowing again, he kissed Rebecca's wrist. "I will place you back in Inga's capable care."

The two women ascended the stairs, Rebecca following several steps behind. Inga could feel her gaze. They reached the top landing and turned right down the wide spacious hall. Ornate gold frames with various paintings of New York and previous mayors lined the wide corridor. Large French doors at the end of the hall opened into a very spacious suite. Overstuffed chairs and an elm coffee table furnished the sitting area in one alcove, two huge elm armoires stood against another wall, and the water closet was lavish, replete with two pedestal sinks and an oversized round cast iron tub. The white porcelain finishes glistened in the last of the sunlight, which streamed in from two high-set windows. A huge bed with thick, highly polished, brass headboard and footboard was centered on one wall, positioned so that the first view from sleepy eyes would be to the enormous corner windows. Here and there, through the glass, taller buildings were visible in the distance above the spring buds of oaks, maples and elm trees that were scattered about the grounds. But there was no luggage.

"Oh, my! John must have brought your trunks to the wrong room!" Inga did her best to display astonishment. She turned to Rebecca. "I shall rectify that immediately. My apologies."

Rebecca's eyes were coolly amused as she looked directly back into Inga's. "After meeting the mayor, I was promoted, was I?"

Despite herself, Inga began laughing; Rebecca joined in.

"Men," snorted Inga shaking her head, then looking quickly at Rebecca to see if she had overstepped.

"Yes, men. Curious but predictably single-minded creatures." The two women smiled again with the knowledge that a bond had been formed.

"Have you ever been invited to dine in the blue room?"

Inga was surprised at the question. She slowly shook her head. "I have but it ended at dessert."

"I would have been astonished at any other outcome," said Rebecca. "We shall see if I even last to dessert."

Smiling at one another again, Inga felt a grudging respect for Rebecca. It was not a feeling she had often for guests of the mayor, regardless of their gender or status.

John and his two assistants struggled through the door with part of the baggage. "Thank you for moving those trunks," Inga told them.

Rebecca pointed. "Set them down over there on either side of the armoires, John."

As soon as the men left, Inga offered, "Milady Marx would you wish me to have a bath drawn for you? Is there anything else you might need? I will be up right away with your tea."

Reaching out, Rebecca gently rested her hand on Inga's shoulder. "While I realize you must follow protocol for others, Inga, when we are alone, please just call me Rebecca. Perhaps we can spend some time together. I've never been to America and going into the city for shopping and lunch would be most enjoyable. I'm sure we can have fun."

Inga was delighted with the suggestion and the invitation. "It would be my privilege to accompany you milady... Rebecca, and I know some fine shops and wonderful restaurants. I think you will find New York quite exciting."

"We have a date then. Perhaps tomorrow, late morning. I need a good night's sleep. Five weeks in the cramped quarters of that ship have worn me thin."

"Midmorning it will be, then. I will have a carriage out front. Let me draw your bath for you, and then I shall leave you in peace." Bustling into the water closet, she began filling the tub, and then moved to the French doors at the entry of the suite, turning toward Rebecca, her arms outstretched on both knobs. She began to close them behind her as she backed out into the hall, then she paused. With a slight giggle, she called out to Rebecca, who stood at one of the windows. "And you shall have a wonderful dinner."

Rebecca laughed. "I shall indeed. And an early and long night's sleep."

March 2, 1855

$\mathscr{S}$EDUCTION

THERE WAS A LIGHT TAPPING AT THE ENTRANCE TO HER quarters. Rebecca swung open one side of the French doors. Standing there was Inga, a conspiratorial smile on her face.

"It's time for dinner with his excellency. I know that you have waited by the door with eager anticipation."

"Actually, I was sitting in the chair, staring out the window and counting the minutes until the clock struck seven." They both laughed.

"You look beautiful, Rebecca. I'm sure some of those fashions are available in New York, though not all. I wish I had the funds to buy one or two dresses like yours."

"Come, my dear." Rebecca put her arm around Inga's waist and began to walk down the balcony corridor toward the stairway. "With your looks and quick mind, I have no doubt that you will one day be able to afford clothing such as this."

Inga ushered her into the blue room. Pale yellow amber light from two wall-mounted gas lamps reflected off the windows, which extended from floor to ceiling in each facet of the curved wall. A highly polished, oak table almost three meters long was centered in the semicircular space. Handsome, carved, high-back chairs with plush, blue upholstery flanked the table, one at either end, and four on each side. Flickering down the length of the table were six candles. Two place settings, one on either end of the long oak expanse, gleamed in the soft light.

"Have a wonderful time, Rebecca—I mean, milady Marx." Inga glanced furtively behind her to see if anyone had overheard her use the less-formal greeting.

Minutes after Inga's departure, the mayor arrived. Rebecca bit her lip to stop the laugh that welled in her chest. His attire for the evening was even more pompous and gaudy than that of the afternoon. *I really should put him in touch with Zachary, Father's tailor.* Smiling sweetly, she allowed the mayor to take her hand, lead her to the table and pull out her chair. As he walked down to his seat, he took care to move the candles so that they were arranged to afford a clear view of her. Smartly uniformed kitchen staff delivered the initial courses on which Rebecca nibbled, forcing herself to appear interested in the mayor's conversation.

By the time the main course arrived, roast duckling with mandarin sauce accompanied by vegetables from the mansion's garden, discussion had progressed only to the point of inquiries by the mayor of the life and economic times in London and dull discourse on the weather in New York.

Focusing on her plate, Rebecca was certain she would surely retch if she had to endure any more of his banal conversation.

Her thought was interrupted when the mayor suddenly snapped his fingers, gesturing to the mousy looking servant who stood off to one side. "Alicia, move my place setting down next to lady Marx." He barely managed to avoid spilling his wine as he pushed back his chair, which nearly tipped over when his ample derriere caught on the armrest. Padding down the table, he pulled out the chair next to Rebecca, sitting down heavily and leaning back with a smug, self-satisfied air. Alicia hurriedly transferred his place setting and overfull plate.

"That will be all, Alicia." He waved his hand dismissively. "I will ring the bell if anything further is required."

The mayor leaned toward Rebecca, reaching across the corner of the table and taking her hand in his, "I was very close to your father. You have no idea how delighted I am that his lovely daughter is my guest."

Rebecca debated whether to pull her hand away, then thought better of it. "Father never told me a great deal about his trip to America. What types of activities did the two of you share when you were together?"

This query precipitated a lengthy reply by the mayor, peppered with obvious exaggeration about this or the other adventurous activity and the shipping business that he had shared with her father. Nonetheless, Rebecca heard several references that piqued her interest.

"So you say my father went west while he was here?"

"Yes, indeed."

"I had no idea! Just to St. Louis or did he go further?"

"No, my dear lady Marx...may I call you Rebecca? And I'd much prefer you call me Ferdinando, rather than mayor."

"I would like that, Ferdinando," Rebecca lowered her eyelids and allowed a beguiling half-smile to spread across her lips. "What did he do in St. Louis?"

The mayor's eyebrows furrowed. "Honestly, Rebecca, I don't know. I did question him several times upon his return. I could not understand what on earth anyone could find to do for six months in St. Louis. However, he never answered the questions directly. He did return with a railcar full of rich furs and skins and a host of other frontier sundries, which were loaded on his ship. He seemed quite delighted."

Rebecca suddenly remembered. "I recall that voyage. I was just a little girl. We had word from an officer friend of ours in the Royal Navy that they had spied *Trader* just a day or two from Portsmouth. I recall standing at the dock in my shawl for almost the whole day as I awaited his arrival. He showed me the skins. The smell was rich and wonderful. I think it was a quite profitable cargo, too. Did Father meet anyone while he was in St. Louis or here in New York?"

The mayor's face blanched in uneasy surprise.

"I'm not sure what you mean, Rebecca. Your father was absolutely devoted to your mother. He loved her deeply. He spoke of her almost as often as he talked about you."

Rebecca shook her head. "No, of all that I am quite sure. Did he make any business acquaintances that you know of?"

"Oh!" said the mayor, relieved. "I know that he spent quite some time with an attorney, what you refer to as a solicitor, when he returned from that one particular venture to St. Louis. I did not feel that Henry's business was any of my concern. The attorney died just a few years ago," lamented the mayor, shaking his head sadly. "Great man. Such a pity."

He reached for her hand, his thumb stroking the top of her wrist. "You appear to have enjoyed tonight's repast. My culinary staff is second to none." Leaning forward a bit more, he spoke in a low, husky tone, "Would you honor me with a nightcap of sherry up in my quarters? The view is wonderful."

She politely placed long outstretched fingers delicately over her mouth, pretending to stifle a yawn. "I am literally exhausted, Ferdinando. It is difficult to explain how arduous the ocean journey was and how interminable the company." Involuntarily, the image of Reuben's green eyes and confident smile flashed across her mind. She willed the vision away. "Inga has been gracious enough to consent to accompany me into the city tomorrow to shop and see the sights. I must get some sleep. But how kind of you to offer."

"Well...tomorrow night, perhaps?" The mixture of disappointment and hope in the mayor's voice was not lost on Rebecca.

"Yes, perhaps tomorrow night. Is that a dinner invitation?"

The mayor's face brightened, "Of course, of course. Seven o'clock again?"

"I shall look forward to dining with you." Reaching over, Rebecca patted his hand, watching with hidden amusement as a scarlet flush crept up his fleshy jowls.

The mayor leaped up to pull out her chair.

"Goodnight, Ferdinando."

"Goodnight, dear Rebecca. Sleep well."

March 3, 1855

*H*ANDLE OF PEARL

LEANING OVER FROM REUBEN'S LEFT, MAE POURED HIM another cup of coffee, bobbing her head and flashing a wide, white smile as Reuben thanked her. "Yessuh." She held out the coffee pot to Johannes with a questioning look.

Johannes' mouth was full of toast and poached egg. Shaking his head, he swallowed hurriedly and grinned. "No thank you, Mae. I am about to float away."

Laughing, Uncle Hermann chimed in, "No more for me either, Mae, thank you." Swiveling his eyes to Johannes, the elderly soldier gave the tall Scandinavian a keen look, "A bit better than kaffee boiled on a bivouac fire. I never liked the way the smell of gunpowder over-whelmed the aroma of the brewing."

In the process of inhaling another enormous bite of breakfast, Johannes stopped chewing momentarily, look-ing sharply at Uncle Hermann. His eyes shifted briefly to Reuben, and then back to the old soldier. "Sometimes just holding a hot tin cup in your hand is a fine thing, Herr Hermann. It reminds you, you are still alive."

Looking from one to the other, Reuben cleared his throat. "Johannes and I are going to take your advice and go down to Wiggins and Booraem Mercantile today Uncle. How far is it?"

"It's a good half-hour carriage ride. You probably noticed the small surrey behind the house by the alley. It's older but clean and functional. Obviously, I have no room here to keep a horse; however, one half mile further down 157th Street there are some larger tracts, and small vegetable farms, each having several acres. My friend, Dr. Kampfmann, keeps my old mare for me. It's an expense, and I haven't harnessed her in more than three months. Of course with this..." he gestured to his leg, "... I haven't ridden in years. Pausing for a moment, he added, "But an old Calvary man has to have a horse."

Johannes blinked.

"There's a halter in the storage compartment of the surrey. Harnesses are in the shed by the alley. If you walk down the road you can lead Gertrude back, get the traces on her and be on your way." Pushing his chair back, he rose slowly using the table for support. "Remember, ask for Wallace," he reminded Reuben, "I've known him for many, many years and we've shared much. He will pay special attention to you."

Several hours later Johannes punched Reuben playfully in the shoulder, chuckling, "I believe, farm boy, you have us lost."

"I have us lost? You were doing the navigating, and you have Uncle's directions. You're supposed to be the worldly fellow!"

"Let's hope your maps are better than your uncle's directions or you and I may be wandering for forty years like your ancestors did."

Reuben laughed loudly, and Gertrude jerked her old gray muzzle up in alarm. Wiping his eyes, his shoulders still shaking with mirth, Reuben gasped, "We could ask somebody."

"Only if she's pretty. I hate asking for directions. Where the hell are we, anyway?" Johannes swung around looking for the nearest street sign "Ah, Beaver Street."

"Very helpful, Viking. That clears everything up."

Johannes exaggerated a sigh. "You said I was the navigator. I have now offered you an exact location. I have navigated! Since we are behind schedule, we should stop for lunch. What about that restaurant over there, Delmonicos?"

His laughter finally subsiding, Reuben shook his head. "No, let's get done what we came to do. The only thing worse than getting lost today, would be losing our way in the dark. Besides, I would like to spend an hour greasing these axles for Uncle. That right wheel is squeaking."

Johannes looked longingly at the restaurant, then pointed, "There's a policeman. Let's hope he knows his way around this maze of streets." He began laughing again. "Just one thing."

"What?"

"You ask him."

Finally arriving at the mercantile, a four-story building of warm, red-brown, pockmarked brick, Reuben looked around bewildered, "Where do we park the carriage? Do we have to go in one at a time?"

Gales of laughter burst from deep in Johannes chest. "You really are a farm boy, aren't you? See that man over there with the uniform? He's a coachman. We leave the surrey with him; he minds the carriage and we go into the store and bolster their ledgers."

"Oh!"

As Reuben was handing the reins to the coachman, an elderly, bespectacled, balding man, with a ragged scar across one cheek, came bustling from the front doors of the mercantile, his eyes moving rapidly from Johannes to Reuben and then to the carriage. A look of disappointment crept into his face.

"I'm sorry; I thought this was Major Frank's carriage."

He began to turn away but Reuben reached out, grabbing his arm lightly. "I am his nephew, Reuben Frank, and this is my friend Johannes Svenson. We're headed west and Uncle insisted we come down here to partially outfit ourselves. Uncle suggested we asked for a 'Wallace.' Do you know him?"

The man spun, a wide smile spreading across his face. "I am Wallace." Looking Reuben up-and-down he nodded, "Yes, yes, I see the resemblance. It is an honor, Herr Frank, to meet my major's nephew. Over the years, he has told me much about you, your father, the farm, and your other brothers." He shook his head sadly. "I believe his leg is increasingly painful. I've not seen him for some months."

"How do you know him?"

Wallace drew himself erect. "It was my honor to serve as his sergeant major. I carried him off the battlefield when he was wounded." He lifted two fingers to the scar across his cheek, tracing it with his fingertips. "I have a memento from that day, too." He fell silent for a moment, obviously remembering the cries of men and horses, and the smoky stench of battle and blood in that moment many years past. "Damn British," he muttered.

His face brightening, he rubbed his hands together. "I am honored to be able to assist you. What is it that you need?" Before either of them could answer, he turned abruptly, waving them to follow.

Johannes and Reuben exchanged glances and a smile as they followed Wallace into the mercantile.

Amazing. Reuben stopped, his eyes moving rapidly around the store. Every conceivable item of mercantile, hardware, armament, tack and frontier merchandise was organized into sections. Balconies of the second, third and fourth floors, each of them extending slightly less from the wall than the floor below, stair-stepped up to the high, tiled ceiling.

Reuben's eyes lit upon a corner with a number of hats on display. Wallace explained, "These new hats are becoming popular in the West and with cattle growers in Pennsylvania and north of the city. They are Army discards—mostly wrong dyes. The Army will only accept dark blue. They are made of beaver felt. The wide brims keep the sun and rain from your face and neck and they can be shaped to your desire over steam."

Reuben held one of the big, brown hats in his hand, liking the stiff feel of its brim and crown, and the texture of the material. He curled the front of the brims toward the center, holding it up at arm's-length and looking at it critically, then trying it on. *Perfect fit.* "I'll take it. Perhaps you could steam just a bit of curl into the front third of the brim for me?"

Wallace nodded enthusiastically.

Johannes pointed to a light tan hat with a narrower brim and a triangular crown not as high as Reuben's. "If it fits, I'll take that one."

Wallace's head bobbed again. "They call those campaign hats. Many ex-military seemed to like them best." He looked at Johannes intently.

The corners of Johannes' lips curled in an almost imperceptible smile. "Do you carry sabers or swords?"

The clerk's eyebrows shot up. "Indeed we do, though not many. We have both 1840 and 1842 military sabers with scabbards. Excellent weapons in the right hands." He looked at Johannes pointedly. "Our swords, unfortunately, are more decorative. I would not recommend them for any engagement."

"If you point me in that direction I'll go take a look. Perhaps you can help Reuben select a pistol. I know what I want. A Colt Army .44 caliber, blued, not plated and four boxes of ammunition. If you can get several of those pistols with varying grips out for me, I'll be over to take a look. I would also be most interested in acquiring an 1852 .52 caliber slanting breech Sharps carbine. If you would also have several of those available for me to heft I would be grateful."

Studying Johannes closely, a slight smile played on Wallace's lips, and there was a knowing look in his eyes.

He nodded, "It would be my pleasure, Herr Svenson." Turning to Reuben, he gestured, "Follow me, young man." They moved toward the back of the store to four long rows of glass display cases, each with three levels of slanted shelves holding a bewildering array of pistols and armaments.

"What do you have in mind, Herr Frank?"

"Please, call me Reuben. Uncle Hermann recommended a Navy Squareback Colt .36 caliber. He said it was lighter, quicker and more accurate than the Colt Armys or Dragoons. "What's that?"

Following the direction of Reuben's pointing finger, Wallace answered, "Holsters, for pistols. They're not yet widely used but demand is growing." They walked over to the line of leather holsters displayed on pegs on the wall. Taking one down, he handed it to Reuben. "This would fit the Navy Colt well. Repeated application of mink oil will soften the leather and mold to the pistol. They are called Slim Jims or Californias, depending upon the maker." He turned the holster over in his hand, peering at it. "Yes, yes, this is made by John Moore. His saddle shop is in Independence Missouri. He just started making these holsters recently. Notice the fine stamping and scrolling. Most people, you know, carry pistols in their waistband or belts. There are advantages and disadvantages to each, Reuben. The disadvantages are, of course, revolvers are percussion weapons and dirt and moisture can get into the top of a holster perhaps affecting the percussion cartridges and the action. Also, you'll notice they hang from your belt. They wobble, and that can slow the time to withdraw the pistol.

On the other hand..." he looked around from side-to-side and lowered his voice, "...I've been told by men who bought these and have become quite proficient in quickly drawing the revolver from the holster that the trick is to sew a leather loop at the bottom of the holster and tie the holster to your thigh with rawhide. Some have even sewn flaps on the body side of the leather, which will protect the weapon when not in use but can be folded back into your belt when the need arises."

Reuben nodded slowly, his thumb tracing the intricate embossing. He liked the feel of the Slim Jim. "I'll take this one. Also, could you bring me a strip of thick leather, a leather awl, mink oil and several strands of rawhide?"

Measuring Reuben's thigh with his eye, Wallace nodded, "About thirty inches long, I think, would be perfect." Wallace hustled off to gather the sundry items Reuben had requested.

Walking slowly down the display cases, Reuben's eyes moved from pistol to pistol. Suddenly, he stopped. Nestled between shiny plated and blued revolvers, and cap and ball handguns of every size, barrel-length and caliber imaginable, was one weapon unlike any of the hundreds on display. Its protective metal coating was soft gray-blue, rather than the typical blue-black. Its handle was off-white, pearl colored, glowing in semi-translucent pearl to cream waves in the light from the high, suspended gas lamps, as if calling him.

Returning with a small burlap sack, Wallace smiled, "I have all your materials gathered, Reuben. Now let me recommend some pistols...." The clerk started to turn.

"No. That one. That one right there."

Wallace followed Reuben's eyes. "It is indeed a Navy Squareback, .36 caliber, just as you were searching for." Wallace paused. "It is very distinctive. This is only the third one that has come to the store in the last eighteen months. Quite expensive, too.

He's trying to talk me out of this pistol—why? "Nonetheless, could you take it out of the case for me?"

Hesitating for just a moment, Wallace walked behind the glass case. Sliding open the rear doors, he reached in, extracted the Colt and placed it on one of the felt pads that were scattered every three or four feet down the countertops.

Picking up the pistol, Reuben spun the cylinder, checked the action and raised it, aiming at the wall. He slipped it in and out of the Slim Jim. Then, undoing his belt he threaded the Slim Jim so that it hung low and just behind his right hip. Holding the bottom of the holster he pulled the gun from it, shoved it back in and pulled it out again. *Perfect heft, weight and feel. The grip fits my hand as if it was made for me.*

"This is my pistol, Wallace." The clerk took the weapon from him slowly. Looking into Reuben's eyes, he carefully chose his words, "Herr Frank, sometimes it is more wise to not stand out."

Reuben returned his stare briefly, then, grinning, motioned with his hand, "Thank you, Wallace. That is my pistol."

Leaning over to Inga, Rebecca whispered in her ear, "I thought you said you'd never been here?"

Inga smiled, intimating in a low voice, "I've never dined in this establishment before, and it is unlikely I will be here again."

The two women were fanning themselves in the humid air as the carriage returned to Gracie Mansion late that afternoon, Inga wearing a mischievous expression.

"What?" asked Rebecca.

"I presume his excellency requested the pleasure of your company at dinner again tonight?"

"Of course. I am simply irresistible." The two women laughed so loud that the driver leaned over to look back in the carriage window to see what the commotion was about.

"Oh dear," chuckled Inga, wiping her eyes with a handkerchief. "I'm sure you know, Rebecca, but it is likely that you could be three feet tall and three hundred pounds and the mayor would have dinner with you every night. That you are as beautiful as you are probably makes him swoon."

Rebecca nodded silently. *Well, perhaps I shall be able to convert the mayor's ardor into something useful.*

CHAPTER
24

March 3, 1855

THE MAP

DESPITE CHEATING FOR SEVERAL HOURS, JACOB WAS down half of his winnings from the *Edinburgh*. Any other time he would have glowered, focused on intimidating his opponents, and been filled with rage over losing, but he was preoccupied. In an earlier hand, one of the other players gathered in a circle on the floor of the rank-smelling, smoky foyer of the rundown tenement, had had an enviable set of cards. The man, a slightly overweight mop-haired fellow, was neither tough nor smart. Despite his meek manner, Micky—as the other players called him—had the intelligence and inebriated fortitude to play those cards, even though his pile of coins and cash had been virtually depleted. Before receiving the fifth card, and making his last bet, Micky hesitated. Fumbling nervously at his lapel, he pulled out a tightly folded grease-stained parchment, which he threw onto the pot.

One of the other players bellowed, "What's this? Where's the money?"

Stammering, Micky tried to explain, "This is worth far more than this entire pot. It's a map to gold." Everyone sitting around the dirty floor laughed.

"A treasure map, is it?" yelled one man.

Another player snapped, "No money, no play."

Fixing his eyes on the folded map framed by the glitter of coins, Jacob's skin tingled. *There are no accidents. I am supposed to have that map.* Looking around the circle, Jacob offered, "If Micky thinks that map is worth ten dollars, I'm willing to let him play." The other players exchanged startled glances. Micky flashed a grateful, pathetic smile. Jacob nodded in return. *If Micky is too much the fool to sense my insincerity, so be it.*

Micky won the hand, upsetting all the players except Jacob. Through the next several deals, Jacob barely concentrated on his cards, instead slipping questions to Micky, who was flushed and counting his money.

"I bet a treasure map is hard to come by," suggested Jacob, passing the whiskey bottle to Micky.

"You have to know the right people," Micky replied in a distracted tone.

Passing him the bottle again, Jacob dug deeper, "Treasure maps are usually of places far away."

Looking up from sorting his winnings, Micky said sadly, "My brother did some trapping and scouting in a place they call Las Coloradas. He had been hired by some foreigners but would never tell me the details. I know he was paid well, but in the end that didn't mean much. He gave me the map." Throwing back his head, he took a long swig of whiskey, blinked, and swiped a tear from one bleary eye with his knuckles.

Letting another hand go by, Jacob asked in the most disinterested tone he could muster, "Why would your brother give you the map?"

Looking pained, Mickey blinked. "You could say he died for the damn map," Micky gestured bitterly at the folded parchment perched on the pile of coins in the center of the circle of players. "When he got back from St. Louis two years ago, he was still carrying an arrowhead in his leg. He almost didn't make it home; it was so infected. He gave me the map the day he died. I am in New York to deliver it."

Mickey won the hand. With a look of relief, he wobbled drunkenly to his feet, belched and swayed. "Time for this lucky man to call it a night."

Waiting for the door to close behind Mickey, Jacob hurriedly gathered up his coins, nodding at the circle as he stood up. "I'm going to call it an early evening, too, mates. I will see you gents tomorrow."

Walking rapidly, Jacob caught up with the heavy man, following twenty paces behind his silhouette, and the shine of Micky's towhead mop of hair in the intermittent gaslight lamps.

Micky turned up an alley, and Jacob pulled the blade from his boot. With a few long strides, he was behind Micky, sliding an arm around his neck. Micky's hands flew up desperately tugging on the forearm cutting off his air. Plunging the knife in the bigger man's arching back, Jacob ripped the blade upward. Micky screamed.

Jacob tightened his arm. In seconds, Micky stopped struggling, and fell to the cobblestones, which quickly reddened with blood.

Rolling the still spasming body over, he rummaged through the dead man's coat until he found the map. Hesitating, he fought the temptation to strip the poker winnings from the corpse, too. *Too obvious a trail once the body is found*, Jacob warned himself. Tucking the thick folds of paper into a pocket, he walked quickly away without a look back.

Returning to his squalid little room in a corner of Samuel's meager flat, he grunted at Samuel snoring drunkenly on the threadbare couch. He lit a candle, his fingers trembling as he carefully unfolded the parchment. Micky's blood had stained one corner. In the flickering light, his dirty fingernail traced the route to St. Louis and then land travel on what was labeled The Emigrant Trail south before Fort Laramie to a place called Cherry Creek and then west over the mountains. A more detailed insert drawn in one corner showed a location marked by an X, labeled *Las Montanas Rojas*.

Leaning back in the chair, he rubbed the stubble on his chin. *I came to America to stay one step ahead of the law in Ireland and England, and now I have been drawn to this moment and to this map.* Taking the double-edged knife out of his boot, he thoughtfully cleaned Micky's blood from the blade.

JACOB WAS ELATED. *I OWE MYSELF A CELEBRATION.* ON his first night in New York, Samuel had introduced him to a nearby brothel. He had taken a fancy to one of the ladies of the night, Mary, an older but curvy wench with all her teeth and a cute little face. *She knows what to do with a man.* In buoyant spirits, he headed for her dilapidated room on the third floor of the house of ill repute.

"Would you like a sip of whiskey, Jacob?" Mary smiled, picking up a flask and a tumbler. "We can take our time, Mister Irish. After you, I have only to return to my apartment and roommates."

Watching her from behind, the warmth of the whiskey spreading through his belly; he felt blood pounding in his ears and in the thickening below his belt. Taking a quick step as she turned around, he knocked the glass from her hand, his lips seeking her neck as he pulled up her dress.

"Jacob!" she gasped, trying to push him away. His fingers found the hot, wet flesh between her legs and her knees buckled. Throwing her on the bed, he ripped off her drawers.

"Let me take my dress off," she complained but Jacob's knees were already between her thighs, his breeches down to his thighs. Grabbing her hips, he lunged into her, Mary groaning in surprise. She strained against him but he had her pinned to the bed and consumed her with rapid thrusts.

"You're hurting me," she cried out. Her words spurred him to greater frenzy.

Jacob scarcely thought of the woman beneath him. "Shut up, woman. I paid my price. I'm going to be rich. I have the map," again, his hips pressed forward, "to the gold and then I'm going to have that redhead for a wife. I'm going to—" he convulsed in primal spasm, exploding deep inside her still struggling body. Groaning, he collapsed on her, sweat dripping from his forehead, a vision of Sarah in his mind.

March 3, 1855

*B*EGUILED

CAREFULLY APPRAISING HERSELF IN THE MIRROR, REBECCA
turned her head left, then right. Gently pulling the fabric of her bodice forward over her shoulders, she
exposed a hint more of the creamy swelling of her
breasts. *That should do it.*

Inga escorted Rebecca to the blue room as she had the
previous evening. This time, however, the place settings
were arranged side-by-side rather than at opposite ends
of the long dining table. *This will be easier than I imagined.*

They had barely begun their first course, baked oys-
ters in a light cream sauce, when the mayor edged closer
to Rebecca, asking in a low, seductive tone, "So, my dear,
is there a man in your life? Have you made any plans for
marriage or family?"

Rebecca nimbly evaded the query. "That is a rather
personal question, Ferdinando. I'm not sure we know
each other well enough...yet."

"Ah, Rebecca I'm just trying to ascertain if my ener-
gies are misdirected. I feel a certain sense of ebullience

when I'm around you. In truth, I can barely keep my eyes off your lovely features. But there's no sense in pursuit if your heart belongs to another."

"Why, mayor, you flatter me. And I must say, your position, surroundings, obvious charm and intellect are most attractive. No one's heart is set for me that I know of, and in truth...," Rebecca added some husk to her tone, "...up to this trip I have not yet met a man with whom I could seriously consider marriage or family. But I am young and there is time. And I will be in America, it appears, for at least half a year. I shall certainly be coming back to New York when I return from St. Louis." Rebecca put on her most demure air, fluttering her eyelashes several times and smiling softly at the mayor, who had taken her hand again.

"It must be lonely traveling by yourself as you are." The mayor sighed. "And I've yet to find a woman to whom I could declare my heart permanently. She must have intellect, charm, manners, grace and beauty, and be from a good family."

Dabbing at his lips with a corner of his linen napkin, he continued, "Frankly, until you, I had begun to despair of ever finding that woman." He began to stroke Rebecca's hand softly. She willed herself not to remove it from the table. The mayor continued, "If there is anything I can do to make your trip safer and more comfortable, and speed your return to New York, I would be delighted."

Slowly brushing the hair from her cheek to behind her ear, she watched the mayor's eyes hungrily follow her every move.

He cleared his throat. "I know you were exhausted last night but may I interest you in that glass of sherry in my quarters this evening after supper?"

"Ferdinando, again you compliment me. I am tempted but I remain without energy. More than a month on the ship has taken its toll on me, I'm afraid. We women are much frailer than you men, you know."

The mayor's face fell but he recovered quickly. "Then may I look forward to supper tomorrow night? And do give some thought to how I might assist you."

"Dinner tomorrow night would be wonderful, Ferdinando. I think I shall retire." As he had done the previous evening, the mayor leaped from his seat to behind her chair, pulling it out.

As Rebecca rose, he leaned forward to kiss her but she turned her chin at the last second so that his lips landed on her cheek.

"Oh, Ferdinando," Rebecca pressed two fingers over her mouth and did her best to look embarrassed. "I shall give your kind offer some thought as I lay in my bed tonight. And I shall certainly look forward to our time tomorrow evening. It may be our last for a while. My train leaves for St. Louis on Thursday, the day after."

"My dear, we have such a short time together. Are you sure? Just one glass of sherry?"

"Thank you. I must get my rest. I just don't feel quite myself yet."

The mayor escorted her to the stairs, all the while, lightly holding her hand. Ascending several steps, she partially turned, "Thank you again for a wonderful dinner and your thoughtful offer of assistance. I am sure your valued help will be necessary in some manner."

The mayor's cheeks jiggled, his body bouncing in that peculiar way on the balls of his feet. "My pleasure, rest assured."

Placing one hand delicately on the handrail, she lifted her dress with the other revealing the backs of her ankles and calves to the mayor. Walking slowly up the steps, keenly aware the mayor's eyes were fixed on her legs, she kept a smile glued to her lips. *Boorish.*

March 4, 1855

*T*HREADS WEST

REBECCA SPENT THE NEXT DAY IN PREPARATION FOR THE trip to St. Louis. She had Inga run several errands for her. In the early afternoon, there was a tapping on the French doors. Inga's voice called out, "I've brought you some tea."

Opening the door clad merely in her camisole and slip, Rebecca smiled. "Come in, Inga."

"Oh, excuse me, Rebecca." Embarrassed, Inga averted her eyes from Rebecca's partially clad figure. "I shall leave this tea and give you your privacy."

"You'll do no such thing. We're both women. We have our privacies but let's face it, there are no secrets. Please come in and shut the door behind you."

Inga did as instructed but Rebecca noticed her face become a shade more pale at the mention of secrets. *Curious.*

"Would you like some tea, Inga?"

"Oh yes, Rebecca, that would be wonderful. How kind of you to ask."

"Seat yourself over here," invited Rebecca, indicating the settee by the windows. Turning her back to Inga, she pretended to engross herself in the tray and teacups.

"Inga, is there anything that holds you in New York?"

Rebecca saw Inga's head snap up in the reflection of the window.

"No, other than I do enjoy this job. I have not been here for long but after many years I finally feel secure. I have fine quarters, decent pay and a steady position. But I have no family and I have never had any entanglements that would bind me to this location."

Rebecca ceased her studied preoccupation with cups and milk and turned to Inga. "Never?" Inga looked down at the floor, and smoothed her hands over her lap.

"Certainly nothing serious and absolutely nothing that involved my heart."

Rebecca turned back to the tray to hide her raised eyebrows. *There is something here that makes me inquisitive.*

Making sure her face was impassive but friendly, she walked over to the settee with the two cups. Rebecca stirred her tea deliberately and slowly. When the light chime of the silver spoon on the edges of the fine china teacup ceased, she bent forward slightly, "How would you like to accompany me on my trip tomorrow? My plan is to try and go no further than St. Louis. I have some family business. I will share some details with you on the train. It is my hope that I can resolve those issues quickly and we can be back in New York in several months. I could use both the assistance and the company. I've given it great thought. I will pay twice the wages you earn here. It might be fun for you, too. We two women could have an adventure together."

Inga's teacup hung suspended halfway between the saucer and her lips, a look of complete surprise on her face. "But I would lose my job here. I could never get permission to go."

Extending her arm, Rebecca patted her thigh and smiled smugly. "I think you very well would be given full permission. Actually, I am quite sure of it."

Inga set her tea down without having taken a sip, staring at her teacup. Rebecca knew her mind was racing.

Raising her eyes, she smiled widely, her features dancing with animated anticipation, as if she was about to share a secret. Rebecca was puzzled.

"Rebecca, it does sound like fun. Do you know that in eight years I have never once really been out of New York City? My biggest adventure was going to New Jersey to fetch a bolt of fabric that no other shop carried for the mayor's then-current mistress. I've heard many of the guests speak of the country between here and St. Louis." Looking out the window, she cleared her throat. "I even heard your father talk about the wild lands that lie beyond St. Louis."

Looking up sharply from her tea, Rebecca leaned further forward. "My father? You didn't tell me that you knew my father."

"He dined occasionally at the Carriage House where I worked. The restaurant was a gathering place for successful businessmen. I remember him because he was most kind and a true gentleman. You do resemble him

in many ways, particularly his strength and resolve..."
Inga held her eyes, "...and cleverness."

Rebecca felt excitement rising in her. "Tell me what
he said. Did you talk for a long time?"

"No. We spoke only in broken minutes when I was waiting his table or when he was paying his bill. The one time
I heard him talk of the great flatlands and the mountains
far west of St. Louis was during a dinner conversation he
had with his attorney." Inga looked around the room as
if someone might be listening. "I know I shouldn't have
stayed to overhear but your father had a strong voice that
was difficult to ignore even when he spoke in hushed
tones, and the conversation was quite interesting, so I lingered at the serving station near their table."

"Well?" Rebecca stamped her foot lightly.

Inga laughed. "Rebecca, you expect more than I can
give you. I heard them talk in bits and pieces about a
red mountain and how beautiful the meadows, cliffs and
creeks were in this place somewhere in some territory
in the far west. I can't quite remember the details. He
talked about great grassy flatlands that went on for miles
and miles and huge beasts called buffalo. I remember
that he marveled at the lack of people, and the hardiness
of the few souls he did meet during his travels."

Leaning back in her chair, Rebecca's fingers absently
moved back and forth across her lips, her mind whirling.
*So he did visit the land. Perhaps there was something to
what he whispered to me in those minutes before he died.*
She had always thought he was a bit delirious at that
point and she had been so focused on holding his hand

and telling him that she loved him that his words had never really taken root, until that very moment as she listened to Inga.

She recalled that dreadful day, the acrid, antiseptic smell that permeated the hospital and the somber hush of nurses she would forever equate with places of sickness and loss of hope. "Gold," he had whispered as he pulled her ear down to his dry, cracked lips. "Not just land, daughter, gold."

Shaking her head, she sat up straight, leveling an intent stare at Inga. "Well, then, will you come?"

"I would love to go on this trip with you. I want to see the country and I know I can be of help. But even with your overly kind wage offer, I really cannot afford to lose this position."

Rebecca waved her hand dismissively. "Do not worry in the least, Inga. The mayor will give you full permission for the journey and you will have your job, perhaps even at a higher pay grade, when you return. In fact, I'll guarantee it."

Inga stood quickly. "If that is the case, then there are less than twenty-four hours until we depart. I must pack. I've no idea what to take."

Rising, Rebecca took her arm, walking her to the door. "Do as I do. If in doubt, pack it. Now be off with you. You have trunks?" Inga turned at the door, exuberant, "I only have enough for one trunk and it just so happens I have one trunk. I'm already halfway packed." Giggling, she jogged down the hall.

Rebecca sat back down on the settee lost in thought. *Ferdinando, my dear, I know exactly how you can render that assistance you so graciously offered.* Smiling down into the milky amber tea, she took a last sip and then rose to prepare herself for dinner with the mayor.

March 5, 1855

THE TRAIN

THE HIGH CEILING OF THE CENTRAL TRAIN STATION OF New Jersey's main terminal echoed with the sound of travelers scurrying on tile floors. Mothers shepherded children. Men wore derbies or coonskin caps and there were the occasional broad brims of western hats.

Standing transfixed by the tumultuous scene, Johannes and Reuben carried only their duffels, the map case and their Sharps rifles, each clutching his long gun sleeved in fringed leather. The electricity of the crowd fired their already heightened sense of adventure. Behind them, a porter hefted Reuben's trunk. A Colt Army pistol was tucked into Johannes' waistband. Reuben's Navy Square-back Colt was snugged into the Slim Jim on his hip, its tapered, scrolled leather sleeve loosely strapped to his thigh with a rawhide tie as the mercantile clerk, Wallace, had advised. He had oiled the stiff skin of the holster but it still had that peculiar light tint of new leather.

The curved black scabbard of Johannes' saber was tied with rawhide to the supple hide which blanketed his Sharps carbine. Watching Johannes deftly bind the sword to the rifle before leaving for the station, Reuben had again recalled his uncle's conjecture about Johannes' possible military experience.

"There it is!" Reuben pointed toward the track. The sign read, *Westbound: Philadelphia, Pittsburgh, Chicago, St. Louis.* Steam was billowing from the engine of the Pennsylvania Railroad train.

Shouting above the din, Reuben bellowed, "Let's go!" realizing Johannes wasn't beside him, he glanced back. His friend had stopped to look down the terminal. Following his gaze, Reuben laughed. Johannes' attention was fixed on a stunning blonde five cars down the track, her form half a head above almost all the other travelers. The crowd momentarily parted, revealing a petite, dark-haired beauty next to the tall, fair-skinned woman.

Rebecca? Can't be! Reuben shook his head.

The New York streets and the bridge to New Jersey had been crowded with pedestrians and carriages. He and Johannes had arrived late. Two sharp toots bellowed from the engine of the westbound train. Taking the few paces back to Johannes, he tugged on the taller man's vest. "Easy boy."

Johannes muttered something in his Scandinavian tongue. Reuben didn't understand the language but the meaning was clear. They both laughed. Hurrying over to a conductor, they showed him their tickets, asking which of the sleeping cars was theirs. He directed them toward the rear of the train. Johannes clambered up the steps, reaching back to drag up the duffels Reuben tossed to the steps. Tipping the porter, Reuben took one last glance down the track as he perched on the bottom step. The tall blonde and the shapely dark-haired woman she accompanied were followed by seven men who lugged trunks and baggage. They moved toward the front of the train. *Doubtful that it's her. Besides, Johannes will certainly investigate.*

Squeezing down the narrow corridor, Johannes grinned over his shoulder, "As soon as we get settled, I think I shall take a walk."

Reuben chuckled inwardly but said nothing.

Finding the compartment, Johannes slid open the pocket door and groaned with disgust. "Don't they have full-size people in America?" Reuben peered around his arm. Their berth was tiny, and the bunks seemed too short for either of them to stretch out fully.

"Well, Johannes, maybe that tall blonde has better arrangements!"

"Yes!" replied Johannes, rubbing his hands together and making a face. "I will have to make friends with her for her bed." His look became mischievous. "Maybe the dark-haired woman with her can sleep in here with you."

Reuben felt himself flush. "What dark-haired woman?"

Johannes slapped his thigh. "Reuben, if I were you, I would be sure to never play poker."

Reuben grunted, looking around the compartment. *The journey would be cramped but this was the most expedient form of travel.*

Reuben sighed as he tried to wedge the duffel and map case under his bunk. The heavy cotton duck fabric of the duffel strained at the seams with the addition of his work coat tucked at the very bottom.

He straightened, his stomach growling. "Why don't we get something to eat? Then you can take your exploratory stroll."

CHAPTER

28

March 5, 1855

*A*T FIRST SIGHT

AFTER SHARING A SLAB OF CHEESE AND HALF A LOAF OF
bread in the dining car, Reuben returned to the berth
and Johannes made his way forward through the parlor
car and then down the long corridors of the train toward
the locomotive.

Standing courteously to the side as other passengers
entered and exited from their berths in the sleeping sections, he hailed a conductor. "There are two ladies who
embarked," he said. "One brunette and the other a tall
blonde, both very attractive."

The conductor looked up from his study of the ticket
of another passenger. He was short and had to raise his
head considerably to peer up past the bill of his cap at
Johannes.

"You are a relative?"

"No."

"A friend?"

"No."

"Do the ladies know you?"

Johannes winked. "Not yet."

The conductor regarded him seriously for a moment, then smiled. "I did notice them myself, indeed, but I'm much too old and besides, the wife would not be happy with that type of thought. The two ladies about whom you inquire are in the next car, third on your left, compartment 310."

"I thank you very much. Would you happen to know their names?"

Shaking his head in amusement, the conductor consulted his manifest. "Rebecca Marx, and Inga Bjorne."

Reaching berth 310, Johannes could hear the muffled voices of the women through the door. Hesitating for a moment, he straightened his shirt and ran his hands back through his thick blond hair, moving it to behind, rather than over his ears. *What's this? She is simply another beautiful woman.* Taking a deep breath, he knocked on the door.

The door slid open and Rebecca stood there. She still had on her traveling clothes.

"Yes?" There was a definite challenge in her query.

Looking over Rebecca's head, Johannes saw the lanky blonde had turned to see to whom Rebecca had spoken. Their eyes met, blue to blue, locking for an extended moment. Johannes felt a skip in his chest. Then the golden-haired woman looked down, her cheeks bright pink, smoothing the front of her dress over her thighs.

"Yes?" Rebecca's tone was a bit harsher.

"I'm traveling with a friend and noticed you two lovely ladies board the train in New York. I took the liberty of requesting the location of your compartment from the conductor."

At the sound of his voice, Rebecca's eyes flickered with recognition. "You were on the SS *Edinburgh*. Your name is Jan or Yahn, I believe?"

"Johannes, Johannes Svenson. Yes, I was on the *Edinburgh*. However, Mistress Marx, I was not aware you were traveling with your beautiful companion on that voyage."

Rebecca snickered. "That might be because I was alone on the ship."

Johannes found himself annoyed with Rebecca. *Reuben is right about this woman.* He desperately wished to respond with a sarcastic comment. Instead, he paused, peering past Rebecca again, and in a most polite tone, addressed the other woman. "Inga?" The blonde's eyes met his again in an evocative but puzzled stare. *She's wondering how I know her name.* The pink turned to scarlet and crept down her throat. "I have always liked that name. I cannot ask you to take a sunny walk in the park but perhaps you would join me for a glass of wine or sherry in the parlor car?"

Inga shot a questioning, hopeful look at Rebecca. The brunette nodded her head. "Do as you wish," she said curtly.

"It will take me just a moment to tidy up."

Johannes smiled at the sound of her voice. "It would be my pleasure to wait outside the door, Inga."

Johannes reached for the door pull but Rebecca's hand had never left it and she slammed it shut.

Several minutes later, Inga appeared. "I shall be back shortly," she called back into the compartment.

"As you wish," Rebecca's voice drifted back.

Moving from the door, they both kept their hands over their mouths to subdue their chuckles. "My name is Johannes Svenson and the conductor tells me yours is Inga Bjorne."

INGA FELT FLUSHED AND WARM. LOOKING UP TO Johannes, she smiled. "You inquired of the conductor?" *I like that he is taller than I. That is rare. I'm acting like a schoolgirl.* "I take it from the lovely introduction by milady Marx that the two of you have met previously."

"Yes, we have. Apparently, I did not make much of an impression." Involuntarily, Johannes' hand reached out and gently brushed one of the long strands of her golden hair from her forehead and cheek to behind her ear. Inga closed her eyes, feeling almost lightheaded at his touch.

"We met shipboard. Or should I say, we saw each other on the ship. I am not sure she ever said a word to me, though she had a few conversations with my friend, Reuben Frank."

"You are traveling with him?"

"Yes, Reuben is a fine fellow, though young. Shall we head to the parlor car?"

Johannes followed behind her as they moved down the narrow corridor. She could feel his energy and his eyes on her body. Trying to still the flutter in her belly, she sighed deeply and Johannes caught the sound of her exhaled breath.

"Is everything all right?"

"Oh yes. I'm just tired."

Entering the parlor car, they chose a small table tucked into one corner. Digging in his pocket, her tall, equally blond companion withdrew a flint sparker, and lit the candle in the center of the little table. It was perched on an iron candelabrum with a wide base so as not to topple from the sway of the train. Watching Johannes' movements, she felt herself drawn to the way the fabric of his thick, cotton shirt rippled across his shoulder as he extended his arm. *Fluid. Athletic.* She looked down at the table studying her clasped hands intently.

Their conversation was effortless, as if she'd known Johannes long before this encounter. She shared with him parts of her life that she hadn't spoken of to anyone for many years, brushing over the several years spent with her uncle, referring to him only as, "a relative with whom I lived for two years who wasn't quite right and made me uncomfortable."

During the course of their discussion, Johannes inquired about what she had done for work in New York. Inga felt a momentary panic. She realized her finger was playing and twirling nervously with her hair. In some way, she felt compelled to tell Johannes the entire story, though she couldn't fathom why. This was information about her very soul.

"I was a waitress and assisted the manager of a very nice establishment, The Carriage, in Manhattan." She willed herself to maintain eye contact with Johannes as she spoke but somehow felt Johannes was aware that this wasn't the whole story.

Unconsciously they had been leaning further and further toward each other during the course of their talk, their elbows supporting the forward posture of their upper bodies. Johannes was clearly about to ask a follow-up question.

Tilting back suddenly, she pointed at the clock next to the window behind the bar. "My goodness, we've been gone more than an hour. Milady Marx will not be happy."

Laughing, Johannes stretched back in his chair, his heels far out to the side of the table and his hands raised in the air behind his head.

"Milady Marx?" There was sarcastic humor in his tone. "A little secret, Inga. There was definitely something between my friend Reuben and milady Marx on the ship. It reminded me of two swordsmen circling before a duel. If you wouldn't mind, don't mention Reuben is traveling with me. I'm sure the two of them will cross paths. This train is a rather small world. You and I can be observers. At least it will provide some amusement."

Inga felt flattered to be invited to share a simple innocent scheme that could be fun and could have no bad ending. Feeling her chest constrict with a guilty surge, she concentrated on her hands. *Ah but my secret is much darker.*

Raising her eyes to Johannes, she bobbed her head, "It will be our secret, then. We will wait until they come across one another."

Moving back up the train, they stopped and faced one another outside the women's berth. She knew Johannes wanted to say something, *and he wants to kiss me.* She realized she was leaning forward.

Placing a hand on either of her arms just below the shoulders Johannes slowly lowered his lips toward hers. Anxiety clutched her, constricting her chest, and she stepped back, just beyond his reach.

"I had a wonderful time, Johannes. I...I'm not sure I've had a talk like that with anyone in quite some time—maybe ever."

He was studying her face intently, a soft smile playing on his lips. "Nor I, Inga, nor I."

Still facing him, Inga reached behind her and tapped three times softly on the compartment door. She heard the deadbolt slide open and Rebecca's cold voice. "You call this shortly?"

The pocket door was ajar just a crack and only the brunette's partially hidden face could be seen. "I'm in my nightgown. Are you coming in or do you plan to sleep in the hall tonight?"

Ignoring Rebecca, Johannes smiled. "Breakfast tomorrow? Dining car? Let's say eight?"

Inga felt that surreal tingle once again. "That would be lovely, Johannes."

Smiling, he pivoted and walked down the passage; Inga watched his retreating form, fascinated with the way he moved.

———◆———

INGA TOSSED AND TURNED FOR HOURS. EVEN THE rhythmic sleep breathing of her traveling companion did nothing to calm her. She buried her face in her pillow. *Rebecca is such a lady; she doesn't even snore.* Listening to the wheels of the train click against the breaks in the tracks, she tried to lose herself in the gentle movement of the car but to no avail. *Should I have told him?* The question wound through her mind a hundred times. Her spirit vacillated between a compelling need she didn't understand to share everything with Johannes, and her worry that he would not be able to assimilate the information. *Would he think me cheap? Soiled? Would he treat me less kindly because of what I have done? Or would he understand?*

Rolling restlessly to her back, she stared at the ceiling, vaguely aware of the dim light from the bright starry night that filtered through the window. The entire situation was dreamlike. *It's all right to have a secret*, she argued with herself. *There's something about him. Much different. I can't risk it. Besides, there's no way he could ever find out.*

Her decision made, she shifted to her side, finally shutting her eyes. As she felt sleep overtake her, she whispered to herself, "A girl must do what a girl must do."

March 6, 1855

ꙨECRETS

Awake with the first tinges of dawn, Johannes lay in his bunk consumed by the vision of Inga's eyes, her smile and her habit of looking down into her hands whenever she was flustered. Their conversation played repeatedly in his mind.

When is the last time this happened? he mused to himself. Sifting through his many memories of women, he could not recall this type of immediate, more than just physical, magnetism. Extending one long arm down to the floor, he groped for his trousers, pulling his watch from a pocket. Six-thirty a.m. He could lie in his bunk no longer. Rising as quietly as he could, he glanced over at Reuben, who lay turned to the opposite wall, snoring gently. Dressing, he slipped into the corridor, found a porter, and with charm and a five-cent tip induced him to furnish a small bucket of hot water.

Returning to the berth, he quietly slid open the door. He used one of the hand towels from the rack above the small pitcher and the small bar of lye soap to sponge his upper body, paying special attention to his underarms. Every once in a while, he cranked his nose to an armpit and inhaled. Splashing water on his face, he looked critically in the mirror, running his hand thoughtfully over his cheeks and chin. He reached over to borrow Reuben's razor, which lay near the pitcher, smirking to himself in the mirror as he ran the blade quickly over his cheeks. *I never could grow a beard.*

Satisfied with the results of his impromptu sponge bath, he took the saber from under the bunk, withdrew it from its sheath and held it. It had a good feel, was well balanced and sliced the air cleanly. With another glance at Reuben, he reached into his duffel, pulled out a whetstone and slowly, being as quiet as he could, began to hone the blade.

The slight rasp of stone on steel caused Reuben to stir. Rolling partway over, he looked at Johannes. "What the hell are you doing?"

Johannes chuckled. "I wanted to put an edge on my saber. I have a breakfast meeting at eight."

Shaking his head, the young Prussian had begun to roll away. At the last comment, though, he shifted his attention back to Johannes. "A breakfast appointment? Oh, I see. Evidently your explorations last night were successful."

"Her name is Inga Bjorne. Delightful woman." Johannes kept his attention on the saber blade.

"A delightful woman?"

"Yes, and even more beautiful close up than at a distance."

Rolling away from Johannes again, Reuben chortled into his pillow, "Wake me when you return."

Johannes was at the table in the dining car ten minutes before eight, drumming his fingers on the tabletop and sipping coffee. He was lost in wondering what the land was like west of St. Louis when he heard her voice. Snapping his head up from the coffee cup, he sucked in his breath. Inga was dressed in a simple but stunning deep royal blue traveling dress. It came down to just below her knees, high for the fashions of the time, and was more fitted around her legs and hips than the standard flare designs worn by most women. The body of the dress molded to her long figure and small but perfectly formed breasts. Johannes noticed the soft mounds of partially erect nipples just below the tips of her long blonde hair.

He almost fell over in his rush to rise and pull out her chair. "I can be uncoordinated at times."

She laughed. The sound of her voice coursed through the center of his being. He shook his head, as if to clear it.

Inga noticed. "Are you feeling well, Johannes?"

He took her hand across the table. Her skin was wondrously smooth and soft and even this slight touch seemed to generate an arc of energy.

"I was just trying to flip a fly off my nose."

Inga giggled, and Johannes laughed as much at his own foolish words as at her response to his lame excuse. Inga ordered tea and they picked up the discussion where they had left off the previous night. Johannes was aware that Inga did not withdraw her hand and their fingers continued to touch.

She told him of her parents and their untimely death, and Johannes made her smile with his comical description of how he and Reuben had met on the ship.

"Have you decided yet?"

They looked up. The waiter seemed annoyed. The dining car was crowded. Several people stood at one end waiting for a table. Johannes realized suddenly that this was the fourth time their server had been to the table to take their order. Three times, he had been dismissed with a "May we have five minutes. We need to look at the menu."

Johannes looked at Inga. "We have held up this poor waiter long enough. What will you have?"

"Two poached eggs, a slice of toast with butter and jam—you do have jam? In a separate serving dish, please. And another pot of hot water."

Johannes glanced up at the waiter. "Exactly the same, except a fresh cup of coffee for me."

As the waiter walked away, Johannes swiveled back to her, extending his free hand to where their fingertips were entwined, and covered her wrist.

"I will share something but you must promise not to say a word to anyone. That means Rebecca, Reuben or anyone, ever."

Inga returned his stare with steady blue eyes. Johannes felt as if he could lose himself in those eyes.

"You have my word, Johannes."

"I was an officer, a captain in the heavy cavalry of the king of Denmark. I served honorably in several campaigns and was decorated. Perhaps I will share that story with you another time. It's not important. What is important is that my father was also in the army. A few years after he was killed, I resigned my commission and I wandered spiritually and mentally..." Johannes bent his head. "...and physically. I am on this train only through a series of quirks. I've been with many women. I managed to get caught with the wife of a very high-ranking minister of the king's inner circle."

"Johannes, you are squeezing my hand."

"Oh, I'm sorry." He loosened his grip. "To compound matters, I was less than conciliatory and respectful to the minister. Through extreme good fortune I knew the magistrate who presided over my case; otherwise, I would be breaking rocks to construct the newest addition to the king's castle, and I would not be sitting here with you, enchanted. Part of my sentence was never to speak of this. Reuben does not even know what country I am from, although he has attempted to elicit an answer from me on many occasions. So now you know of certain of my vices and my fall from grace."

Inga's eyes misted slightly. "Johannes...we all have our past. In many ways this journey west is a new beginning for me, too." Her face had a pained expression. She opened and shut her mouth several times as if in a search for words. "I must tell you..."

At that moment an attractive young woman swished by the table, her hips swaying with slight exaggeration that swung the bottoms of her bright scarlet dress with black velvet trim from side-to-side.

Johannes eyes followed her, "Why some women dress like that has always perplexed me. It simply makes them look like tarts."

Johannes looked back at Inga. A slight frown furled her eyebrows. "I'm sorry, Inga. You were about to say?"

Pulling her hand away from his, she glanced at the wall clock, "Only that I should be getting back to milady Marx. She is still grumbling about my extended absence last night, and she was none too pleased about our breakfast this morning."

Slapping his leg, Johannes laughed loudly. "The same reaction I had from Reuben but what do they know? I have a great idea," he continued. "Reuben has a stubborn pride and I think without some devilish conspiracy between you and me, he might make an effort to avoid Rebecca once he knows for sure she is on the train. I will plan to bring him to the dining car at seven-thirty. Do you think you could lure Rebecca there shortly after that?"

Inga's tense expression relaxed slightly. "I'm quite sure I can."

"Want to have lunch with me? If the waiter will serve us again."

"I have a number of things to do for milady Marx today, Johannes but I will see you tonight."

Johannes felt it wise not to push. Inga still seemed troubled and her tone had changed perceptibly. He lifted his arm, bent his elbow, drew the back of her wrist to his lips and kissed it slowly. He was pleased that the pink color at her collarbones spread upward through her neck into her cheeks. He went behind her, slid out her chair and gave her arm a gentle squeeze as she rose.

"See you tonight."

Inga smiled faintly back over her shoulder but said nothing.

March 6, 1855

ⲀUNT STELLA'S SHOP

IT WAS MIDMORNING WHEN JACOB AWOKE. HIS EYES fixed, unseeing, on the filthy brick of the tenement next door, barely visible through the grimy window. His violent tryst with Mary somehow only whetted his appetite for Sarah. *I need to formulate a plan. I know the end goal; the trick will be getting there.*

Rising, he rummaged through his sparse belongings, picking out the cleanest clothes. "Samuel, you drunken son of a bitch, do you have a razor in this hole?"

Hours later, holding a small bouquet he had stolen from a street side cart, he knocked on the side door of Sarah's aunt's sewing shop. He looked down at his hands, annoyed that his fingers were fussing with his shirt buttons. The door was opened by Sarah. A white linen blouse clung to her slender form, and a soft wool tweed skirt accentuated her waist, her petticoats adding flare to her hips. Her eyes were red and watery. *She's been crying.* She stepped back, startled to see Jacob in the doorway.

Jacob bowed slightly, "I was in the neighborhood. I thought you might like these."

She smiled cautiously, hesitating before she reached for the blossoms, "Why thank you, Jacob."

Looking past Sarah, Jacob rapidly surveyed the dress shop. The space, brightly lit from the storefront windows, was cluttered in a semi-organized fashion with fabrics and sewing materials. Several women were selecting materials and looked at drawings. Hats hung here and there and scraps of cloth decorated the cutting tables. A newfangled sewing machine nestled in one corner. *A cozy business, though not highly successful.*

Sarah was silent. "May I come in?" he asked, his gaze returning to her.

Looking quickly behind her, and then apprehensively back at him, she shook her head. "We are very busy, Jacob. I am not sure this is a good time."

The familiar angry tightness welled in Jacob but he forced himself to be pleasant. "Now Sarah, I have come a long way to say hello."

Aunt Stella, overhearing the conversation at the door, left an elderly patron with an "Excuse me; I'll be right back," and bustled over.

"Aren't you the kind man who helped my niece find her way here?"

Bowing slightly again, Jacob took her hand and quickly brushed it to his lips. "Yes, ma'am."

Stella blushed. "You flatter an old lady. Well, come in; come in. Sarah, why don't you fix some tea? I have to get back to my customer and then I will join the two of you," Aunt Stella's voice trailed off. She floated cheerfully across the shop toward a frumpy older woman chirping, "Isn't that a wonderful color? ..."

Jacob turned to Sarah. "I wanted to stop in and see how you were getting along."

Her cheeks reddening, she bit her lower lip. "I've been helping my aunt and trying to get settled. Come in, I'll make tea."

Settling himself uncomfortably in one of four small chairs in the alcove parlor off the main shop floor, he murmured "Thanks," as Sarah handed him a small porcelain teacup. The tiny vessel was lost in his big hands.

Taking the silver flask from his shirt pocket, he poured heartily into the cup. "Hope you don't mind," Slipping the flask back in her pocket, he leaned forward. "Something bothering you? You seem upset."

A tear ran down her cheek as she answered in a quavering voice, "It's not quite what I expected. My aunt works very hard and the shop pays her living but there is simply not enough business for two here. I hate to be a burden. I'm really not sure what to do."

He regarded her carefully. *I thought it would have taken longer than this, at least several visits. But O'Shannahan knows an opportunity when it arises.* Keeping his voice soft and off hand, and his eyes locked with hers, he asked, "Have you heard anything about the West?"

"You mean, St. Louis?"

Jacob smiled. "No, Miss Sarah, further west than that—Las Coloradas, the western Kansas Territory, the Rocky Mountains."

"Oh, I've read about those. They are like the Alps. Aren't there Indians? Are there any cities?"

"I've talked to folks. There are small settlements, some forts far apart and there's a place called Cherry Creek. It's not like New York but it's a big town in that part of the world. Things are just getting started there. I have a friend in the mining business. Did you know there's gold out there?"

Her eyebrows rose, and her eyes widened with interest. "There is?"

"There is. Better yet, it's a brand new land with lots of opportunity for people to build brand new lives. People like you and me."

Sarah blinked. "I have heard that St. Louis is growing rapidly. Are you asking me to go west with you?"

To his dismay, Jacob found himself slightly flustered. Concentrating on his teacup, he shifted in his chair, then rose quickly, stepping to the edge of the alcove parlor. Staring out into the shop, he shoved his hands in his pockets.

He turned to face her. "That hadn't occurred to me. But, now that I hear of your situation, I thought I'd share what I've learned, friend to friend. I am going out there the end of the week—on Saturday, in fact. I'd be happy to make certain you arrive there safely. It's not a journey a lady wants to make on her own even if you wish to go no further than St. Louis."

Sitting further back in her chair, she dropped her hands from her teacup and clasped them tightly in her lap. "How would that work?" Sarah's voice was soft but with a suspicious edge.

Jacob looked her in the eye, willing himself to keep his gaze steady. *She does not trust me...yet.* "I'm sure we could provide for separate arrangements. I would enjoy your company and I would protect you."

Avoiding Jacob's stare, the redhead, turned her head toward the dress shop and Jacob followed her gaze. Her aunt was doing her best to convince the now solitary customer that a hideous blue taffeta was perfect for her.

"How long would the trip to St. Louis take? How would we get there? I don't have much savings."

"There's ways to earn money along the way. We could chip in for common expenses and each of us would pay our own ticket for the train to St. Louis. That would be the cheapest, fastest and most comfortable way."

"What happens in St. Louis?" Sarah asked, staying focused on the alcove opening, as if in hope that Aunt Stella would arrive soon to rescue her.

Jacob shrugged. "From there, the journey gets more difficult. If you wished to continue west, we could maybe tie in with a wagon train. We probably wouldn't reach Cherry Creek until early summer."

Snapping her gaze away from the shop, her eyes widened. "Two or three months? But, how long just to St. Louis, Jacob?"

"It's a big country Miss Sarah, with big opportunity. I think the train takes four or five days from here to St.

Louis, so your trip would be much shorter." Jacob said slowly, emphasizing 'your trip,' knowing that any further push would merely heighten her resistance. *One step at a time.* "Well, think about it. Thank you for the tea. May I call on you tomorrow?"

Standing, she pulled down the sides of her skirt with her hands then looked up and answered, "If you wish," in a tone that lacked enthusiasm.

Jacob bent slightly from the waist. "Tomorrow, then."

March 6, 1855

$\mathscr{A}$ DIFFERENCE OF OPINION

AS JACOB EXITED THE SHOP, HE WAVED AND SMILED AT Stella.

A customer left, and her aunt hustled back to the parlor. "What a nice young man. What did he want?"

Sarah conveyed the conversation to her aunt.

Stella was silent for a minute, apparent worry shadowing her eyes. "Oh, Sarah, I feel so bad. You have traveled so far. When I wrote that last letter before Thanksgiving, I was much busier but now there's not enough business here to keep us both working. With this new Singer sewing machine, my increase in production has run headlong into a drop in business. This country and this city are very uncertain right now. The slavery issue, talk of war, the upheaval at city hall with the mayor having his own police force that fights with the other law enforcers—well, it all makes people reluctant to spend." She sighed heavily.

Looking down at her lap, Sarah blinked, fighting another of the waves of disappointment she had been contending with since her arrival.

Shaking her head mournfully, and waving her hand at the shop, Stella continued, "One of the first things many seem to cut back on is finer clothing. You noticed right away that I no longer have an assistant."

"It's fine, aunt, really. I understand. This is not of your doing. I will admit to you that for some reason, I have wanted to go west eventually. I read about St. Louis, even in England. It has grown eightfold or more in ten years, and they have even started laying railway tracks west of the Mississippi, though I understand there is no bridge yet." Pouring more tea into her cup, Sarah paused, deep in thought. "Perhaps 'eventually' is now, Aunt Stella. Events transpire for a reason. Perhaps St. Louis is where I am meant to start my shop. I get the feeling, even in the few days I have been in America, that one has opportunity if one works hard and knows a trade. It is one of the reasons I so looked forward to coming here."

"You may be right, dear—there may be no better place to build a life and make something of yourself. But let us talk of the pragmatic. Would you be comfortable traveling with Jacob? Do you trust him? An unmarried woman traveling with a man is bold, even for these times."

"I have my reservations, Aunt, and no, honestly I don't fully trust him but what's the worst that could happen? He is rough and a bit odd but he has given me no indication that he is violent. Sharing traveling expenses would save money, and I will need every penny to establish myself in St. Louis. If matters become untenable, I can always part company and switch trains at one of the stops...," Sarah pursed her lips, "and I know how to take care of myself. Father taught the whole family how to shoot a pistol. I have a revolver in the false bottom of my valise. I will hide the money I sent you the same way."

Aunt Stella shook her head. "This worries me, child. You will be alone with a strange man, though he does appear to be very nice. He does not seem rough to me. He brought you flowers..." she paused, her features tightening as she reached some decision in her mind, then continued "...but none of that is important. In thinking about it, I recommend you do not travel with him or any man. It is simply not proper."

Her shoulders slumped and she was silent again. Then she shook her head, "It is all my fault. It's just not proper." Stella fussed with the sugar cup and rearranged the teaspoons on the table. "I should accompany you."

Reaching over, Sarah patted Stella's arm. "You and I know that you can't make the trip. You have your life here—a business and customers who depend on you. The idea of my own shop intrigues me, and St. Louis is at the edge of the frontier. It must be very exciting, with many new people coming and going, all of whom have to have clothes. But I shall make no decision until I talk to Jacob tomorrow and you and I discuss the situation further. With Mother gone, your opinion, support and approval are very important to me."

Shaking her head sadly, Stella blinked back tears. "I have placed you in a terrible situation, niece. I am sorry. But please consider that nothing mandates you depart on Saturday, and the extra costs of traveling alone rather than sharing expenses cannot be that great."

Sarah noticed that her aunt moved more slowly, and had aged in many ways. They had not seen one another for years. It might well be another very long time until they could again spend an evening just talking. I do not want my own anxiety to interfere with the little time we have together. "I will weigh my alternatives carefully, aunt. Now, let's make supper and chat. I shall tell you about Emily, and Mother and Father's graves, side by side in a very beautiful corner of the city."

March 6, 1855

REUNION

REUBEN WAS ENGROSSED IN PRACTICE WITH HIS COLT revolver. His fascination with the weapon since first seeing it at Wiggins and Booraems had not diminished. The soft blue-gray of the barrel was perfectly offset by the pearl grip. *A blend of art and power.* He practiced drawing it from the Slim Jim, sometimes aiming with his arm extended, and at others sliding it quickly from the holster and pointing from belt level using his faint reflection in the window as the target.

The stiff leather of the holster was softening with repeated doses of mink oil, and beginning to mold to the trigger guard and cylinder. His draw seemed to be smoother as the leather became suppler.

The Sharps rifle lay on a blanket folded in thirds lengthwise on the bunk. He planned to get familiar with the feel and operation of that weapon, also.

His right hand dangling loosely inches from the holstered Colt, he faced the window. The pistol's pearl handle glowed muted and wavy in the reflection of the glass, its creamy sheen accentuated by the black of night outside the train. Taking a deep breath, he drew, his hand a blur in the glass surface, the Colt appearing as if conjured in the reflected image, the menacing, unwavering eye of the barrel pointing at his chest. Reuben smiled. *Getting a bit faster, too.*

The door slid open with a bang. "I am back from my afternoon reconnoiter," announced Johannes. His eyes slid to the Navy Squareback still in Reuben's hand, and to their reflection in the window. "Windows don't shoot back," he said dryly.

"Just practicing." Reuben was suddenly embarrassed. He put the Colt on the bed next to the Sharps. *Time to change the subject.* "I am sure the tall blonde was part of that reconnaissance. Is that all you think about? Women?"

"She is infinitely more tangible than a reflection. And, what about the princess?" Johannes teased.

Reuben had no retort to the friendly taunt.

Rubbing his stomach. Johannes looked at the weapons on the bunk, then shifted twinkling eyes to Reuben. "It's almost seven-thirty. My belly is growling, and you can play with your toys later. Our first order of business should be to get some food. Aren't you hungry?"

"Now that you mention it, I could use some supper," Reuben covered the weapons with the blanket, making sure the door was locked as they left.

The two men sauntered from one swaying car to the next until they reached the mostly empty dining car midway in the train. As their order arrived, the far door of the car swung open. Johannes' fork froze between his plate and his gaping mouth as in sashayed the tall blonde.

Leaning toward Johannes, Reuben whispered, "She is stunning!"

"Shh! She'll hear you!"

Smiling at them, with a coy directed nod at Johannes, she chose a table next to theirs, taking great care to sit facing them. Reuben was not surprised at the distinctive Scandinavian accent when she ordered, pointing out the place setting next to hers to the waiter, obviously giving him some additional instruction.

"You can close your mouth now," Reuben teased Johannes. "Go on, go say hello."

"Why, thank you for your advice. Perhaps I will introduce you." Grinning, his friend pushed his chair from the table and walked to her.

Reuben watched, thoroughly amused. *They are striking next to one another, both tall and fair.* Bending over, Johannes spoke to her in a Scandinavian dialect. She giggled, blushing deeply as he sat down next to her. They began speaking earnestly in the arresting singsong of northern Europe. The waiter returned, filling their coffee cups, and setting a fine silver teapot down in front of the vacant chair. Shifting in his chair, his friend waved to Reuben to join them.

Neither of them looked up as Reuben took the few steps to their table. Reuben stood, waiting patiently until Johannes turned to him.

"This is Inga Bjorne. We come from the same area. Her country is our neighbor state,"

Reuben felt one eyebrow rise, "And where might that be?" Flashing him an irritated glance, the tall man spoke in German, "Can't you see I'm busy here? Very busy."

Inga admonished Johannes in impeccable though accented German, "Johannes, that is no way to talk to your friend." Flashing a dazzling smile at Reuben, she continued, "Does he do this to you often, sir?" Despite the guttural nature of the language, her voice resembled a happy wind chime in a light breeze.

Jerking in surprise, Johannes almost fell off his chair.

Reuben bowed before sitting down. "I am Reuben Frank. It's delightful to hear you soften the German language with such a lovely voice."

"Yes, yes, she does speak beautifully," stammered Johannes.

Their conversation was interrupted by the sound of a woman clearing her throat. "Am I intruding?"

Reuben looked up into the arrogant scowl of Rebecca.

"This is my mistress, milady Rebecca Marx," offered Inga in a gracious tone.

Standing, Reuben nodded at the brunette. "Mistress Marx."

"It seems we are all going west, though I'm surprised to see you on a train." Rebecca's voice was contemptuous. "It is an expensive form of travel."

Inga appeared dismayed. "Do you know each other?"

"Mister Frank and I met on the ship. He assisted me with my luggage." Her scornful look refocused on Reuben. "Are you certain you won't let me pay you for your services?"

Reuben looked at her for a moment, smiling tightly. Bending forward, he pulled out her chair, making a sweeping gesture with one arm. "Your chair, madam. Thank you for the offer but we will manage without taking money from a lady."

Rebecca stiffened.

Reuben remained standing and turned to Johannes. "Shall we return to our meal and leave the ladies to their privacy?"

Whispering a few last words in a Scandinavian dialect to Inga, Johannes picked up his coffee cup. She giggled and said something in reply. Returning to their own table, Reuben asked, "What did she say?"

Johannes' eyes danced with mirth. "She said she was very surprised to see that her mistress could actually be interested in a man."

Reuben's fork had been halfway to his mouth. Lowering it, he shook his head. "Viking, you are a rascal. And you are wrong about Mistress Marx."

Johannes looked at him blankly. "I am?"

"Yes!" Reuben starting to laugh. "She is not a princess. She is a glacial queen!"

From the corner of his eye, Reuben saw Rebecca's head swivel sharply toward the sound of their guffaws.

March 7, 1855

*T*HE BAGGAGE CAR

THE TRAIN CHUGGED WEST. JOHANNES WAS OFTEN missing from their compartment, and Reuben had no doubt as to his whereabouts. Inga had totally captivated him. Reuben passed the time studying his maps and continuing practice with the Colt. His draw was increasingly smooth and fast but he worried about accuracy. *I shall have to practice as soon as I have a place to shoot,* he told himself. *Johannes is right. Reflected images don't shoot back.*

He read several journals on the lands and mountains west of St. Louis, obtained before they left New York. He had read enough to know that the Rockies were arid. He would need a lot of land for grazing. He made lists of provisions and supplies that they would need. *I will try to hire one good hand for the new ranch before leaving St. Louis. A scout, familiar with the territory and the mountains and handy with a gun, would be best. I can probably organize the rest when we reach the Rockies—ranch hands, a cook, and the purchase of breeding stock and bulls.*

*There was much to learn. A cattle empire here would be
far different from the small, lush farms of Europe.*

At other times, sitting on his bunk and thinking, he
recalled his uncle's admonitions, comparing them to his
experiences. The many Americans he had met were pleasant, even helpful but he sensed an independent spirit and
underlying aggressive nature that were rare in the more
tranquil societies of Europe. *There is no doubt that at
some point I will have to fight to protect what is ours.*

Casting a snide look at Johannes, Rebecca left
the women's compartment to go to lunch. Standing
together, Inga and Johannes watched the rolling, heavily
wooded landscape flow to the rear as the train sped
steadily west. The track curved gently and their shoulders touched. Johannes felt heat course through his
body and a current pulse in his fingertips. Putting his
arm around Inga's shoulder, he turned her to face him.
The front of their bodies lightly touched. Her face
looked almost fevered; her parted lips glistened moistly
and her eyes were half-closed. Drawing her tightly to
him, he kissed her deeply.

They melted together, the contours of their tall, athletic frames molding perfectly. Johannes felt dizzy with
want. "Come with me," he whispered, taking her hand
and stepping out into the corridor.

He looked both ways, and then deeply into Inga's eyes
with a voice-less question.

Inga swallowed, and nodded, "Yes."

He led her forward to the baggage car directly behind the engine, deftly unlocking the door with his pocket-knife, and sliding it shut behind them.

INGA HAD NEVER BEFORE KNOWN RAW PRIMAL DESIRE. She felt light-headed, almost dizzy but she knew with certainty that for the first time in her life, she truly wanted a man — this man.

Without a word she pressed Johannes against the side of the car, feeling the heat and wetness surge in her loins as his hands slowly traced her breasts. Watching his hands caress her she marveled at how quickly her nipples became taut and visible beneath the fabric of her frock. There was a white-hot need in her belly, and somewhere deep in her mind she kept hearing a voice: *Oh my God, oh my God.*

She heard herself gasp as he slid one hand up the inside of her thigh and pushed the hardening in his breeches against her hips. Deftly loosening the string holding up her pantaloons, his hand slid down the smooth skin of her abdomen. Wherever he touched her she could feel fire and tremor.

His probing fingers slipped gently into her. Inga felt her legs buckle and she clung desperately to his neck with one arm, roughly loosening the buttons of his pants with the other. He sprang free and she closed her hand around him, softly stroking his length.

Sinking to the floor, their long legs intertwined. Orgasmic tremors coursed through her belly as he sank deeply into her. The whole of her body quivering. She cried out, wrapping her legs around his hips, her arms desperately winding around his heaving back, completely consumed with a passion she had believed she could never, would never, experience.

They remained locked together for half an hour, their breathing ragged between long passionate kisses. Tenderly brushing the blonde strands from her face, Johannes' lips traced the pulsing in her throat. Closing her eyes, she wondered if this were a dream, wanting the perfect feel of his skin and weight on her to never end. Reluctantly, they finally arose and began to dress. Inga fixed her bodice and straightened her skirts.

Johannes was flushed and there was a glazed look in his eyes. Gathering her in his arms, he whispered into her hair, "I suppose you and Rebecca will stop in St. Louis?"

Shaking her head, she murmured, "No, Johannes." She ran her fingertips down the length of his upper arm. "Although not her original intention, milady Marx has decided to head west from there. All the way to the mountains. We are headed initially to Cherry Creek. And I am delighted."

Deep inside her belly, she could feel her body absorbing his seething explosion and her abdomen pulsed with currents of heated energy. She knew her face glowed. Through a film of impassioned tears, she looked into his eyes, "I...I have never felt like this."

Kissing her slowly and passionately, his lips trailed from hers to the side of her neck below her ear. "Ah, Inga, it is new to me, too. And wonderful," he sighed.

"And utterly surprising. I am so glad fate has ordained us to meet and have a similar destination."

She laughed quietly into his shoulder. "I wonder how milady Marx and Reuben will react when they learn this train may not be the end of their association."

Looking at her thoughtfully, Johannes intimated, "You know, Reuben is anything but the simple immigrant Rebecca thinks he is. He is landed gentry and intends to establish a large cattle ranch for his family."

Tipping her head back from his shoulder, Inga smiled. "I knew when I first saw him that he was not a commoner. I'm not certain that there's anyone that my mistress does not consider beneath her. I think, though, the more I get to know her, the more I feel that she has another side."

"What do you mean 'another side'?"

Inga shrugged. "She's like every woman. She wants a man but refuses to admit it. There is a definite current between her and Mister Frank. I wonder if we could somehow facilitate some higher level of contact between them? It might be highly beneficial to our own relationship."

Johannes regarded her with admiration. "You do think things through, Inga. It would absolutely benefit our possible travel together." Johannes' voice was wistful. "What caused Rebecca to suddenly decide to go beyond St. Louis?"

Stroking his cheek with the back of her fingers, she thought for a moment. "I don't know, my love. It has something to do with some land her father left her." She closed her eyes as he nuzzled her, relishing the pulsing in her abdomen.

He buried his nose in the curve of her shoulder and neck, breathing in deeply. "Ah, Inga, I love the smell of you."

"Oh, Johannes, and I you. I want to see as much of you as I can."

"I like your idea, Inga. We should make a plan. It would be good for them and for us. I don't think we should tell them we know they both plan to travel past St. Louis to Cherry Creek. Each of them is way too stubborn. They might actually go out of their way to choose different routes or means for the journey."

"I am sure we can manage to keep their courses parallel." Resting her head on Johannes' shoulder, her voice broke, "Johannes, please believe me. This is the very first time in my life that I have truly made love."

"Inga," he said, pushing her away just enough to see her eyes. "The same is true for me." He smiled. "And that is quite something." His look was one of tenderness and delight at her words but mixed in his expression was a faint trace of puzzlement. Inga's heart lurched. *He is wondering if there is a deeper meaning to my words.*

March 7, 1855

ENCOUNTER

REUBEN WAS LOST IN THOUGHT AS HE MOVED TOWARD the parlor car. *A glass of brandy and the smell of tobacco is what I need.*

He was crossing the exterior separation between dining and parlor when the train lurched. Stumbling forward, head bent, he tried to regain his balance. A woman just emerging from the opposite door fell into him, her head lowered as she tried to keep from tripping on her skirt. Grasping to steady themselves, they clung to each other. It was then that Reuben recognized the dark hair and fine clothing. *Rebecca!*

She tried to step back but he held her tightly. He felt suddenly, magnetically drawn to this woman, the smell of her perfume the feel and fit of her in his arms. *Much softer than I imagined.*

Lifting her head, her usual haughty look was instead an expression of disbelief. She was disarmed, at a loss to regain either her balance or her composure.

The lonesome echo of the whistle sounded, and Reuben felt the rush of evening air. The train regained a smooth rhythm and their bodies swayed together, in unison. The moment was hypnotic. Lowering his face toward hers, blood roared in his ears. Closing her delicate eyelids, she raised her face to him. Their lips met, warm, soft, moist and demanding. Responding with passion, pressing her hips into the thickening in his pants, her tongue worked its way deep into Reuben's mouth. Slipping his hand to the small of her back, he drew the arch of her body closer, molding her form to his. Her breath was coming in ragged gasps, and then she abruptly pushed him away. She steadied herself, smoothing her disheveled hair.

"Well!" she blurted.

Reuben grinned at her, "Well, what?"

"Well," she repeated, stamping her foot, "I thought you were a gentleman."

"And I, Mistress Marx, thought you were a lady. How delightful to find that you are also a woman."

Stamping her foot again, she tried to pivot away, almost falling. "This is utterly wasted effort, Mister Frank. After this train reaches St. Louis, we shall never see each other again. You took advantage of the situation and I shall not forgive you!"

Reuben felt the smile slipping from his face. "I have not apologized, Rebecca—I assume I may now call you Rebecca—nor will I. Contrary to your protestations, you did indeed kiss me back. Apparently, much to your own dismay."

Her mouth curling derisively, she snapped, "A typical commoner, Mister Frank. You have never been around real ladies. Of course, you would not know how to treat them, and you certainly are unable to ascertain what you call a response was my simple attempt to disengage from an awkward situation. I say again, you are no gentleman, Mister Frank!"

Reuben's elation fully dissipated. "I am when circumstances call for me to be one. You appeared to be a woman who wished to be kissed."

"You were sadly mistaken, sir."

"Mistress Marx, you would do well to cease your judgment of people based on appearance or your own immature and inexperienced assumptions."

"Oh!" There was no mistaking the wrath and dismay in her voice. *It is likely no one has ever addressed Rebecca Marx in this way.* "Oh!" Rebecca stomped her foot again, suddenly drawing back her hand to slap him but Reuben caught her wrist.

"Rebecca, that type of behavior is not acceptable, particularly by one who proclaims herself a lady." Stepping back, his jaw clenched. "My apologies if you were affronted in any way."

"This is not worth further discussion." With her chin disdainfully in the air, Rebecca brushed past him, disappearing into the car from which Reuben had just come.

Reuben was angrier then he could remember in some time, he could not help but remember the evocative way Rebecca's breasts had pushed against the tight cloth of her dress. *Heaving with indignation? Or something more?* He stood for a while longer allowing the cool rush of air to take the heat from his face but the memory of her lips remained firmly etched in his mind.

March 7, 1855

THE DECISION

THE NEXT DAY, HUMMING "THE WEARING OF THE
Green," Jacob purhased a new shirt. *Need one anyway
and even had a bath,* he thought, smiling to himself. The
previous night had been a good night for poker and
after his visit to Sarah, he had enjoyed another hour of
brutal possession of Miss Mary. *Play my cards right and
soon enough, that will be Sarah.*

After their session, the tart had drawn a hot bath for
him. He planned his return to the dress shop this day to
coincide with closing time to avoid the interference of
customers. Along the way, he heisted another bunch of
flowers from the same hapless vendor.

Greeting him at the door of the shop, Sarah's smile was
reserved but genuine as she thanked him for the bouquet.

"Tea?" she asked over her shoulder as she led him
back to the parlor.

"Yes, please." Jacob stayed several steps behind her
admiring the movement of her hips. "I like your dress."

"Why thank you, Jacob. I designed it myself and
sewed it just before coming over from England."

"Well, Miss Sarah, I don't know much about these things but I would say you have a definite talent."

Sarah blushed, obviously pleased by the compliment. Jacob liked the way the reddening of her face accentuated the freckles over the bridge of her nose.

Drawn to the parlor alcove by the whistle of the kettle, Aunt Stella smiled at Jacob, "Jacob, how pleasant to see you back again so soon. What's this I hear about you going west?"

"I hear the West is a land of possibility. I have good contacts out there in the gold mining business."

Hesitating a moment, Aunt Stella became serious "My concern, Jacob, as you can understand, is that Sarah be accompanied in a proper manner. It's important that her reputation not be tarnished. I am also anxious that she have someone to help her find work as a dressmaker when she arrives. I don't want her to spend her entire inheritance to get there and have nothing left with which to start a new life."

Jacob felt a sudden keen interest at the word "inheritance," but he was careful to show no reaction. "It would be my honor to escort your niece if she would like to make the journey to St. Louis. I'm headed there, anyway, but perhaps if she stayed here in the city with you it would be a safer course of action."

Aunt Stella made a show of moving sugar and spoons around the small tea table. "There, there," she clucked. "Would you like milk in your tea, Jacob?" She stirred her tea slowly, obviously collecting her thoughts.

"Sometimes a person, even a woman, has to take a path that is a little less customary." She sighed and her lips quivered slightly. "I did that myself coming here years ago. The journey killed my poor husband. I've heard some great things about the West. My friends and I talk about it. Often there are stories in the paper. It has become crowded here, and there is great competition. It's difficult for a new dressmaker to get established. The wages for a simple seamstress are minimal. If I were younger, I'd make the trip myself."

"For someone as established as you are, it might be a bad business decision. But I'd be glad to escort you both if you'd like." Reaching over, Jacob offered Aunt Stella the sugar.

"That's very kind of you, Jacob." Aunt Stella sighed again, slowly shaking her head. "If I were younger, without this shop..." Her voice trailed off.

Sarah had left the table to tend to a plump, middle-aged patron. The customer left. Locking the shop door, she turned over the "*Open*" sign that hung in the glass, returning to the tearoom and sitting quietly off to the side, her face pensive. Realizing Jacob had spoken to her, she looked at him blankly.

"Have you given the trip some thought? I plan to catch the New York Central train west on Saturday morning. Do you wish to accompany me?"

Her hands pulling nervously at her collar, Sarah looked at her aunt, who gave a slight negative shake of her head. Finally, she said, "I'll go as far as St. Louis. St. Louis is growing, and I will stop there."

Staring at her niece, Stella's face paled and her lips parted in surprise.

Struggling not to appear overly elated, Jacob nodded his head. "Shall I meet you at the train, then?"

Aunt Stella protested. "I insist that you collect Sarah here and help her to the station."

"Of course, of course," he stammered. "What a careless mistake on my part. I thought the two of you...well, I didn't know. Sarah, if you will give me your fare, I'll purchase our tickets today."

"Yes, Jacob, I shall get the money for you after tea." She studied her hands, which rested in her lap, then looked up. "Have you seen Mister Frank since arriving in New York?"

"Mister Frank?" Jacob was puzzled.

"Yes, Reuben. Reuben Frank."

Jacob felt his cheeks warm and his eyes narrow. "Oh, Reuben. The Prussian farm boy? I did not know his last name was Frank. No, I have not. Why?"

Looking away from his sudden, very intent stare, Sarah's voice was soft and wistful, "I was just wondering."

Sarah's aunt began to speak "I think..."

Better not let her muck up the works. Standing suddenly, Jacob bowed to Stella, "Mistress Stella, it was a pleasure to share tea with you.

"But..." the older lady stuttered.

I shall take good care of your niece. Sarah, if you would be so kind as to fetch the train fare, I shall be on my way. Our departure will be at nine, and Saturday is the day after tomorrow."

CHAPTER

36

March 8, 1855

$\mathcal{D}$ANGERS AHEAD

RECLINING ON ONE OF THE DIVANS IN THE PARLOR CAR, Reuben forced his mind from the encounter with Rebecca and sipped his brandy. He didn't smoke but he liked the smell of pipes. The aroma always reminded him of his father and Uncle Hermann. He also found surreptitious eavesdropping on tongues loosened by tobacco and alcohol informative. Johannes sauntered in with his face cracked in a wider than usual toothy grin and his hair slightly disheveled. A pink hue colored the normal fair cast of his Scandinavian skin, and there was a faint circular red smudge on his neck.

"Your breeches are undone," said Reuben dryly.

"Oh! Must have caught my trousers on a door latch,"

The two men laughed as Johannes fastened two buttons on his pants. "Let's go back to our compartment," Reuben said. "There's something I want to show you."

Licking his lips, Johannes glanced at the bar. "Can we discuss the matter over a drink?"

Reuben looked around the car. "No, there are too many eyes and ears here."

Back at the sleeping berth, Reuben pulled out the leather map case. Carefully, he rolled the maps out on the bunk, weighting down the corners with their pistols, and the length of the bottom of the top parchments with their rifles.

Johannes frowned at the spread out parchments framed with weapons. "I hope that is not an omen."

"Come on over here." He motioned to his friend, ignoring the comment.

Hunching over the maps the two men looked at the territory west of St. Louis. "I shared these with you at Uncle Hermann's but it is time to review them in detail. Here is the route we need to take toward Cherry Creek. It is called the Mormon and Emigrant Trail. We will follow the Missouri River, and then the North Platte to Fort Kearney. Out here, we will swing south before Fort Laramie and follow the South Platte to Cherry Creek. From Cherry Creek, we head southwest into the mountains. It will be a very long journey, with lack of water, extreme weather, no law, maybe trouble over this American slavery issue and Indians upset that their treaties have been ignored."

"What's the good news?" Johannes asked with suppressed mirth.

"The good news is that you and I will get fully outfitted for the journey to the mountains in St. Louis. When we reach the mountains we will hire some help, locate cattle to purchase, and then we're going over the Rockies to right here." Reuben punctuated his comment with a punch into the map.

Johannes peered closer. "If you would remove your hand, Reuben, I could see what the hell you were pointing at."

"Oh," Reuben chuckled, moving his fist.

Johannes read the words on the map. "Tell me more of *Las Montanas Rojas.*"

"As I told you at Uncle Hermann's, it's a set of three reddish-colored mountains in a range called the San Juans. Most of the features were named by the Spaniards before they lost it to Mexico, and then Mexico in turn was defeated by the United States and Texas. The Americans call the area Red Mountains. Supposedly, one of them has some type of red stone cliffs with strange interspersed hard rock formations. Along the base of the cliffs is a creek, which flows down to the Uncompahgre River you see on the map. The cliffs come down in big grassy plateaus. On the other side of the mountain, there is scattered timber, which is supposed to be great cattle range, good south sun for the winter, many springs and grass as high as your waist. Also, some smaller creeks and level areas, which we might be able to farm for winter hay."

"How do you know all of this? You haven't been there, have you?"

Reuben straightened up. "Of course I haven't. My father hired a scout through Uncle Hermann. He gave him a two-year commission. His job was to find the best area for cattle, based on a set of requirements my father and my uncle wrote down for him. This is information we got from his letters, and he drew these maps, which he also sent to us."

"That's it?" asked Johannes. "We're going on a five-month-long journey, to an area that I hear is like the Alps, in a country where half the citizens dislike the other half, filled with hostile Indians, all based on one man's assessment? How do you know what you're going to find when you get there?"

Reuben felt his jaw set. "If you have something better to do, you can certainly back out now."

Johannes' head jerked up. "I was bringing up the obvious, Reuben. I made a deal. I keep my agreements and I think that I'd better be around to be your rear guard." His lips slipping into a sly grin, he added, "And maybe protect you from that dark-haired woman too, the princess." His tease broke the tension in Reuben's chest and he sat down on the bunk.

"I will have to tell you of my encounter with Rebecca between the train cars."

Johannes' eyebrows shot up with anticipatory delight. "Oh? Rebecca? A rendezvous with the princess? What happened with Mistress Marx?"

"But first, one more thing about Las Montanas Rojas."

"And that is?" Johannes' impatient tone clearly indicated he wanted to hear about Rebecca.

"One of the scout's letters said something about potential gold in the area. He was supposed to have sent back a third map but it never arrived. Uncle Hermann told me he died. Killed by Indians."

He gave the map to his brother in St. Louis, who then supposedly headed to New York. Despite his best efforts, Uncle Hermann was not able to locate the brother."

"Gold?" echoed Johannes. "I am not sure if that is good or bad news. Gold seems to bring out the worst in men."

"Yes," responded Reuben, "and cows can't eat gold, either."

37

March 9, 1855

*I*NNOCENCE STOLEN

THE EXPENSE OF TRANSPORTATION FOR SARAH ANGERED Jacob but he found a dowdy buggy for hire, rationalizing it was a small price to pay to get what he wanted.

Arriving at Aunt Stella's shop slightly after nine the morning of their departure, he found Sarah waiting inside, her trunk packed and ready to leave.

He smiled at Sarah's aunt. *She looks very agitated.* Invoking his most charming demeanor, "Stella, what a lovely dress. That fabric is perfect for this bright sunny day."

"Why thank you, Jacob. That is very nice of you to say." Her eyes bored beseechingly into his. "Now, please, take good care of my niece—she is very special to me and her sister back in England. We entrust you with her well-being. Hopefully, you will have time to help her get settled in St. Louis before you proceed west for your mining business."

"Don't worry, Stella; Sarah's care is foremost in my mind. Sarah, that dress is perfect on you. I haven't seen you in green before. You ready?"

Her lips forming a tight smile, Sarah nodded without a word. She was very pale.

Aunt Stella and Sarah hugged a tearful good-bye, and then Jacob assisted her into the open cab. Cracking his buggy whip, the silent, surly driver forced the sullen, slightly emaciated horses into an unenthusiastic clip-clop of hooves, which echoed off the sheer walls of the buildings on either side of the street. Waving from the doorway Aunt Stella dabbed at her eyes with an embroidered handkerchief.

"Write me, dear Sarah," she cried out.

THEY REACHED CENTRAL STATION AFTER THE FERRY across the East River. People milled on the street unloading bags from many different types of horse and oxen-drawn carriages, buggies and wagons. Couples and families were hugging and waving farewell to one another all around the curb and entry to the station. Jacob made two trips back to the buggy for their bags and Sarah's lone trunk. The driver offered no assistance.

Clutching her satchel with the secret compartment tightly to her chest she waited for him a short distance from the train. The porter loaded Sarah's baggage and Jacob's small greasy duffel into one of the sleeping cars. Sarah hesitatingly climbed the steps into the car throwing a last uneasy glace at the throng that ebbed and flowed on the platform. Jacob climbed up, taking her hand in his and they walked down the passageway of the car, checking the numbers of the compartments. He stopped at door 1204, car twelve, berth four. Holding open the door, he smiled, "After you, Sarah."

A small closet was situated next to the door. Two bunks, one on either side, hung from the sidewalls. A tiny washbasin with a pitcher secured by a fabric thong perched below the window on a narrow table that doubled as a shared nightstand. People on the platform outside were waving. Wisps of steam scuttled by the window. The car lurched slightly. Sarah turned to Jacob, wide-eyed.

"Are we leaving?" she stammered.

"Yes, Sarah, we are. That green really does suit you," said Jacob, his hands on his hips.

"This is my compartment, then?"

Jacob shook his head slowly. "This is our compartment."

Sarah took a step back, a cold trepidation stealing through her.

"But...I thought you were going to have your own compartment. That's why I gave you the money to purchase my fare."

Jacob shrugged. "They were all out of other compartments. We'll have to share. But the money we have saved will come in handy later." Jacob flashed a smile.

Sarah took another step back.

"Of course, I'll be a complete gentleman. I'll fetch us some water."

Watching the cityscape begin to speed past the window, she tried to think. She had never felt so alone and vulnerable. The image of Reuben slipped into her thoughts. She bit her lip.

Returning with a tray of breads, cheeses and water Jacob seemed full of a strange energy. "I'll go fetch some wine for us." He left again.

Sarah heard the lock turn in the door after he closed it. She suddenly felt nauseous. He returned with a bottle of red wine and two goblets. "Make sure those don't fall over," he said, pouring one goblet to the brim. "Have some wine."

Perching on the edge of the bunk, she clenched her hands so tightly in her lap that her knuckles were white. She still wore her coat.

Jacob closed the door and locked it again, the dead-bolt making a loud click in the small space. He handed Sarah the untouched glass of wine.

"But it's not yet noon," she protested.

Jacob leaned forward over her. "Drink it up."

Her shaking hands grasped the glass, spilling a few drops as the train hurtled down the track. She took a sip. Jacob leaned against the door.

"Finish it up, woman."

Raising the goblet to her lips, she took another large swallow.

"All of it," he insisted.

They had left early for the station. Sarah had been too excited and nervous to eat. "But, Jacob," she protested, "I have not had any breakfast. This will go right to my head."

Jacob walked slowly over to her and took away the wine.

"Let me help you take off your coat."

She hesitated, then rose uncertainly. The train swayed and she was thrown against him. His arms slid around her waist and he pulled her into him, his lips pressing against her neck.

"Jacob!" she said sternly. Rising up the bodice of her dress his hand cupped her breast. A jolt of fear coursed through her. Struggling against his grasp, she opened her mouth to scream but Jacob smothered her lips with his, pinning both her hands behind her back with one arm. With his free hand, he untied the top bow of her blouse, slipped his fingers through the open fabric and below the camisole.

Feeling the strength leave her legs she gasped, "Jacob, no!" The tiny space began to spin.

Growling out a knowing laugh, he ripped the fabric of her blouse down to her waist. Sarah was shocked. *This can't be happening. Not to me.* She felt like an observer who was simply watching some strange man and woman. She felt faint.

"I have wanted you since I first saw you standing there in the wind on the ship," Jacob whispered in her ear. Sarah felt her heart pound. His hand began lifting her skirt and petticoats, a few inches at a time. His forefinger stroked upward against the thin fabric of her drawers and her inner thigh. Desperate, Sarah wrenched her shoulders from side-to-side in an attempt to get her arms free. He tightened his grip. She opened her mouth to scream but Jacob quickly covered her lips with his hand, pushing her backward onto one of the bunks. "Shh, woman; don't fight. You'll like it."

His fingertips were inching below her waistband. She opened her mouth again to cry for help but reaching over to the pitcher stand, he grabbed one of the cloth napkins, shoving it roughly between her teeth. With a violent effort, she tried to turn her body but it was too late. She gagged. Her entire body was trembling and her thighs shook. His rough, whiskered face scraped her cheek. One of his hands stayed between her legs. Her arms were pinned between the bed and her back. She felt his lips on her throat, jumbled thoughts flitting through her mind.

The delicate fabric of her drawers ripped as he stripped the cloth from her hips. His breeches were down around his knees. She tried to push against him but he crushed his frame to hers. He grinned, then grunted, his hips bucking back. She convulsed in pain. Disgust and horror welled through her. Tears streamed down her cheeks. The train rocked side-to-side. The goblet of wine crashed to the floor, sending a spray of deep red splashing against the window.

March 9, 1855

METAMORPHOSIS

SARAH LAY STUNNED, HER SHOULDERS HEAVING WITH each retching sob. Outside the stained compartment window, daylight faded. Jacob had roughly removed the rest of her clothing and had taken her repeatedly. The whole day was a nightmarish blur. Each time she tried to convince herself that nothing had happened, that this was all just a terrible dream, she was reminded of the awful reality by pangs in the tender apex of her legs. Jacob snored next to her, naked from the waist down, his arm tight around her waist. He had even accompanied her, one of his hands like a vise on her arm, on each of her two trips to the toilet that served their set of berths. Each time they encountered another passenger, the increasing pressure of his grip hurt and bruised her bicep.

As the hours ticked by, her horror, shock, pain and denial began to yield to a white-hot anger. *This animal has taken my virginity. My trust. My innocence. Forever.*

Curling into a fetal ball, she attempted to ignore the sore burning below her hips and the angry constriction deep in her chest. Trying to will the rhythmic motion of the train and the tracks to calm the bitter contempt that consumed her soul and induce sleep was futile. There was no bottom to the depths of the growing rage clogging her throat, tugging viciously at her gut, swirling like an angry storm in her head, filling her heart. Staring fixedly through the gloom at her valise, she visualized the pistol that lay in its secret compartment.

Jacob left early the next morning, again locking the door with the key. Springing from the bed as soon as the lock clicked, she sparingly but hurriedly used the water in the pitcher, and with dampened napkins and the remnant of her torn undergarments, cleaned herself as best she could. Opening the false bottom of the valise, she drew out the revolver, wiping it with the tattered remnants of her torn clothing to impart the energy of her shame to the dull, dark blue steel and give it purpose. Placing the weapon on the bed within easy reach, she put on clean clothes. A feeling of detachment pervaded her like a protective cloak. Drawing herself up on a bunk facing the door, her back to the corner of the compartment, she wrapped her arms around her knees and pressed them against her chest. Rocking slowly back and forth, the pistol in one hand, she waited, every sense alert, marveling at the cold clarity of her thoughts.

Returning several hours later, Jacob fumbled with the lock outside the door, speaking in apparent good humor, "I have some food for us, woman. Won a bit of money from some fools who think they are poker players." Backing into the berth, he was focused on shutting the door, one hand holding a tray of cheese, bread and apples. Leveling the pistol at the center of his back, Sarah steadied the barrel with both hands on the grip, her trembling forearms resting on her knees. She waited for him to turn around. *I want to see your face, your eyes—I want you to know.*

Sliding the door shut, Jacob turned, his eyes on the tray. Sarah pulled back the hammer. The distinctive metallic click of the mechanism engaging seemed unusually loud in the small area.

Jacob looked up, startled, his smug smile vanishing instantly. He froze. "Now, Sarah, you don't want to do this," he said in a low, soothing tone.

The world seemed to pause. Sarah's vision narrowed to only the cocked hammer and barrel of the pistol pointed squarely at the stocky figure in front of her. She felt nothing but grim satisfaction at the look of fear in Jacob's eyes. No sound reached her ears but his voice and the inner palpable pounding of her own heart.

"Yes, I do," she said in a voice that seemed somehow separate from herself, and pulled the trigger. Jacob hurled himself sideways to the right, almost simultaneously with the surprisingly subtle pop of the shot.

For a moment, Sarah thought the bullet had felled him but he rose frantically, cursing, "You bitch!" He put his right hand to the blood seeping into his sleeve several inches below his left shoulder.

Sarah began to fumble with the pistol in the surreal moment. The cylinder would not advance, and she struggled to cock the hammer again, watching her hands as if from another body. Everything seemed to be in slow motion.

Pausing only for a split second, he leapt the few feet to her bunk, his right hand stretched for the pistol as Sarah struggled with the weapon. Landing squarely on her, his weight jammed her into the corner with full force, knocking the breath from her. Wrestling the revolver away from her, he stood, glowering as she gasped to regain her breath. His tone was deadly, "If you ever try anything like that again, wench, I will break your neck with my bare hands and throw your body off the train. Now get up, get some water from the pitcher and clean my arm."

Jacob raped her brutally that night, covering her cries with his hand. "Hurts does it, lassie? Well, my arm hurts, too."

He began to develop a pattern. He would leave mid-morning after taking her to the water closet. He was generally gone several hours, then he would return with food and usually with coins or small bills that he would add to his money pouch. The pistol had disappeared. Sarah contemplated requesting help from another passenger or the conductor but realized it was his word against hers. *Besides, the shame of this wretched situation; no one will believe we shared a compartment by mistake.*

The third day of the trip, she waited a few minutes after he had left the compartment and then opened his duffel, pawing its contents with violently shaking hands. *There is no doubt he will make good on his promise of killing me if provoked but I need something to give me leverage.*

Under the dirty shirts and old cloths, she discovered a large folded piece of parchment paper. It looked old and worn. Carefully opening it, she held it up to the light of the window. She was startled. *This seems to be a map to a gold deposit.* There was a reddish-brown stain in one corner. *Where had he gotten it?*

Sitting on the floor in the narrow space between the bunks, she reviewed her options. They had been through Philadelphia. She could try to escape when the train stopped in Chicago but she was a virtual prisoner and the authorities were far less likely to believe a woman. *It will be my word against his and with each day that passes greater doubt would be cast on my version. He will be difficult to shake. How can I keep the map and be rid of him? How long can I stand the thought of him next to me everywhere we go, and his vulgar touch?* The map indicates the gold is somewhere far west of St. Louis. Is the revenge of my honor and justice worth it?

"Las Montanas Rojas," she muttered to herself. *Perhaps I can steal the map and safely lose myself in the dense population of St. Louis? But that is not where the gold is.*

Meticulously replacing the map just as she had found it, she whispered grimly to herself, "The opportunity will arise, Mister O'Shanahan." Staring at her valise, she wished fervently her revolver was still concealed in the bottom. Closing her eyes, she gritted her teeth and clenched her fists. "I will wait, be patient and play the game well. You owe me, Jacob. And I shall collect."

March 11, 1855

T. LOUIS

LYING ON HIS BACK ON HIS BUNK, KNEES BENT, HANDS clasped behind his blond hair, Johannes rolled his head toward Reuben. "Can we please find a hotel with beds I can straighten my legs in?"

Sitting on the edge of his bunk, Reuben looked up from oiling his Slim Jim, and grinned. "Worse comes to worst, there's always the floor—that would be an improvement over this cubby hole."

"You have a point, my Prussian friend."

"And..."

"Yes?"

"Think of the room you'll have to stretch out under wagons and stars for the next two months."

Johannes fixed his eyes toward the ceiling and grunted.

Reuben and Johannes disembarked as Inga and Rebecca were emerging from five cars down the track. Walking toward one another through wafts of steam slipping down the track from the locomotive, Reuben noticed the intense stares exchanged between Johannes and Inga. "Careful you don't walk into a post, Johannes."

Reuben was delighted to be off the train and in St. Louis. *The last time we really stretched was Chicago.* His good humor was dampened, however, as he returned Rebecca's coldly aloof gaze. "Where will you be staying?" he asked in a polite voice.

"That's none of your concern," Rebecca snapped, her eyes dropping to his lips. Reuben wondered if she was thinking of her passionate response when he had kissed her between the train cars.

"Well, for the sake of those two," Reuben nodded his head toward Inga and Johannes, who had drifted a bit to another spot on the platform, "we should at least know where the other is staying."

"I imagine you're staying down in the river district?" she said.

Reuben felt his jaw tighten. "Actually, we have a room at the Southern Hotel at Fourth and Walnut."

Her eyebrows lifted in astonishment but her voice was sharp. "How did you manage enough money for both a train and a fine hotel?"

Before Reuben could reply, Johannes and Inga returned. Inga had overhead Reuben's last statement.

"That's where we're staying, too!" exclaimed Inga. She clapped her hands together and seemed to take a little jump. She shot Rebecca a look that said, 'I told you so.' Rebecca flashed back a baleful stare.

Johannes cleared his throat, "Well, let's get a carriage together."

Reuben threw him a warning glare. "I don't think there's enough room for the four of us and all the ladies' luggage in a single carriage."

Rebecca's shoulders drew back and she turned away. "Come along, Inga. Find us some porters. Though Mister Frank seems fixated with my trunks, I have heard no offer of assistance from these two." Bestowing a dazzling, parting smile upon Johannes, Inga hurried after Rebecca.

Johannes turned to Reuben, obviously perplexed. "What was that all about?"

"Just having some fun at her almighty's expense. Let's get our bags."

"I think she likes you." Johannes tried vainly to make his tone serious.

"Then I would hate to see how she acts towards someone she dislikes."

The next morning Reuben cast a half-open eye toward Johannes' unslept-in bed. An hour later, he was in the lobby, vibrant with a crowd of finely dressed men and women seated at scattered round tables having breakfast and coffee. Reuben chose a table centered in a broad beam of sunlight spilling invitingly through one of the large, high windows. Stretching in the bright warmth, he studied the other people gathered for breakfast.

A woman's voice jolted him out of his survey of the dining area. "Gentlemen usually rise and pull out a chair for a lady."

Reuben was shocked to see Rebecca standing by the other chair. Her well-tailored dress accentuated every supple, inviting curve of her figure. Though she attempted to cast her usual superior air, Reuben felt some other indefinable energy. *The same sensation as when we kissed on the train.* Bolting to his feet, he bowed slightly, motioning with his hand for her to be seated.

"Thank you." Rebecca's nose was slightly upturned; her shoulders squared back, stiff and straight. "Inga tells me you're going west to Cherry Creek."

"Yes, we are." He volunteered nothing else.

Her eyes dropped to his chin, and then fleetingly to the tufts of hair poking from his open shirt collar, and then up to his lips. She smiled disarmingly. Reuben felt a stir in his loins. *She's about to play me for a fool,* he warned himself.

"It just so happens we are going to Cherry Creek also," she said, busying herself with a rearrangement of the utensils in front of her.

"I thought you had some business pertaining to your father that you had to attend to here in St. Louis." Reuben's fingers were tapping on the tabletop.

Rebecca started. "You remember our conversation back at Castle Garden?"

"Yes or perhaps Johannes is not the only one who tells tales out of school," Reuben said.

Rebecca smiled. "We shall have to have a talk with our people."

There was a moment's silence; their eyes met, and the two of them began laughing uproariously.

People at the tables around them rotated in their seats, staring at them. An old lady who sat near them leaned over to her companion and said in a tone they were not meant to overhear, "I suppose when you make that striking a couple, you think you can do what you wish."

"So, they must take breaks from their romantic escapades at least long enough to share a few sentences," Reuben teased.

"Well, at least someone is experiencing romance." Rebecca subconsciously ran her tongue along her upper lip.

"We do make a fine-looking couple," Reuben said.

Rebecca dabbed at tears of laughter with her napkin. "Do you really think so? I've never imagined myself as part of a couple."

"I wonder why not?"

"I've never had the time or the opportunity or found a man in whom I was even slightly interested."

"When do you plan to leave?" Reuben asked, purposefully absorbing himself in his coffee cup.

"We don't know that yet. I understand from the concierge that the wagon trains leave periodically this time of year. But it's important to be in with the right class of people and to have a good captain."

"Wagon master," Reuben corrected.

Rebecca paused. "Wagon master.... Yes, I've heard it's important to have the right wagon master to remain safe. Have you found an appropriate situation?"

"Have you?" he countered.

"No. We have no inkling of where to begin. I rather hoped that you could assist me."

Deep within him, something turned over. *I have been right all along. This woman does not and has never cared for me. I doubt she cares about anybody unless they are of some specific use to her.*

His chair legs made a loud scraping squeak on the marble floor as he rose abruptly. "It seems your attitude changes when you need something."

"Reuben...I—"

"We would be happy to assist you." Reuben cut her off, keeping his face impassive and his voice steely, "We are beginning to get ourselves prepared this morning. There is a group being organized to leave within the week. I'll have Johannes keep Inga abreast of our progress."

Rebecca's eyes widened at the sudden change in his demeanor. "Thank you, Reuben."

"If you'll excuse me." Reuben quickly left the table. Glancing back from the foot of the stairs, Rebecca still sat at the table looking after him, her expression one of perplexed surprise.

March 15, 1855

#

SARAH KNEW JACOB WAS KEEPING A WATCHFUL EYE ON her. During each stop along the route, he remained in the compartment with her, the door locked and window shades pulled. Her wrist was still black and blue from his vise-like grip when they had switched to the Illinois Central train in Chicago for the last leg of the journey to St. Louis.

He wore a light jacket to cover the bloodstains in his shirt where the bullet had pierced his arm. Watching him dig out the small mound of lead with a stiletto he had pulled from his boot, Sarah purposely did not warn him to heat the blade with matches before he performed the procedure.

His advances were less frequent. He was doing well at cards, which seemed to keep him in relative good humor. His first act each time he returned was to shove his winnings in his change bag. If he wasn't too drunk, and passed out first, his second was usually to command her to take off her clothes. After the fourth day, she

forced herself to become more compliant and less resist-
ant, though she remained rigid at his touch. The strategy
seemed to work. During the last several occasions they
had coupled, Jacob had changed his position and become
less rough when Sarah complained he was hurting her.

Sarah's one escape was the changing nature of the
countryside. She was startled from one particular
moment of reverie watching the land transform, when
Jacob had stood behind her, putting his hands lightly on
her shoulders and rubbing them in a clumsy but almost
gentle way, "Aye, it is a beautiful landscape with not so
many people. I think we might like it in the West."

Sarah was startled by the sudden thought that Jacob
had started to care for her a bit. *Perhaps in some twisted
way, he respects me for trying to kill him.* She had no further illusions about what sort of man Jacob was, and she
was no longer innocent. She stowed the realization for
future use.

IT WAS A PLEASURE TO STRETCH HER LEGS WITHOUT the
confines of the train and to feel space around her when
they disembarked in St. Louis.

"Had some good winnings on that train, woman,"
Jacob boasted. "If there are even bigger fools in this
town, we will be well outfitted for our journey west."

He hadn't asked her about her money and she said
nothing. Jacob found a seedy hotel, the Planters Inn, on
the northeast side of town. The room had an odor but
its bed was semi-clean. They had barely entered the

room when Jacob suddenly pushed her face down on the bed. The old mattress sagged in the center and creaked as he lifted her skirt and petticoats and pulled her drawers down to her knees in one adept motion. Sarah had no leverage in the concave springs. Her cries were muffled in the mushy wool of the blankets as Jacob spread her thighs with his knees and entered her from behind. A few thrusts and he grunted, then relaxed. He stood up, buttoning his pants.

"I'm going out. We need money for supplies and passage." Sarah still lay face down but raised her shoulders from the bed.

Turning her teary face toward the blurred stocky figure, the fiery thought of revenge, which had sustained her to that point, vanished. "I don't want to go to the West. I will stay in St. Louis."

Jacob's hands paused at the last button of his breeches. "Woman, you have little or no money and you know nobody here. You're going with me. You have no other choice."

Sarah rolled over and sat up, her body wracked with sobs. Jacob's fingertips rubbed the stubble on his chin. Striding to the bed, he sat beside her, putting his hand on the small of her back. She flinched.

"You know, Sarah, there are many bad people out there. They could take advantage of you. I will keep you safe. And...and...I like your company."

She looked up at him incredulously, "You like my company?"

Withdrawing his hand from her waist, he said gruffly "Yes, I like your company. Let me show you something that will cheer you up. I have a plan." Glancing furtively about as if spying eyes filled the tiny hotel room, he reached into the breast pocket of his coat and drew out the worn and tattered document that she had found days earlier in his satchel.

"There's gold out there and I have a map."

Wiping the tears from her eyes with her wrists, she pretended surprise. "A gold map?"

"Yes, Sarah. This is our perfect hand. Four Aces. We will be rich."

"Oh, Jacob," Sarah forced a smile. She knew Jacob would mistake her reaction as one of interested excitement. He would not suspect the sudden rush of power she felt, now that she was certain how important this map and the gold were to him. Her hopeless panic of a few minutes before vanished. She felt a resurgence of the calm cold that had permeated her emotions after the first rape.

Her gaze was drawn to the reddish-brown stain in the corner of the map. "Where did you get this map? How do you know it's real?" She felt a jolt as she realized the red smear in the corner of the old parchment was dried blood. "What is that stain?"

He ignored her questions. "We get along well, woman. I will take care of you. Besides, we fit together pretty well. I notice you've begun to like it."

Sarah's lips pursed tightly but she said nothing as Jacob grabbed his hat, shoved the knife in his boot and headed toward the door, calling back over his shoulder, "I'm going to go fleece some money and find out about how we get west from here." The door slammed behind him. Sarah sighed in relief at the sound and at the realization that he had not locked it.

She remained on the bed. She had spread her dress over her legs but her drawers remained bunched around her ankles. *Yes, you owe me, Jacob O'Shanahan.*

Wanting to indulge herself for the few hours she had alone, she walked to the door and locked it. Closing the curtains on the windows, she sat in the single threadbare chair, pausing every few minutes to listen for footsteps outside the door. Emptying the contents of her satchel, she opened the secret compartment. She removed only five cents, the cost of a bath. She didn't want Jacob to find even a spare dime in her purse. Her nose wrinkled at the pungent smell of their sex and she recoiled. She couldn't wait to wash the odor of him from her body. Dressing quickly, she hurried down to the hotel bathhouse.

The hotel's common bath area was separated into male and female areas. The women's section was planked rough, weathered wood. Its tile floor was slick, much of the floor covering cracked with age. There were four tubs separated into cubicles only by thin cotton curtains. Plump matrons with aprons scurried back and forth with pails of hot water. A warm, moist, mist hung in the air suspending a pleasant though pungent fragrance of soap and perfume. Sitting in one of the chairs by the door, she waited for a tub to free up. A cheery attendant, sweat rolling down her florid face and her gray hair stringy with the humidity, wallowed over to her, "All set, missy," she said with a smile. "How hot would you like your water?"

"Hot. Hot as I can bear," she said.

Luxuriating in the steaming water replete with bubbles, her body finally relaxed but her mind stayed active. Jacob's disclosure of the map had triggered a series of disjointed thoughts. *Will my plan work? His debt to me is far more than just money.*

She was back in the room several hours later feeling more like herself than at any point since the first horrible hour on the train, almost a week before. Jacob sauntered in a half hour later.

"Jacob, I've decided to go west with you."

Looking up from his money pouch, the stocky towhead beamed at her. "I knew you had sense in you, woman." Shifting his eyes toward the door, he lowered his voice. "But remember, this is our secret. Not a word to anyone about the map."

"Not a whisper, Jacob. This will be our secret."

CHAPTER

41

March 15, 1855

MONEY FOR THE JOURNEY

FEELING PARTICULARLY GOOD ABOUT SARAH'S AGREE-ment to accompany him west and her interest in the map and gold, Jacob explored the grimy streets around the hotel. He whistled to himself as he walked. *Getting a tad sweet on her, are you, Mister O'Shanahan? And she on me?"*

Inquiring from a group of men loitering at a bar entrance, he learned the locations of several good card games. Singling out one of the unkempt group whose clothing was more tattered than the others, he motioned him away from the group.

Pulling the flask from his pocket, he asked if he knew about wagon trains west. The man's tongue played over his lips when he saw the silver container.

Eyeing the scalloped silver of the container, the man offered a sullen "Yes."

"A drink for a name," said Jacob.

The man took a long swig. Jacob had to wrest the flask from his hand. "That's enough, mate."

"If you're headed west from here like those other fools, I hear the best wagon master is that son of a bitch they call Mac."

"Mac?" Jacob repeated.

"For Macintyre. He's a Mick!"

"Well, that should make him a fine fellow. Where can I find him?"

The man belched. "He's usually down by the livery stables over on the west side of town at the end of Fourth. Down by the river south of the steamboat wharfs. They ferry across there because the river is shallower. I hear he's putting together a train now. Another drink?"

"That bit of information wasn't worth the first drink," snapped Jacob harshly. Backing away from the man, he walked down the street. *I will inquire further at Six Mile House and Kraft's Saloon, the bars those slobs recommended for the best poker games and easy marks.*

Six-Mile House was bursting with roughly dressed, unshowered people, mostly men, virtually all armed. *That boot knife is of little use here. I've got to get me a pistol.* Thick putrid cigar smoke curled around the vertical log posts supporting the second floor. Mirrors behind the long bar reflected all shapes and sizes of glasses, pumps and cheap whiskey bottles. Calling for drinks and elbowing for position around the bar, women in low-cut gaudy dresses and rouge with brightly painted lips sat on customer's laps. Raucous piano melodies strained futilely against the clamor. A steady parade of couples stumbled drunkenly up the stairs to the second floor. Periodic curses echoed above the cacophony of the overall din. Spotting several circles of men far in the back corner playing cards, he moved in that direction, shouldering people out of the way.

The poker tables were full. Drooping over one of the tables was a smaller young man, his nose swaying from side-to-side over his pile of chips and the line of empty shot glasses in front of him. Though the man was dealt into every hand, he had not picked any cards; instead, the player to the man's left reached over before each hand and threw the man's ante into the pot.

Pushing his way to the young player's side, Jacob roughly shoved his shoulder. "You're done playing."

Turning slowly, keeping his elbows planted on the felt of the poker table not to fall out of his chair. The man slurred, "Shit, no I ain't."

"Shit, yes, you are."

Grabbing the man by his collar, he threw him to the floor, seating himself in the vacant chair. The table fell silent. Jacob was sorely tempted to stash some of the drunken man's chips. *I'm being watched too close. Never pull it off.* Sweeping the chips off the table with his forearm, they bounced and rolled around the drunken form on the wood planking, he snapped, "Never seen an Irishman before? Deal."

RETURNING TO THE ROOM SEVERAL HOURS LATER, HE stumbled from the door, throwing his money pouch on the bedside table where it landed with a heavy metallic thud. Pretending to be asleep Sarah held her breath, as she felt his eyes on the curve of her hips and buttocks, hoping he was half-drunk and too tired. Shaking off his boots and muttering, he crawled into bed with his clothes on.

"I've got everything fixed now, woman," he mumbled brokenly to the opposite wall.

He began snoring loudly. He reeked of whiskey and tobacco smoke. Facing away from him, Sarah opened her eyes, and relaxed now that she was certain to be spared his touch. Reaching carefully over, she took a few coins from the pouch. *He won't have any idea how much he had actually won.*

CHAPTER

42

March 16, 1855

STANDING WITH JOHANNES IN THE DUSTY SIDE STREET, Reuben was grateful for the comforting press of the pistol holster tied to his thigh. Everywhere around them, there were rough-looking characters. *This is certainly the fringe of the frontier.* Some men wore coonskin caps, scalp belts dangled from the waists of many. Each of them was carrying a Sharps, Enfield or Greene rifle. Some had pistols in their belts, usually ball and cap, and fringed knife scabbards hung low off of their waistbands. The end of the 4th Street alley overlooked the Mississippi River, one half mile downstream from scores of riverboats, their high black single or double stacks belching steam and smoke. Side paddle wheels glistened wetly in uneven cadence from the boats mooring or departing the levee, headed to or from the channel in the center of the wide expanse of river.

At the end of the alley were makeshift corrals, some with oxen, others with mules or horses, most of which looked well-tended. To the side of the corrals perched a large, low, building of aged wood. Gusting off the river, an eastward wind stirred dust devils. Swirling and dancing along the street, their whirling edges dissipated as they made contact with the buildings.

Making their way toward the sign that said *"Livery Stable,"* Reuben's eyes soaked in details and people, particularly a tall, buckskin-clad figure leaning against the side of a building, watching them over fingers that were rolling a smoke.

"This must be it." Johannes' voice diverted Reuben's attention from the lanky frontiersman. In the open stalls at the front of the building and just inside the door, five blacksmiths were industriously shaving horses' hooves and fitting shoes. Broad-shouldered Morgan and Quarter horses, bred to pull and haul, whinnied in the stalls. At the end of the stalls, there was a table of sorts, made from a door set atop some hay bales, empty wooden water barrels serving as seats. A short but very broad, muscular man with red hair, mustache and thick curly beard sat on one of the barrels. The weathered etchings on his face and his biting blue eyes below shaggy, red, eyebrows were animated. He was emphatically waving some papers in his left hand, pointing them repeatedly at a smaller, unshaven, sallow-faced man sitting on another barrel.

"I'm going to buy fifty of your sorry animals, and I won't pay more than five dollars a head."

He had a deep, thunderous voice. Though Reuben and Johannes were now standing by the makeshift table, the red-haired man didn't give them a glance. Staring pointedly at the other man, his whole body pushed forward. He punctuated the air with a stab of his finger at the recipient of his words. "And that's my final offer."

Each time the red-haired man gestured, the other man winced and lowered his pale, thin, pinched face, his look darting more than once to Johannes and Reuben, as if to seek help. The little man finally squeaked, "Okay, Mac. You can have the damn horses for five dollars a head but I expect an extra trunk-load of pelts when you come back."

Mac's shoulders relaxed. Reaching out a massive arm, he clapped the man on his shoulder, almost knocking him from the barrel.

"That's my boy, Seymour," he bellowed. "Have them here tomorrow afternoon. I aim to get this circus started daybreak three days from now."

Seymour started to walk away. "And Seymour..."

The little man turned. His hands were shaking and his face was white. "Nothing lame or sick or I will shoot 'em and you'll replace them for free. Or else I might shoot you instead."

Seymour nodded and scurried for the open end of the livery.

Turning his attention to Reuben and Johannes, he eyed them silently for a few moments. *We are being sized up.*

"What can I do for you lads?" His tone was uninterested. Johannes and Reuben stood relaxed. Wanting to make it clear the appraisal was mutual, Reuben waited to answer. "We're headed to Cherry Creek, western Kansas Territory," said Reuben.

"I know where Cherry Creek is," Mac snapped. "Do you have your own wagon or will you be needin' one?"

"We'll plan to purchase our own horses, a set each. We'd like to travel with the train for protection. We can help with the hunting and moving that herd you just bought if they are replacement teams. However, we do have some friends. They are ladies."

"Really? Ladies?" Mac shook his head, rolling his eyes, and looked up to the ceiling.

"They will require a wagon," Reuben said evenly.

"Is that so?" Mac rubbed his great, red beard with stubby fingers, studying Reuben closely. "How will they pay?"

"Cash, up front."

"Give me your hands," demanded Mac. He grabbed Johannes' hands first, twisting the palms upward. Releasing them with a mutter of disgust, he grasped Reuben's next. He held them for a while, looking into Reuben's eyes.

"You've worked on the land." It was more of a statement than a question. "Livestock?"

"Cattle," Reuben replied.

Mac sat back down. His eyes dropped to their revolvers. "Know how to shoot?"

"We do."

"Fine, then. There's some things men on horseback can help with. You'll pay for your own supplies and provisions. You'll give me work equal to my full fee, which is one hundred dollars. If you've lied to me and you're worthless, I will leave your sorry asses for the Injuns or the buzzards, whichever gets you first. Your lady friends owe the one hundred dollars but I'll throw in a wagon for them. Going to need an extra rig to haul pelts back from Cherry Creek, anyway. But the team is your problem. I won't charge you anything else except for feed for the horses."

The wagon master stood up.

"You've got yourself a deal," said Reuben firmly. They shook hands, Mac's weathered countenance breaking into a smile.

"I'll choose a good wagon for your ladies. I think a Prairie Schooner will be easier for them to handle than a Conestoga. Daybreak, two days from now. I won't wait."

Pausing when they emerged into the dusty sunlight of the alley. Johannes glanced back at the livery. "Now that was an ox of a fellow. I like him."

"Yes, I think he is someone to ride the river with."

"Ride the river with?" Johannes' tone was puzzled.

Reuben took off the new, wide-brimmed, western hat he had purchased at Booraems, running his hand through his hair. "Something the scout wrote to my father in one of his letters. I think it means he can be trusted."

March 16, 1855

COMEUPPANCE

RISING EARLY, JACOB TOYED WITH THE IDEA OF TAKING Sarah before he left but he was anxious to line up their passage west. He had extracted directions from one of the poker players to the livery stable where Mac the wagon master conducted business.

Reaching the dusty alley, he glanced at the barely legible 4th Street sign that flapped in the wind. *Glad they use numbers rather than words on these street markers.* He took a moment to reflect on the impressive sight of scores of steamboats upriver. *Bet there are some damn good games on them.*

He began the dusty walk down the narrow street toward the river. Men were lounging in the shade of buildings or sitting on crude log benches following his progress. Jacob felt uneasy. These men in the frontier outfits radiated a cold, suspicious energy toward him, as if they somehow sensed his sordid history. Trying to ignore them, he marched into the livery, wrinkling his nose distastefully at the smell of hay and manure. Ignoring the industrious work of the blacksmiths, he focused instead on a big, redheaded, bear of a man shouting orders at the other end of the barn. Walking over to him, Jacob held out his hand.

Turning cold blue eyes on him, he looked him over once, then again. Leaning to the side, he spit out a chew of tobacco. Some of the brown juice caught in his beard. He didn't take Jacob's hand.

"Are you Mac?" Jacob asked. "I am."

A silence ensued, Jacob restlessly shifting his weight from one foot to the other. One hand played with the gold pieces in his pocket.

"I hear you're heading up a wagon train going west."

"I am."

There was another silence.

"I have things to do here man, so if you have something to say, spit it out." Shifting his eyes from Jacob, he began to read some papers on the table.

Jacob clenched his jaw. *This asshole thinks he's God.* Gaging Mac's powerful shoulders, he decided to say nothing confrontational.

"Me and my fiancée are looking for passage west."

Mac looked up with a frigid stare. "You bring your own provisions and ammunition. It will be two hundred dollars."

Jacob had heard that Mac typically charged one hundred dollars. He tried to return the intense look from Mac but couldn't.

"Does that include a wagon?"

Mac's eyes flickered. "I'm all out of wagons."

Jacob leaned forward, feeling heat flow to his face. "You mean you're charging two hundred dollars, and that doesn't include a wagon?"

"Aye, and we're leavin' two days from now. At daybreak. If you're not there, we're not waitin'." Ignoring Jacob again, Mac looked back down at his paperwork, then he leaned to his side and spat another tobacco chew to the dirt floor. "One more thing. It's cash in advance."

"We'll be there," Jacob clenched the hand in his pocket. It shook slightly as he handed over the money. "Where can I get a wagon?"

Mac did not look up. "Talk to the tall man down at the corrals."

"How much should I pay?" pressed Jacob.

Raising his head, the red bearded wagon master's eyebrows were furrowed, and his eyes annoyed. "Whatever he charges."

Dropping his eyes to his papers, he gave a dismissive wave with one hand. Jacob spun, taking long quick strides toward the livery entrance. Mac shouted after him, "Make damn sure it's a good wagon. If you're broke down, you'll be on your own. Your scalps will be on a tipi pole and coyotes will feast on your livers."

Walking back down the street, he could feel the terse anger in the muscles of his neck and shoulders and the boil in his gut. A man whose vision was obscured by a large sack of flour over his shoulder didn't see him. Jacob shouldered him, sending the man staggering off the boardwalk.

I need a bar, any bar, a couple of shots of strong whiskey and time to think. He gritted his teeth. With his winnings, he had plenty of money but he was loathe to spend more, particularly with Mac.

It was late when he returned to the cramped hotel quarters. Though furious about having to spend eighty dollars on a wagon and a team, he thought he had bought a good stout rig and the horses seemed healthy to his untrained eye.

Bursting into the hotel room, he waved at Sarah. "Woman, come downstairs. I want you to see this fine wagon I bought just for you."

Sarah was staring out the window from her seat on the edge of the bed. She blinked but didn't move or turn.

"That was thoughtful, Jacob," she said.

"By the way, I've told everyone you're my fiancée."

Sarah smiled sweetly. "Thank you, Jacob, for thinking of my dignity."

Jacob stared down at her, feeling his brow crease suspiciously. "You feelin' okay?"

"I was a bit nauseous this morning but I am better now. Thank you, Jacob, for being concerned."

Jacob scratched his head, then shrugged. "Come on, we need to get ready. We need provisions and a pistol. I threw that antique of yours off the train. I spent some time in a mercantile. I think I will get me one of them five-inch, short-barreled .44 revolvers that that Frontier Army Company just came out with. I can keep it in my coat pocket. And we have to be down there at the crack of dawn in just two days. The wagon master is a mean son of a bitch."

"Then perhaps we should wait for another wagon train."

Whirling in the doorway, Jacob shook his head vehemently, "No. There are very few. We're going. The next set of wagons might not leave for weeks. I don't want anyone to beat us to the gold!"

March 17, 1855

PREPARATIONS

STOPPING AT THE HOTEL'S FRONT DESK, REUBEN WROTE out a quick note, then handed it to the bellhop along with two bits.

"Deliver this to Miss Rebecca Marx, please, Room 430."

The bellhop's eyes widened at the tip. Minutes later, Rebecca was walking toward him across the foyer, hips swaying, her form-fitting dress shimmering over the curves of her body. Her dark hair tumbled down her neck, ending in slightly curled wisps at her shoulders, contrasting provocatively with the bright red color of the fabric. The creamy swell of her breasts peeked from the frilly trim of the low neckline. Men's heads turned. Despite himself, Reuben drew in his breath but he remained hunched over the counter with his shoulder to her.

Reaching him, she smiled guardedly. "Shall we get a table and have some tea?" she offered.

"I have things to do."

Rebecca drew in her breath, a look of disappointment flitting momentarily across her features.

"I've arranged your passage. You'll be furnished a wagon. I will select a good team of four for you. Typical is two but better to be safe. You can pay me back half for the horses and we will split them when we reach Cherry Creek. Johannes and I will be on horseback. We will assist you as necessary. In return, we would expect to stow our supplies and duffels in your wagon."

"Inga will be delighted," Rebecca responded smoothly. "Thank you, Reuben. How much is this going to cost?"

"One hundred dollars and I would estimate your share of the horses at ten to twenty dollars." Reuben eyed her dress. "I would limit the finery you bring. There's not much room, and traveling light will be critical...."

She began to speak but Reuben held up his hand. "I'm not done. Do you have any idea what provisions are needed?"

Thrusting her chin forward, the brunette drew herself to full height. "I am sure Inga and I can figure out what is needed."

Reuben laughed. The slight flush he had noticed in her face when she walked up began creeping down to her collarbones.

"Well, if you decide you need assistance, let us know by this evening. Just over two days is not a great deal of time to get ready for a journey of this type."

"Reuben." Rebecca extended her hand, letting it rest lightly on the forearms he had crossed over his chest. "Do you wish us to not be on the same wagon train? Will we be an imposition?"

Reuben was dismayed at the look in Rebecca's eyes, her words and her tone. The giddy feeling of camaraderie the day before rushed back, along with self-annoyance. *Damn, get yourself under control.* Taking a deep breath, he ran his thumb gently over a solitary tear that had begun to form at the corner of her eye. Her eyes closed and she rested her cheek lightly on his hand.

"No, Rebecca. I don't mind. We can all help one another. This is not a trip to make without friends or for the fainthearted."

"I know, Reuben. I am not sure there is anyone else I could say this to. I am a bit frightened. This is all new to me. I am very much out of my element. Inga and I are very happy you and Johannes will be traveling west with us."

Reuben cleared his throat. A strange, pleasant tightness troubled his chest. "It's new to us too. We will be fine, though it will not be easy. We can all contribute, as long as you aren't so stubborn."

Rebecca's nostrils flared. "Oh, you must be teasing me. I think that might be the pot calling the kettle black."

"You need to begin preparations," said Reuben gently. "Let's get Inga and Johannes organized."

"I will go talk with Inga right now." Rebecca touched his arm again, her eyes studying his. "Thank you again." She turned, heading for the stairway.

Reuben walked briskly toward the entrance. *Now where is that damn Johannes?* He felt a bounce to his step and he realized that the tune he heard someone humming was his own.

"JOHANNES, HERE ARE LISTS I MADE UP ON THE TRAIN. Buy one and a half times the amount of each item. I am under no illusions. It is doubtful that Rebecca and Inga will have the slightest notion of how to outfit themselves. Then, why don't you bring the wagon Mac has provided for them back up to the hotel and help Inga pack it properly. The two of you can coordinate the supplies together. We will keep our goods in their wagon."

Johannes rubbed his hands together. "It would be my pleasure, Reuben."

Reuben laughed. "No, Johannes, we need less pleasure, and much more concentration. Three hundred miles from St. Louis will be an inopportune moment to realize we did not bring an important item. Make sure we each have at least two hundred and fifty rounds of ammunition for your Colt, and see if you can find the same for the rifles. Buy an extra two hundred rounds for my pistol, if you would—I need real firing practice."

Johannes stood at mock attention and saluted. Despite his attempt to be comical, Reuben noticed the salute was exact. *Johannes did have military experience.*

REUBEN RETURNED TO THE DUSTY STREET LEADING TO the livery stable that afternoon. *I need one trail-savvy hand for the journey west and the ranch. Even better if he knows Indians and the mountains. The rest of the men I can gather in Cherry Creek or one of the trading posts.*

Stationing himself against the weathered brick of a smoke shop on the opposite corner from 4th Street, legs crossed, arms folded across his chest, and the wide brim of his hat pulled low, he watched carefully. A medium height, thin man perched on the second rail of a corral fence at the end of the alley, talking to the horses. A number of horses had come up to the man and were crowding close to him, gently pushing against each other for his attention.

He recognized the tall frontiersman who had caught his attention when they first met. He was leaning against a corner of a building like the day before, and again appeared to be rolling a cigarette. Two knives hung from the tall, lanky man's belt, and another was slung across in back in a leather scabbard. A brace of pistols, one cap and ball and one newer revolver rested crosswise behind his buckle, and a well-used .54 caliber Sharps rifle nestled in the crook of his arm. The man had an air of quiet confidence. Keeping his eye on the buckskin-clad figure, Reuben nodded to several men who walked by but spoke to no one.

He moved down the boardwalk toward the sinewy man building the smoke. The man lit the cigarette, watching him approach. Reuben stopped a few feet away, and the two men sized each other up in silence. The frontiersman had not changed his stance. He continued to lean against the side of the building, taking another draw on the cigarette with an air of ambivalence. Except to drop briefly to Reuben's Colt, his stare never left Reuben's face. Weathered crow's feet crinkled from the corners of the man's bright green eyes. Two heavy purple scars ran across the man's cheek from under his eye to above the jawline. Reuben's gaze lingered on his cheek.

"Bear," the man said, matter of fact.

Reuben studied the scars more openly. "What happened?" The man's eyes narrowed at Reuben's accent.

"I ate him."

Reuben laughed. "My name is Reuben."

"Reuben what?"

"Frank."

"Prussian?"

"Yes," replied Reuben feeling mild surprise. "How did you know?"

"The way you speak American."

There was another long silence as the two men regarded one another.

Blowing smoke out of his nostrils, the frontier man reached into his buckskin jacket, pulling out a tobacco pouch. "I am Zeb. Smoke?"

"No, thank you. Who is that thin fellow down at the corral having a conversation with the horses?"

Without turning, Zeb responded, "Thomas, Mac's wrangler."

"Are you going west?"

"Yep. Going back west. Plan to trap some more beaver. You?"

"Yes, we are."

"We?"

"My friend Johannes and I. We'll be riding on horseback. I need to buy eight good horses, in fact. We have two acquaintances heading out with the train too but by wagon."

Bending over slowly, his shoulder still resting against the wall, Zeb spat. He wiped his mouth with the back of his hand. "Johannes? Must be the tall blond fella you was with the other day. Mac said something about two single women going. That be the others?"

"Yes."

Zeb straightened up slightly but his features remained impassive. "Greenhorns can get themselves into trouble out there," he gestured to the west, "and women can be bad luck. Thomas will steer you to some good horse-flesh." He smiled, chuckling low in his throat. "That bastard must have been a horse last go round."

"Perhaps you can help us not be greenhorns. The ladies will not be a problem. They are capable and smart. And they can cook." Reuben's mind flashed on an image of Rebecca in the red dress. "Or they can learn to. Do you know the mountains southwest of Cherry Creek?"

"I trap out that way, though you most likely ain't goin' that far. My nineteenth or twentieth season, I've lost count. What's a fella like you goin' out there for?"

"You look like a man who has common sense, a quick wit and would honor your word. I sense a toughness, too. I'm headed out to establish a cattle ranch and I need a good man who knows the country and the ways of the land," Reuben paused, "and who can fight, if need be."

ZEB WAS SURPRISED. *SOUNDS LIKE AN OFFER OF SOME type.* He remembered the young man from the previous day. It was his walk, faster than most, the air of quiet surety and the way he seemed to take in everything as he had moved down the street toward the livery with his tall blond companion. With the question pending, he took his time to study the younger man's medium but solid build, and the lack of dust and sweat on the broad-brimmed hat. He let his eyes linger on the holster that cradled the six-gun. It was slung low and slightly behind Reuben's right hip, snugged comfortably to his leg with a rawhide thong. The leather was new but well oiled, beautifully stamped, and the lighter, rough scrape marks on the front of the holster lip testified to repeated draws of the weapon. *Been practicing.*

"Them one of them Slim Jims I have heard tell of? Pretty fancy."

"Yes."

Raising his eyes back to Reuben's, he stood upright from the building wall, spreading his feet and facing Reuben head on. "You askin' me to work for you?"

"Yes."

Shaking his head, he began rolling another smoke, somehow annoyed at the younger man's offer. But, he was curious. "I ain't worked for no one, except back when I was fifteen. Where exactly are ya headed? Do ya know?"

The young Prussian hesitated, then spoke slowly and deliberately. "I have some maps but we are eventually bound for near where the Kansas and Utah Territories meet toward the southwest flank of the mountains. A place called Las Montanas Rojas. You may have heard of it as Red Mountains."

Zeb forced himself to keep his focus on the cigarette half-built in his fingers but a good portion of the tobacco tumbled from the rolling paper when his hand jerked slightly at Reuben's words. Cursing, he slowly sprinkled more leaves on the paper. "Yep, I heard of the place. What's the pay? And I do plan to trap, no matter what, and I don't take orders from no one."

"Supplies, board when we get some buildings up, and five dollars a month. And trapping on the side would be fine."

"And I don't have to deal with any damn cows?"

The young man shook his head. "No, others will handle the livestock."

"And I don't have to stay in any buildings ya might put up?"

Reuben smiled, obviously amused. "You can live under a tree if that's your preference."

Taking a drag on the cigarette, Zeb's mind worked quickly. Contemplating the half-smoked butt for a long moment, he flicked it with his thumb and middle finger out into the dirt of the alley. Watching the smoke curl blue-gray into the air, he ran his fingers down his long mustache, and made a decision.

"You got a deal for now, Mister Frank. We'll see how it goes longer term." Zeb held out his hand, which Reuben shook firmly.

"I'll go talk to Thomas on those horses. See you after we ferry across the river the morning we leave. You can begin our instructions then."

Zeb nodded. His thumb and forefinger smoothed the end of his mustache as he watched Reuben stride down 4th Street, sunlight glinting on the pearl colored handle of the Colt as it swung slightly in its holster on the young man's hip.

On the Eve of March 18, 1855

WESTWARD

ONE THOUSAND MILES SOUTHEAST OF THE THIN WISPS of smoke curling from the tipis of a small village of Oglala Sioux along the south fork of the Powder River, and three hundred miles northeast of slave hovels on a sprawling plantation in the Oklahoma panhandle, a number of curious onlookers watched the prairie schooner being loaded in front of the hotel on 4th and Walnut Street.

Johannes had hired some Chinese immigrants to transport Rebecca and Inga's luggage and the supplies through the hotel and to the wagon. They were busily sorting supplies and baggage on the curb next to the wagon. Reuben came out for a last check before the items were loaded into the prairie schooner. All six of Rebecca's ornate trunks were in the street. His tall blond friend shot him an exasperated glance, rolling his eyes.

Reuben shook his head. *That woman is incorrigible.* He charged up to Rebecca's room.

Answering his loud knock, the smile she had been wearing as she swung open the door quickly disappeared. "Your eyes shade to gray when you're in a dark mood," she said.

"To hell with my eyes. We discussed the need to travel light, Rebecca. Six trunks are not needed out West. If you spend an extended time, you can have them shipped later."

"Every day here is an extended time. I need my belongings with me. That's final." She walked away.

"The extra weight is wear and tear on the wagons and the horses," gritted Reuben, thrusting his face forward, and clenching his hands at his side.

Turning toward him from halfway across the room, her nose elevated, she snapped, "I am quite sure there is some type of society out there, and I will require decent attire. I don't take orders from you, Mister Frank."

Reuben felt the veins in his neck pop and a hot flare in his cheeks. He slapped the door so hard the doorframe quivered. "This topic is not open to discussion. Go down there and choose what you need that will fit in two trunks or by God, I will unload all six of them on the street!"

Walking briskly back to him, Rebecca thrust her face just a foot from his, her hands on her hips.

"No one talks to me that way! You will do no such thing."

Reuben edged closer, pointing at her.

"You have thirty minutes to shift those trunks. I want to get the wagon loaded in daylight. Get some porters and Inga to help you. The hotel will store the other four until you return. This trip is not some countryside picnic in the rolling hills of Devonshire. I will not let your selfish lack of common sense jeopardize us or others on the wagon train."

Her arms rigid and her breasts heaving, Rebecca stomped her foot. "Who put you in charge?" she stuttered through clenched teeth.

"I did." said Reuben simply. "Thirty minutes." Wheeling from her, he opened the door, slamming it behind him, and walked down the hall.

Wrenching the still vibrating door open, Rebecca jumped into the corridor. "How dare you!" she shouted. Guests in the hallway turned, surprised and curious at the commotion. Reuben gave them a cold glance. He heard her door again slam behind him.

Returning to the growing mounds of supplies and bags on the curb, he found Johannes shouting orders in his Scandinavian tongue and gesturing wildly, surrounded by the coolies who were equally animated and jabbering in some oriental dialect. Rebecca's voice floated down from several floors above his head, "Reuben Frank, you are a rude, impossible man."

Reuben looked up. Rebecca was leaning out her window. As soon as she knew she had caught his attention, she quickly withdrew from the window, shutting it with a crack that could be clearly heard on the street.

"You better find Inga and get those trunks arranged or I will throw them in the street!" Reuben yelled up at the empty glass.

March 18, 1855

Dawn on the day of departure was a brilliant palette of indigo in retreat to the west and blossoming fire orange to the east. The Mississippi had a slight chop from the morning wind, the surface ripples reflecting the burgeoning day in a shimmer of color. The east side of the river was a scene of frenetic activity. The forty-one wagons in the train contained several childless couples and a number of families. There were two steam tugs, each dragging its own barge across the river. The barges were just big enough to accommodate several wagons and teams. On the west side, the wagons that had already been transported were grouping in single file, pointed west toward the Rockies a thousand miles distant. Mac's shouted directions boomed over the murmur of the river and the chatter of the pioneers. The whinny of horses, bleat of oxen and bray of mules echoed across the water.

By later morning, all the wagons were across the river and the wagon master had the train fully organized. He put Inga and Rebecca's wagon third in line, where there was less dust. Johannes was driving the wagon to teach the women how to use the lines and brake. His horses and the two extra mounts Reuben had purchased were tied to the back.

Twisting in his saddle Reuben searched for Zeb. Far behind the last wagon and a quarter mile to the south, he picked out a figure on a painted horse leading three mules. *As I would have expected*, he mused. He turned his attention back to the front of the train.

Mac was up toward the first wagon astride a stocky, red sorrel that matched him well, cursing as the excited horse shook its head and pranced sideways.

"Reuben, check those last wagons and make sure they're ready. Let's get this damned show moving. We're already late!" Mac bellowed.

Reuben's horse was agitated, too. "Easy, Lahn." Reaching down, he patted the blond neck of the big Palomino. The gelding snorted, shaking his head, and stomped a dance in a quarter circle. Wheeling the muscular horse, he cantered toward the rear of the line of wagons. He was not yet used to the deep trough of the western saddle, a far cry from the European tack he was familiar with but he liked the feel of the heavy leather footing underneath his hips. As he passed the rigs at the center of the train, he was shocked to see the attractive redheaded girl from the *Edinburgh* sitting on the driver's bench of one of the wagons. *And that bully from the ship, Jacob, is with her.*

Sarah had a heavy shawl over her shoulders, appearing cold and unhappy in the cool of the spring morning. Jacob seemed to be busy with the brake. Reuben caught Sarah's eye. She seemed as startled as he but there was something other than simple surprise in her look. Smiling widely, she waved. Reuben pulled down on the brim of his hat in return.

The coincidence of Jacob and Sarah on the same wagon train, and the apparent fact that they were a couple, was troubling. *Not her type at all. Very off.* Reining up in a swirl of dust at the last wagon, a Conestoga, he shouted, "Ready?"

The thickset man with a ruddy face who drove grinned widely. "Let's go!" He had just unfurled a several-foot-wide American flag from a pole he had lashed to the side of the wagon at the front rim of the curved canvas top. The colors looked old to Reuben. They snapped in the wind, and he felt his eyes widen. "That is a version of the United States flag I have never seen. Thirteen stars in a circle on the blue? What does that mean?"

The driver beamed proudly. "This here...," he gestured, "was the flag my great-grandpappy carried in the revolution. That's just eighty-odd years ago, ya know. Family has been in Virginny since the sixteen hundreds. It was the first flag of this country—called the Betsy Ross circular. There ain't many of 'em around anymore. We usually just fly her on July Fourth but we figgered what we're doin' is about as big as then, so—'cept for bad weather—this cloth is goin' to be full-view to God and country all the way to the Rockies. I aim to fly it on a big tall post before I set the first foundation stone for our homestead."

Next to him, his buxom wife smiled and nodded. Two round-faced little girls peeked from between their mother and father.

Reuben was not fully sure of the man's meaning but decided he could find out more later. Easing Lahn alongside the wagon, he fumbled in his shirt pocket. "Do you like jerky?" he asked, leaning from the horse, and holding out the treat to the children. They hid their faces, giggling. "Come on, take it," Reuben coaxed. Taking a bite himself, he smacked his lips. "Umm, good." Laughing shyly the older girl extended a pudgy hand and took the dried meat. "Fine children," Reuben said.

Their mother smiled. "That's Becky and Eleanor. I am Margaret and this is my husband, Harris." Becky and Eleanor were chewing contentedly on the jerky. "Perhaps you would join us for dinner one night, Mister...?"

"Frank. Reuben Frank. And yes, that would be my pleasure. You can tell me more of the flag story."

Turning in his saddle, Reuben raised himself high in the stirrups, waving his hat in the air. Far to the front of the line of wagons, he heard Mac roar, "Move 'em out!"

TO BE CONTINUED...

Threads West
An American Saga

THE SAGA CONTINUES...

Book Two of the *Threads West,* An American Saga Series

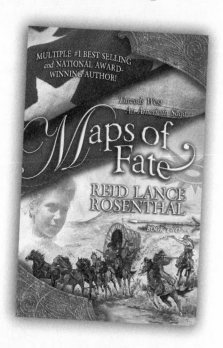

PREVIEW
Maps of Fate—Book Two

THE *THREADS WEST, AN AMERICAN SAGA* SERIES continues with the second novel, *Maps of Fate*.

Maps of Fate builds the suspense of this epic series as the dark history and elusive promise of the *Threads West* parchment maps play out through the personal filter of each of the characters you have come to know and care for in Book One. They are propelled from one adventure, danger, romantic twist and encounter to the next, each challenging experience hurtling them toward their destinies. Lethal surprises overtake some of the *Threads West* personalities when they are forced to defend their lives, their loved ones and their honor. New characters color the tapestry of the tale with their dark hearts, lost souls, cruelty and hopeful innocence. Others, newly free and in search of family, a sense of place and their slice of America, catapult into the story.

They begin to build a nation whose essence is in transition, their lives shaken by events and convergences with other souls they could not foresee. An elderly black couple sets their life sails for winds of freedom. An Oglala Sioux family struggles to cope with the foreshadow of lands and culture forever changed. Mormons stream west in the Great Exodus escaping persecution, and searching for Zion. A black-hearted renegade is unknowingly catapulted by his tortured past into possible redemption.

Torrid passions and bittersweet ironies unfold in harrowing trials and joyous triumphs that give rise to the next generation of compelling characters in the series.

You will recognize the characters that live in these pages. They are your neighbors, your family, your co-workers. They are you and they are us; the threads of many lives—both men and women—from different locations, ancestry, social and financial backgrounds, faiths and beliefs. They are personalities forged on the anvil of the land, woven together by fate and history, and bound by the commonality of the American spirit into the tapestry that is our nation.

A surprising convergence of events in *Maps of Fate* sets in motion the thrilling, yet heartrending conclusion of Book Two, setting the stage for the continuation of the saga in Book Three, *Uncompahgre—where water turns rock red*. As the tale continues, readers will grow ever more spellbound by the passionate meld of the American spirit with the souls of the generations, the building of the heart of the nation, and the powerful energy and beauty of the western landscape.

To be continued...

Excerpt from Book Two, *Maps of Fate*

URPRISED

THERE WERE MORE AND MORE INDIANS NOW INSIDE their circle, splitting the pioneer firepower from the outside of their shield of wagons. The two wagons in the river were burning. Johannes and another man were dragging Thelma and the doctor through the creek. The corpses of two pioneers and two warriors drifted downstream bobbing in the current like lifeless logs. Sarah stood stupefied; her knees trembled. The sweat of heat and fear ran down her temples in grimy streaks. Smoke from the burning canvases, dust, and gray puffs of gunpowder rendered everything surreal, softening the apparitional shapes of the wounded and bodies strewn in grotesque positions. The guttural whoops of the attackers, screams of petrified and dying animals, and moans of pain echoed among the wagons and the sharp sounds of gunshots.

Sarah held the Sharps in one hand, breech open, ready for loading, frozen in shocked disbelief. The scene was incomprehensible. Through the haze of the battle raging around the wagons, she saw the shadowy figures of Mac, Reuben and Johannes sprinting to a breach where the Indians had pulled over one of the smaller rigs. In that gap, Zeb, a knife in each hand, and two other men from the train, struggled in mortal combat with an increasing number of lance and tomahawk wielding invaders. Reuben and Mac each carried two rifles. Johannes had his carbine in one grip, pistol in the other. His saber scabbard slapped against his leg as he ran.

Sarah saw him look over his shoulder and could barely make out his shout. "Behind us!"

Johannes wheeled, ghostlike in the brownish gray cloud that enveloped the conflict, and stood calmly erect, his pistol extended.

He fired once from the Colt. The rider of the horse bearing down on the three jerked violently from the impact of the .44 caliber slug, then somersaulted backward over the rear of his steed. He lay unmoving, barely discernible in the groundswell of dust.

Sarah's eyes quickly searched the nearby wagons. Jacob had disappeared. Her mouth fell open when she saw Harris wrestling with a much smaller Indian who was obviously after that heirloom American flag, hanging ripped, tattered and limp in the semi-opaque heat. Disbelief knifed through her numb detachment. *What type of people are these who risk their life for a piece of old cloth?* Below Harris, Margaret wielded her musket like a club, keeping another attacker at bay. Two men ran through the din to assist her.

"Sarah, load the damn rifle!" came Rebecca's frantic shout. Sarah jolted back to reality. Trying to control the trembling that had overtaken her body, she jammed the cartridge into the Sharps with shaking fingers, then handed the long gun to Rebecca who, in turn, gave her the Enfield she had just discharged. Rebecca turned, rested the receiver and forestock over the lip of the wagon and swung the muzzle as she found another target.

Without looking back, Rebecca commanded in a loud voice, "Inga, reload that Enfield. Quickly!"

Pressed against the side of the wagon box, Sarah fumbled in the saddlebag Rebecca had draped over the wagon wheel for the next round. She heard a whisper in the air, like the sound a small bird makes on a calm, peaceful evening in the stillness just before dark. Then a sudden, hollow, resounding *thud*. A woman's voice cried out in pain.

To be continued...

Excerpt from Book Two, *Maps of Fate*

REVELATION

REBECCA SMILED TO HERSELF AS SHE WALKED AWAY from the wagon and entered the scattered trees that separated the circular encampment from the river. She reached the edge of the river, drew up the hem of her skirt and shook her head at the tiny explosion of trail dust from the fabric. Leaning her Sharps against a cluster of boulders, she checked carefully for nettles before easing herself down in a small grassy nook between the rocks. The circle of wagons was not more than two hundred feet away but she felt almost as if they did not exist. She was alone in a vast empty space on the edges of the Big Nemahaw, five thousand miles from the expansive city she called home, or *had* called home. She furrowed her brow at the thought.

Above the gentle murmur of the river current where it caressed the shore, she heard the faint crackle of the campfires, occasional laughter, and the clang of stirring ladles chiming dully against interiors of the great iron pots suspended from tripods as supper was prepared.

Every so often, muted male voices cursed softly in unison with snorts of horses and the low brays of oxen as men carried water buckets to the stock. Downriver, the diffused steel-gray curtain of dusk stole toward her like a phantom from the east, gradually swallowing the golden waves of the prairie grasses visible in breaks in the mixed deciduous cover. To the west, the last rim of retreating sun blazed in an orange glory, its rings of shallow red, then fading pink and pale yellow, bidding farewell to the day in concentric arcs of flaming color.

The vastness, the emptiness, the sheer space enveloped her. The promise of tomorrow, etched in the direction of the dying sun, stirred a feeling of excitement. She sighed almost reluctantly at the remnants of disappearing blue as the evening sky darkened. She tried to remember home—her bedroom, and the cobblestone street lined by similar stately row houses outside the great front door of their elegant London abode. *I wonder how you are, Mother?* She closed her eyes and lifted her face to the cooling breeze to focus on the memory of crowds, city noise and fine linens but the images remained distant, as if from a long ago dream.

To be continued...

Excerpt from Book Two, *Maps of Fate*

$\mathscr{P}$ROPHECY

SHE FELT THE FIRE IN THE SMOOTH CARESS OF HIS FIN-
gertips as they traced across her breast, lingered on her
erect and pulsing nipple, then continued down her hips
and came to rest lightly, longingly, on the concave valley
of smooth belly between her hips. The smell of him, and
of them, mingled with the fragrance of sunbaked sage.

Her heart pounded, a strange tingling heat permeated
her loins and she could feel the blush in her face. This
was a feeling she'd never known, could never imagine,
could barely absorb on so many levels. She swept a soft
palm over the cords of muscle in his arm. She was consumed by a desperate wanting, a deep primal need that
overrode her butterfly fear of the unknown. She gasped,
her hips writhing involuntarily as he lowered himself
gently onto her. A momentary stab of pain was followed
by an overwhelming wash of pleasure, which enveloped
her being as he slowly, carefully, began to sink into her.

She groaned, a muffled cry equally grounded in passion, trepidation and longing. He stopped, tenderly

brushed a calloused thumb slowly across her forehead and down her cheek and looked deep into her eyes, "Am I hurting you?"

She felt the tears welling in the corners of her eyes. She bit her lip and shook her head, her full answer to the question an ever-tightening wrap of her arms around his shoulders, the increasing instinctive bend of her knees, and the firm plant of her heels against the muscular flesh of his buttocks, drawing him in. *"Please... please,"* she moaned.

To be continued...

Excerpt from Book Two, *Maps of Fate*

RENEGADE

BLACK FEATHER WAITED UNTIL CROW AND THE GIRL were one hundred yards away on the other side of the wagon. He climbed on the wagon seat, reached into the bed and dragged the front half of the mother's body from behind the canvas. He checked quickly to make sure the canvas top blocked the girl's view. His blade flashed in the sunlight and moved several times in a saw-like motion, its sharp edge making a swishing sound like a rough finger drawn back and forth across wet parchment. Black Feather rose, scalp in one bloody hand and the silver-red knife dripping in the other.

Hoisting the prize in the air, his bronzed arms lifted high, he tipped back his explosion of long, dirty, brown hair, shook the scalp and the knife at the blue sky that seethed with morbid pink-hued memory and screamed in triumph; his muscular torso etched against the morning gray, his silhouette framed to the south by Longs Peak and to the west by the Rawah Range. Around him, the unkempt members of his renegade band had gathered. They, too, raised their rifles and bows to the sky, joining his bloodcurdling howl.

He jumped from the wagon directly into the saddle on the stallion. "Men, strip everything of value. Don't forget the food, and do not fight over the scalps. We won't torch. Smoke would be dangerous." The band scattered with whoops and shouts except for Pedro, his lieutenant, who rode up beside him, awaiting orders.

He turned in his saddle and spoke sharply to him in Spanish. "Pedro, after the men have stripped the wagons, get the girl and bring her to me. Bind her wrists. Wet the rawhide first. I want it tight but not so that it marks her. She is mine."

Pedro puffed out his chest. "But we always share..."

Black Feather's fist, clenched around the hilt of his knife, struck out, delivering a meaty backhanded blow to Pedro's face. The paunchy man's voice died in a gurgle as he fell from his horse. Black Feather glowered down from the stallion as the fat man rolled back and forth on the ground, clutching his bloody nose and whimpering in pain. Black Feather watched with impassive detachment.

"One more word Pedro, and your scalp will join those of the white eyes on my belt. If I tire of her, perhaps I will give you a taste or perhaps I will kill her."

To be continued...

Excerpt from Book Two, *Maps of Fate*

$\mathscr{S}$TRENGTH
OF CONVICTION

ISRAEL MADE A FIST AND SLAMMED IT ON THE TABLE
but with no real force, "And, that new law I told you
'bout just now—it made Kansas a territory, and its
free—no slavery—and it ain't much more than two or
three days' walk."

He rose from the table, bent down on one knee in
front of her, reached out his calloused, once powerful
hands and wrapped them around one of hers. "Look at
me, Lucy. Have I ever told you wrong?" Lucy's eyes held
his. She shook her head slowly.

"That's right. No, I ain't. And I'm telling you, I don't
read so good but I've done read and overheard enough
to know slavery ain't gonna last forever. It might be over
sooner than you think. The trick is, we might be too old,
and if all the darkies get free all at the same time, it's
gonna be rough. Most folks like us don't think like I am
talking. The massuhs don't want us to have these
thoughts. That's why they say we aren't allowed to read.

I'm telling you woman, we need to get out ahead of what's going to happen. We don't want to be where there's gonna be armies or worse yet, a bunch of godless bad men pretending to be armies like them Quantrill and Brown fellas you heard them talking about. They is in the paper, too."

Lucy looked at him intently. She blinked rapidly and another tear trickled down the roundness of her opposite cheek. "Even if what you say is true, Israel, there's nothing we can do. This is all much bigger than us. It will all just be like before. Everything we do, everything we are, everything we have, our lives, will always be decided by others."

Israel reached up both hands, pressed them gently against either side of her face and held her head steady just inches from his own. "You're wrong, Lucy. We got four things way bigger than the white man's armies or the massuh's rules. You got you; I got me. We got each other. And we got the Lord. Ain't nothin' bigger. No one can take our spirit from us." He paused and looked earnestly into her eyes. "If we don't do something with these gifts the Lord done give us, then we got no one to blame but us. Let me read you something."

Israel stood carefully, pushing down both hands on his raised knee to lift his other leg off the floor. He went to the door, opened it a crack and looked out. He made his way to the window and carefully surveyed the flat, wavy, undulations of the countryside, and the main house several hundred yards distant. He moved over to the bed, which was little more than a raised wooden platform topped by a thin mattress with strands of straw poking out from a threadbare cotton cover, overlain by several tattered, dark wool blankets.

He reached under the mattress and drew out a folded piece of old, ragged, brownish-yellow newspaper. "You know what this is?" He shook the paper, which crinkled in the stillness of the shack. "This is a printing of the Declaration of Independence. You know, July 4, when they have their picnic and such. This here paper is what happened when some white men decided they wasn't going to be slaves of other white folks in the seventeen hundreds. And this applies to all citizens of the United States of America and that's what we are part of."

Lucy shook her head again, "But that's the point, Israel. We ain't citizens."

"By God, we are. This paper says so and there's a bunch of folks that agree with it. I've been reading about—hold on a minute—let me find it." Israel carefully unfolded the paper, its brittle, compressed pieces reluctant to separate. He fumbled his spectacles onto his nose with one hand and held them there, "All men are created equal and endowed by their Creator with certain inalienable rights..." he bent his head closer to the print "...life, liberty, and the pursuit of happiness."

Israel slowly took off the spectacles, thoughtfully refolded the paper and slipped it carefully far back under the mattress. He turned to face his wife again. "Lucy, 'all men' means us! I think it's high time that Lucy and Israel grabbed their share of that 'equal' and that 'liberty'."

To be continued...

Excerpt from Book Two, *Maps of Fate*

$\mathcal{S}$PIRIT WHISPERS

TURTLE SHIELD AND POINTED LANCE HAD REACHED them now, each of them with a hand on either arm of Brave Pony, who sagged weakly over the neck of his horse. Eagle Talon walked to them. "Lower him down to me."

He gathered up Brave Pony in his arms and carried him over to the taller grass at the base of the cottonwood, laying him down gently, then examining the wound closely. The injured brave's eyes fluttered open. "Perhaps it is my time to meet Wakan Tanka."

Eagle Talon was concerned. There was puss forming around the uneven edges of both the entry and exit of the bullet wound that had pierced his friend's side. He was sure the shell had not touched anything vital but infection could kill just as easily.

He grabbed Brave Pony's shoulder and squeezed it hard. His friend's eyes opened again, "Are you trying to break my shoulder, too?"

Eagle Talon laughed with a humor he didn't feel. "You see, you feel pain. This is not your day to die. You will have to wait to see Spirit. You're stuck with the four of us for many winters."

Turtle Shield and Pointed Lance came running up, their hands full of young plantain leaves. They looked with concern at Brave Pony, then at Eagle Talon, with the question in their eyes.

A minute later, they heard a low shout from Three Knives. "Water. Plenty of it!"

"He will live," he answered their voiceless query. "Three Knives, get the water over here. I will prepare the poultice." Using a rounded rock, he pounded and mashed the broadleaf plantain to shredded fibers. Three Knives joined them from the willows, carrying two small buffalo bladders. The tough membrane was damp but watertight. "Three Knives, give him some water."

Eagle Talon stripped off his shirt and made a shallow leather bowl within a circle of rocks he assembled. He looked up at his friends, "Walks with Moon will have my hide for this. She made the shirt for me just this winter."

The three warriors laughed, "I'm sure you will find a way to make her smile, Eagle Talon. It is well known in the village that if we can't find you, you are under the robes with Walks with Moon."

Eagle Talon chuckled and shook his head. "Winters are cold and long. One must stay warm somehow." They all laughed again, even Brave Pony, although his laughter was mixed with a hacking cough.

Eagle Talon carefully stirred the plantain, adding just a bit of water at a time. When it was a fine, mushy, fiber paste, he had Three Knives and Turtle Shield roll Brave Pony to his side.

"Three Knives, bring me some of the gunpowder for your musket." Three Knives looked at him, initially not understanding. Then his eyes lit up. "A good idea, Eagle Talon." He ran to his mustang and grabbed his powder horn.

"This will hurt my friend." Brave Pony nodded his head, gritting his teeth. He sprinkled gunpowder into both bloody red holes, then worked the tip of a finger in from each side, Three Knives adding powder as Eagle Talon packed the wounds. Brave Pony groaned through clenched lips.

"Bring a flint."

"Here." Pointed Lance reached into a small, beaded leather pouch that hung from his neck and handed the flint to Eagle Talon. Holding the flint close to the wounds, Eagle Talon struck the flint once, then again. A spark caught and an explosion of fire seemed to leap from both bloody apertures, diminishing to gray smoke and the acrid smell of exploded gunpowder and burnt flesh. Brave Pony stiffened and bit into the meaty part below his thumb until it nearly bled.

"Now I will put the poultice on, and you'll feel much better." Eagle Talon applied the poultice lavishly, pushing into both sides of the wound. He sat back on his heels and sighed. Shaking his head, he cut a sleeve from the shoulder of his shirt, then cut it again, longitudinally. Turtle Shield and Three Knives held Brave Pony's shoulder up so Eagle Talon could bind the two strips tightly around his friend's midsection, over the poultice.

Brave Pony stifled a groan as they sat him down. "I thought you said I would feel better." They all laughed, and Brave Pony smiled. "I do feel better. Spirit will have to wait."

UNABLE TO MAKE FAST TIME, THE SUN WAS LOW IN THE sky when they topped a golden ridge. The rolling country undulated in waves of spring grass, as does a pond in the wind.

"There they are!" exclaimed Three Knives.

Eagle Talon nodded and took in the scene, searching for Walks with Moon's graceful figure. Sixteen tatanka carcasses lay scattered across a wide valley, the nearest almost five or six arrow-flights from the furthest. Some were already just partial bones and remnants of flesh. Teams of women and older children worked on others, fleshing the great bloody hides, as others removed chunks and strips from the mountains of meat, cutting it carefully for storage, salting and smoking. Others sloshed around in great piles of entrails, removed from the carcasses soon after death so that the meat would not spoil. The saving of hide, fat and bone would come later. Camp dogs slunk around the edges, snatching whatever scraps they could.

Silhouetted on the higher hills all around the valley, braves stood guard over this ancient ritual—the difference between life and death for The People. Three

Cougars pounded up the incline toward them, smiling. "We've done well. This was the second herd. We took fourteen in the first one and sixteen from this one. It was a great gathering of the brothers—probably thirty arrow-flights wide. He pointed out the mile-wide swath of trampled grass that receded up and down the hills, disappearing northwest into the twilight. His eyes fell to the scalps and his face grew somber. "That is the good news but there is other news."

Three Knives cast a nervous glance at Eagle Talon. "What?"

"I was instructed to tell you that the council wants to meet with you as soon as you arrive. You're not to go to your lodges first." He looked down at the ground, hesitating, and then up at them again. He leaned forward and in a voice barely more than a whisper, "It was Flying Arrow himself who gave the instruction."

The five braves looked at one another. Eagle Talon swallowed. We shall get Brave Pony to his lodge. He is too weak to attend the council meeting. Tell Flying Arrow we will be there immediately after."

Three Cougars nodded, wheeled his horse, and with a shout, headed down the ridgelines toward—Eagle Talon supposed—where they had set up camp for the night, away from the valley of their dead brothers and the predators that would surely visit in the dark.

To be continued...

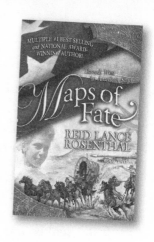

One saga, five generations of unforgettable
characters and—through their eyes—
one hundred seventy years of America brimful
of history, adventure, sensuality and intrigue.

You will recognize the characters
who live in these pages.
They are you. They are us.
This is not only their story. It is *our* story.
It is *Threads West, An American Saga.*

The gripping, sizzling reads of the *Threads West, An American Saga* series unfold over the course of five eras:

1854 to 1875—The Maps of Fate Era
Book One, *Threads West, An American Saga*
Book Two, *Maps of Fate*
Book Three, *Uncompaghre—Where water turns rocks red*
Book Four, *Moccasin Tracks*
Book Five, *Footsteps*
Book Six, *Blood at Glorieta Pass*
Book Seven, *The Bond*
Book Eight, *Cache Valley*

1875 to 1900—The North to Wyoming Era
Book Nine, *North to Wyoming*
This era includes five other novels

1900 to 1939—The Canyons Era
Book Fifteen, *Canyons*
This era includes five other novels

1939 to 1980—The Coming Thunder Era
Book Twenty-One, *Coming Thunder*
This era includes five other novels

1980 to present—The Summits Era
Book Twenty-Seven, *Summits*
This era includes five other novels

An American Saga

The *Threads West,* *An American Saga* series now Honored with Thirteen National Awards!

A Sweep of the Major Categories!

THE THREADS WEST SERIES IS THE PROUD RECIPIENT of thirteen national awards as of the date of this printing, including Best Book of the Year award or finalist designations in the categories of Western, Historical Fiction, Romance, West/Mountain Regional Fiction and Design! Thank you readers, and USA Book Review Awards, Next Generation Indies Awards, Independent Book Publishers Association—IBPA, Forward National Literature Award, International Book Awards, and Independent Publisher Book Awards (IPPYs).

Winner
- (BEST) Western 2010 and 2012
  (USA Book News Awards)
- (BEST) Romance 2011
  (Next Generation Indies Awards)
- (BEST) Historical Fiction 2011
  (IBPA—Ben Franklin Awards)
- (BEST) Design 2011 (IBPA—Ben Franklin Awards)

Silver Medalist
- (BEST) Regional Fiction 2012/West/Mountains (IPPYs)

Finalist
- Historical Fiction 2012 (USA Book News Awards)
- Historical Fiction 2013 (IBPA—Ben Franklin Awards)
- Romance 2011 (Forward National Literature Awards)
- Romance 2011 (International Book Awards)
- Romance 2010 (USA Book News Awards)
- Best Overall Design 2013
  (Next Generation Indies Awards)
- Best Cover Design 2011
  (Next Generation Indies Awards)

Be part of the Threads West Stampede!

Hop on board the Threads West Express! The adventure and romance of America, her people, her spirit and the West is comin' down the tracks at ya! Keep your ear to the rail for upcoming specials, excerpts, videos and announcements *only* for Threads West Express members!

Sign up to receive insider information, updates and contests at:

www.ThreadsWestSeries.com

Follow the conversation and participate in the games and promotions at:

www.facebook.com/ThreadsWest

Have questions or comments about the series? Contact us at:

ThreadsWest.Media@gmail.com

Shop the Threads West Express!

As a thank you for buying this book and being a part of the Threads West Stampede, we invite you to join the Threads West Express team. Send us your comments/feedback and receive discount coupons that can be used at the Threads West Express store!

Canvas Tote Bag   Limited Edition Prints   Photos of Threads West Country

Or shop at:
www.ThreadsWestExpress.com